# ONE HELL OF A NIGHT IN MEXICO

## SUNNI ELLIS

D & T
PUBLISHING

*To my best friend Desiree, for alpha-reading every single thing I've written over the last twenty years...including the poetry.*

*"It's like this, in Mexico there are three deaths, when the heart ceases to beat, when the body*

*returns to the soil...and when there is no one left to remember you. I promise you, amigos,*

*nobody in Almas Perdidas will ever forget you." ~ Archbishop Declan McQuade*

# 1

SUNDOWN IN ACUNA WAS A SKULL-CRUSHER. Damn rotters had moved through less than an hour ago. Dogs were still howling at the mess they'd left behind. No matter, the gunslinger had them, dead to rights. He'd catch up to them quick enough.

He killed some time picking off stragglers down at Julio's Cantina. Julio's had probably been an okay place before the swarm. Now it was a tangle of desiccated corpses. The bartender, Julio, caught a bullet in the fold of his right eye and jackknifed over the bar, loosely clutching a fifth of Mezcal. The gunslinger gripped the bottle and slid it from his grasp. Eyes rolling to the back of his head, he took a long pull and coughed, "Gracias, amigo, don't mind if I do. You won't be needing it where you're headed and that's a damn shame. A bottle of this, trust me, you can dance."

A brittle rain scratched at the windows, muted by the low grumble of gathering thunder. There might be a slim chance to keep ahead of the storm, but he had to ride now. He tossed the butt of his cigar into the bottle and watched it fizzle out, then reloaded. On impulse, he extended a long, sharp talon and scraped a message deep into the bar, "Creed Goodnight - Gun For Hire - Wire El Paso".

Creed ran the horde to ground right about the same time as the whole damn sky unhinged. He was packing a deadly accurate Colt Peacemaker in a leather holster slung low at the hip and tied to his thigh to facilitate clean quick draw access. Fast was fine, but in most cases it all boiled down to firepower. His weapon of choice was usually the shotgun concealed under his duster, but neither prepared him to face off with a rampaging storm.

Teary eyes pinched half shut with sand, he licked his dry, cracked lips and scowled up into a greenish-black bruise of horizon, unraveling by the second. Instinctively, he dodged left, missing decapitation by a gnat's hair as the weathered WELCOME TO WHISKEY LICK sign flew past him to join a wicked vortex of dust and debris lashing the desert.

Of all the cursed bad luck! He'd been on their ass for months. Now, he was stranded all to hell with the rest of the rotters until the squall either claimed him or moved on. He

had read somewhere that Socrates held all men's souls to be immortal, while the souls of the righteous were both immortal and divine. Big talk coming from a suicide. He wouldn't swear to it that vampires even had a soul, but he was sure as hell immortal. Chances were he'd survive this crapshoot, one way or another. A smug grin played at the corners of his mouth, "Fuck you, Socrates."

The gunslinger had long since made peace with being undead. In fact, you could say it stacked the deck in his favor. He could ride for days at a time in relentless pursuit, fend off most any incarnation of hungry predator, and take down zombies with his bare fists. Truth be told, vampires have no real quarrel with zombies at all, but a job is a job. Daywalkers like Creed had a lot of free time and zombies are slow and stupid. It was almost too easy. Before some jackass unlocked the gates of Hades, zombie hunting was the only thing keeping the bar tab current, with a little extra to keep him in blood whores. He wasn't getting rich, but it kept his appetites satisfied, all of them. Creed could get pretty hungry.

Scowling, he shoved a fist deep into his pocket and fished out a crumpled REWARD poster, deliberating one more time. Eight hundred dollars for a renegade horde-smiting sounds like real good money until you figure in a legion of pissed off demons, spawned in the breakout. Hell, this whole damn rathole reeked with the sickish stench of sulfur and decay.

Mexico, that's where the trouble started. It never fails. When the dust kicks up in Mexico, they sneeze in Texas. Any fool, dead or otherwise, knows that you don't just unhitch the Gates Of Hell without expecting a few devils in the exodus. So, when a pack of lesser demons got a notion to cut loose and wreak a little havoc along the border, they needed something fleshy to ride before hooking up with insurgent hordes headed north. Humans tend to be frail creatures. After a week or so of diabolic possession, decomposition sets in, making it a hard stretch to separate the hellspawn from intended targets in an infestation.

Throw a cadre of these skin boys into the mix, and the mob he'd been dogging had escalated to ridiculous numbers. He might as well save his bullets, he'd be taking on an army now. Mean mojo to be sure, but he was meaner. He reckoned on sweetening the odds with the dynamite packed inside his saddlebags. Most things die if you set them on fire.

The reward purse was the first shot he'd had at serious cash in a good while and when fate throws you a bone, it's best not to haggle the fine points. Besides, he was owed for the time he'd spent picking sand out of his fangs since leaving El Paso. Now that he'd caught up to the horde, he'd be damned if a little bad weather was gonna jinx the deal.

An urgency of dark, churning skies spit torrential sheets of pounding rain that sliced at his face in icy needles. Creed snarled, swiping at the thick, dripping tangle of silver-blonde hair falling into his eyes. On a different day, this whole ruination would have been done and dusted before the blood was dry. His thoughts were cut short by a savage gust of wind pitching in from the west, fanning the increasingly hectic tension of a town already dancing on the brink of a grave.

It took a full five seconds for the high-pitched shriek to register. Suddenly, lightning scraped the sky and a massive twister surged forward in the flash. Droning banshee wails sent the gnarled husk of a hackberry tree crashing through the window of a Dry Goods store at his back, littering the street with chunks of splintered bark and shattered glass. He marked the distance at about five hundred feet. That was good news. If the tornado stuck to that trajectory, it would clip the outskirts of Whiskey Lick and head east.

A livery stable at the far end of town caught his eye. He'd always held trust to be a liability, with the sole exception of Cuchillo, a surly behemoth of a stallion, black as a raven's wing. The ramshackle stables might not be the safest option, but at least they could both hole up inside while the storm passed. Creed spurred the stallion and slid low in the saddle, giving him the reins to run. They broke loose in an unrestrained gallop, weaving wildly in the cross-currents. Seconds later, the gunslinger skidded to a stuttering dismount in front of the stables, barely avoiding twisted remains of a stagecoach heaped up in the middle of the street. Two young females, hookers by the look of them, lay stretched out beside shabby trunks and satchels scattered haphazardly in the mud. Colorful satin dresses and frilly lingerie billowed and swirled in the air, swept up by the whipping winds.

Judging from the grisly condition of the women, and that of the horses as well, Whiskey Lick was probably a walking bone-yard by now. The bodies smelled of sulfur. No surprise since they were mutilated beyond recognition. Hell, let's not sugar-coat it, something gutted these girls like a trout. They'd bled out from the thoracic cavity while the organs and soft parts were eaten away. Deep striations on the the head, neck and extremities indicated that the carcasses had been chewed on for quite a spell afterward.

Creed flinched involuntarily when a gore-crusted skin boy threw himself forward from the wreckage, shuffling spasmodically. Demonic bastard, it had to be at least six foot eight. His face was swollen and pasty, quicklime white, with bulging, heavy-lidded eyes sagging in folds over a ragged hole where a nose should have been. Sensing a food source, he moaned excitedly, mouth gaping open like a milk bucket. An eyeball rolled from the blackened tongue and landed in the muck with a wet splash.

The gunslinger was really starting to hate these uppity devils. Veins swelled at his temples as adrenaline raced through his body and crept up his spine. He pressed forward and growled, "Time to pay up, sumbitch." A thin trickle of cigar smoke snaked upward into his flaring nostrils. Creed leveled the shotgun and fired twice, shattering the brute's legs. Indifferent to the keening screech of the wind, he watched with the cold detachment of an executioner as the wretch writhed on his back, surviving limbs pumping up and down in violent spasms, smashing into the ground with sustained fury.

Right about then, the squall intensified, making a whiny, ghoulish sound as it raged. He gritted his teeth in annoyance, then dropped his soggy cigar into the skin boy's nose cavity, grinding it under a boot heel until brains seeped out into the mud. Shoulders tucked, he braced against gale force winds and tugged hard on the unwieldy stable door. It creaked open on tired hinges, just wide enough to lead Cuchillo inside.

The smell hit him first, a sweet, musty odor of straw and leather with undertones of blood and kerosene. Dust filtering in through the aging wood, swirled in an anemic half-light, exposing a long, narrow walkway between a series of stalls cluttered with body parts and clumps of gore-streaked hay. Shelving structures in back stretched up to the rafters, stockpiled with supplies and kerosene lanterns. Best guess, Whiskey lick served as a swing station for the stagecoach line. Yeah, he would have been real fired up about stumbling across that amount of kerosene, if not for a voracious flurry of carnage spewing up on his left.

Creed grumbled in a low, threatening snarl, "Aw, hell no." It was shaping up to be a real shitty day. Another prostitute, pinned and squirming on the ground, gurgled incoherently while a couple of rotting cowboys and a sheriff's deputy feverishly peeled back stringy shreds of lace and flesh. He stared regretfully at the long strands of sleek, auburn hair stuck to the whites of her saucer-shaped eyes. Her rich brown skin, now graying in patches, had already begun to stiffen, drawing thin lips away from her pearly, blood-stained teeth. What a waste of talent.

Impassively, he slid the Colt from its holster and pumped a bullet into her forehead. A forced smile stuck to his face, he hissed venomously, "Where are your manners, boys? Try and show a little respect for the dead." They responded by tearing what was left of the victim into small strips. His shoulders twisted into a lopsided shrug, "Yeah, I kind of thought you'd say that." He fanned the pistol, firing three shots at point blank range.

Creed's lips curled into a hostile sneer as he scanned the room for any more dirtbags who might decide to give him trouble. Confident that he could relax for a minute, he paused to reload and caught the glint of a ruby ring still stuck to the finger that had swollen around it. Doubtless, it must have flown off during the ruckus. He picked the finger up and tasted the blood, then shook his head sideways with a half smile.

Pushing aside thoughts of hunger, the gunslinger sparked a match with his thumbnail and fired up a cigar, savoring the calm that always perched in the eye of a storm. Startled by an unexpected rustling in one of the stalls, he focused on the sound. Gripping the pistol in his free hand, he kicked the gate open, growling, "Talk fast, asshole."

He could barely make out the outline of a small, delicate form crouching in the darkness. She quickly began humming shaky snatches from some dancehall tune, between gasps of rapid breathing. The sweet scent of sex and lavender was intoxicating. A small sigh escaped her lips and she slowly leaned forward, extending a dainty arm from the shadows. It was smeared with dark red blood, clotted like cranberries in the fang marks. Seized by instant cravings, Creed lowered the Colt. This girl was a blood whore. Hell, they all must have been. Damn rotters, no appreciation for the finer aspects of appetite.

The little minx was buck naked. She'd probably sensed his presence and stripped down in the darkness, waiting. He stared shamelessly at her shivering body, his deep emerald eyes gleaming hungrily, then sunk his fangs deep into her soft, pulsing wrist. After a brief drink, he pulled back with a practiced restraint. If there was any chance to walk away from this, she'd be needing her strength.

Creed was struck by her sultry innocence. A wild mane of flaming red hair curled at the edges of a flawless, blue-eyed, baby face, a sure sign that she was new to the game. But what the deuce was he gonna do with a woman in a dogfight like this? Gently stroking her glossy hair, he tipped her chin up with his fingertips, "Listen sugar, you're real pretty and all, but you're a serious complication right now. Now, be a good girl and put your clothes back on. When this storm lets up, I'll be making a lot of noise. Take advantage of the confusion to head west. Try to put as many miles between you and this hellhole as you can." He tipped his hat and smiled, "I must say, it's been a pleasure, ma'am"

Her sparkling eyes rolled upward with an amused stare. She ran a tongue across her pouty red lips until they glistened wetly, separating just enough to draw him closer, and

whispered, "Will you kiss me just once if I promise not to follow you?"

The gunslinger nodded patiently. "Sure, honey. Just one,

okay?" He knelt down and pressed his lips to her full cushioned mouth, getting a shock that pounded through his skull in waves. Her kiss was like molten lava. It shot all the way down to his toes and lingered at the edge of his skin in aftershocks. Creed braced himself as the girl clung to him like a shadow, squirming and caressing in all the right places. He couldn't shake her loose, but by then he didn't want to.

A sliver of moon, pale and sickly, stuttered reluctantly in the sky like a wraith. Jagged veins of lightning spiderwebbed along a blackened bank of low-rolling clouds where the storm was shifting east. Keeping the Colt clenched in his fist, Creed yanked the stable doors open. Brain-dead rotters, the kind that can smell the wounded from a mile away, were starting to crawl from darkened doorways and piles of debris. A few already prowled the street like jackals, oblivious to the fiery holocaust in their near-future. Withered eyes scoured the darkness for the next piece of meat.

He licked an index finger and held it up into fierce, chaotic winds still gusting up the empty street. It was worth sitting out a tornado for velocity like that. A few calculated bundles of dynamite and a lot of kerosene might be enough to tip the odds in his favor, but he had to move fast, before the rest of the skin boys decided to join the party. As a rule, he stepped wide of demons. It was hard to tell if they meant to stake you or cut you in on the action. Even so, the lack of mutual respect was wearing parchment thin and some rules just begged to be broken. He wouldn't lose a wink of sleep watching them all burn.

The gunslinger pulled a fresh cigar from his pocket and thumbed a match, only half-surprised when the stallion spooked. Cuchillo whinnied, pacing nervously and shaking his head. The little sweat-soaked hooker had squeezed back into a tight black velvet corset and petticoats. He gave her a critical once over, frowning with bemused curiosity, then laughed. From the look of things, she'd been busy trying to add horse thief to her list of skills, with little success.

Creed spun the Colt back into his holster, and slipped the reins from her trembling hand. Gently stroking the horse's mane, he whispered softly, "Easy now, boy. That's it. Nice and easy." He waited until Cuchillo had calmed down, then turned to face the girl. "Okay, honey, you can ride with me as far as El Paso, then you're on your own. Got it? What's your name?"

A nervous, cornered look crept into her eyes, lasting a second before she composed herself. "You seem like a nice man, mister. I haven't run across a lot of nice men in my line of work. When you've been roughed up as many times as I have, you don't waste time waiting around to make sure." There was a slight catch in her voice, then her tone went dull and flat. "My name? Does it matter?"

His stony, piercing eyes gripped her in a merciless stare. "Maybe. I may need to know what to put on your grave marker if everything goes south. Don't get me wrong, honey, I might seem like a nice man, but if you try to steal my horse again, I'll look a lot different to you."

Underneath the constant whine of the wind there was another sound. It was vague at first, intensifying as it drew closer to the stables. There was no mistaking that indistinct shuffle of shaky legs. A menacing rumble of rusty throats, mewling and moaning, built slowly in a grapevine of feverish clamor. Cuchillo snorted and pawed at the ground, ears pinned back by the hellish chorus. Numb with panic, the girl whimpered, covering her ears against the bellowing groans. "They're out there! They're coming for us! Please, mister! We've gotta get out of here!"

Creed thrust both hands into his saddlebag, gingerly removing the twenty-one sticks of dynamite concealed inside, then grunted, " Yes ma'am, we'll be on our way, directly." Before she could protest, he bundled them in groups of three, peppering the room with explosives. A tight, humorless smile tugging at the corners of his mouth, he soaked each of the stalls with kerosene until it trickled out across the floorboards in rivulets.

Uproar in the street rose in pitch, becoming a wailing screech as the rotters tightened into a ravening mob. Creed hooked a boot in the stirrup and vaulted into the saddle, sweeping the shivering girl up behind him. It was time to throw the dice. Either the rotters were gonna burn, or he would. One way or the other, he'd be done chasing this moldering horde. Mostly, he was just sick of the stench of sulfur. He drew deep on the cigar. Red glint from the tip contorted his features into a mask of merciless resolve as he hurled it back over his shoulder.

At once, stacks of hay burst into flames with a dull roar. Floorboards began to buckle and swell with the increasing heat, igniting sparks in the aging wood that ran up the walls and blossomed into a sheet of fire in the rafters.

Without warning, rotters breached the stable doors, creating a draft that sucked the blaze right out of the walls, blasting it back at the greedy mob. Parched, shriveled bodies combusted like dry tinder. Within seconds, scathing winds shot around the burning bodies in rapid bursts, blanketing the horde in a smoldering inferno of white-hot cinders. Most crumbled to blackened ash, dissipating in the updrafts. Stragglers, reeking of grave rot and burning flesh, shambled off, groaning and wailing in a fiery, chaotic dance.

Cuchillo reared up, smoke curling in his singed mane. Creed tensed, trying to focus while the panicked hooker clawed her fingernails into his waist, screaming hysterically. At once, the stallion snorted and lunged forward, muscles rippling in his massive legs. Cuchillo danced back and forth in the churning winds, sidestepping bodies and wreckage as they raced in tandem with a meteoric rush of fire and dense, scalding smoke punching its way up the street.

Wood and metal shriveled, wrinkling around the burn until charred facades slid down the collapsing storefronts like syrup off a sundae. Blinding and white-hot, heat lightning forked through the blackened night illuminating a legion of skin boys slithering out from the burning buildings.

In that frozen moment before the pack closed in, the demonic rumble of growls and snarling was eclipsed by a violent series of ear-splitting blasts. The rickety stables heaved and exploded into geysers of flame and molten debris, erupting outward in every direction. Swift and brutal, a spontaneous inferno engulfed them all. Shrieks of loss and outrage escalated to skull-shredding howls of pain. To be trapped inside a human host after death meant a straight shot back to Hell. Threats and curses tapered into silence as fragile skin crisped and blistered, spewing chunks of clotted blood like magma. The host bodies melted, staining the ground bright red before seeping thickly into jagged fissures in the earth.

Cuchillo picked up speed at a thundering gallop, hoofbeats ringing in a pounding wave of dust. Creed half-turned in the saddle and bellowed, "Adios, boys. Give Satan my regards." Smoke and dust swirled and twisted in the turbulent winds, stinging his eyes and nostrils. He'd sensed movement in the holocaust behind them, but it was hard to be certain. Squinting harder into the dense miasma, he slowly slid the Colt from its holster.

Three hulking silhouettes emerged from the firestorm with a cocky strut. Flames licked at their clothing, but the bodies remained mostly intact. That could mean only one thing, they were Fallen. Creed had run across a Fallen before, but he'd never gone up against one. He hoped he wouldn't have to now. Rotters and demons were predictable, but if the stories were true, these Fallen bastards packed an arsenal of angelic muscle and speed.

Merciless and driven, the Fallen dropped to all fours and bounded straight for them in a malignant surge of unchecked rage. Within seconds, they flanked the fearless Cuchillo on either side, snapping and snarling like wolves taking down a stag. Creed gritted his teeth and barked at the screaming hooker, "Shut up, girl, and hold on," but it didn't matter. Vicious talons raked into her abdomen and she let loose a wavering shriek of agony. He stretched back, grabbing for her hand as it slipped from his waist, but her sweaty fingers slipped through his grasp. When he heard bones snap as they dragged her from the speeding horse, he lowered the Colt and put a bullet between her horrified eyes. She disappeared in a tumble of petticoats and long red hair.The Fallen dropped back, ripping at her corpse in a savage frenzy that lasted only seconds before their human bodies finally combusted.

It was hard to figure how long Whiskey Lick would continue to burn before settling into ash. Creed hurtled away from the firestorm, into a dead flat of Sonoran Desert as far as the eye could see. As darkness buckled, bone white slivers of moonlight broke through the heavy cover of smoke. The air was cool and crisp against his skin. He could almost see the night winds rushing past giving life to patches of tall grass still sparkling with rain from the storm.

He came across a steep stone outcropping where he could view his handiwork from a distance, and dismounted. Heaving from exhaustion and smoke inhalation, Cuchillo drank deep from a puddle of water collected in the rock. Creed reached inside his duster for the Mezcal he'd stolen from Julio's and raised it to Cuchillo, letting his smile tighten up around the edges. "Here's to us, old friend. Fuck those rotters." Stretching the last drag from his smoke, he flicked it at a wind-bitten crow circling overhead, then threw his head back and drained the bottle.

Cuchillo stood patiently while the gunslinger stuck a fresh cigar between his bloodless lips and struck a match. He knelt down, swiping at the sweat and ashes on his face with the sleeve of his coat. What kind of questions would the law dogs in El Paso be asking when he showed up to claim the reward? Smiting is hard work and some things just need killing. He regretted nothing, except the hooker. It was a damn shame about her, but he'd done the only thing he could to make things easier. All things said, it was a clean smite and he'd earned every nickel of that eight hundred dollars.

Creed climbed back into the saddle and scanned the desert for signs of pursuit. It stretched empty for miles. Whiskey Lick was nothing more than a grim line of rubble, rising up like a tombstone in a heavy pre-dawn fog that magnified the phosphorescent orange haze shrouding it. Flames danced in the distance as plumes of thick gray smoke swallowed the sky.

The melancholy whistle of a freight train sounded in the distance, discordant, like the hollow baying of hellhounds. For a moment, hesitation flickered in his feral, green eyes. Heaven might work in mysterious ways, but it was safe to say that Hell could be a real sore loser. His jaw stiffened. He hadn't counted on throwing Fallen into the mix. The concern faded quickly and something else took its place. He let his eyes squeeze shut and grinned big. He'd beat them, damn right. Sure, they probably slipped the flesh before torching out, but it would be a while before they found another body to ride. Plenty of time to get back to El Paso and get paid.

# 2

---

EL PASO WAS PRACTICALLY a ghost town at seven in the morning. Creed swatted the cigar smoke away from his face and let his eyes flicker to a makeshift gallows outside the sheriff's office. Two poor bastards dangled from the end of a rope, jerking stiffly in the wind while vultures tore at their flesh. A third noose swung empty beside them. Wanted posters, smeared with dark, curdled stains, were pinned to their shirts beneath festering wounds where the hearts had been crudely torn out. While not too concerned by the ghastly corpses, it was the empty noose that prickled the hairs on the back of his neck. If these law dogs had cooked up some scheme to cheat him out of the reward purse, they'd best think again. The whole damn street was fetid with the coppery taste of blood and a good bit of time had passed since he'd last eaten.

He wrapped the reins around his saddle horn and dismounted, tethering Cuchillo to a hitching post out front. The stallion whinnied and lowered his head, nuzzling Creed's shoulder. Creed scowled and stroked his matted mane, grumbling, "No call to worry, boy, you earned your pay. It's apples and oats when I get back."

Sheriff Quinten Chance was a serious man with a serious gun. He was a risk taker and as any poker player can tell you, a skillful gambler is the nerviest and deadliest man alive. Creed had dealt with him before. He also knew that Chance was expecting him. The smell of coffee was strong enough to peel paint off the walls, the gunslinger could smell it from the street. He drew the last few drags off his cigar and flicked it at the gallows, then walked inside.

A pudgy, unshaven deputy leaned against a gun rack in the corner. Another nervous, spoon-chested law dog perched on a cot against the left wall. This one rubbed a sweaty hand on his shirt then locked it around his pistol in a white knuckled grip. Sheriff Chance was squeezed in back of a wide, oaken desk, behind stacks of paperwork. The bars of a cell were visible in a room behind him.

Chance didn't look up right away, thumbing through a pile of wanted posters instead. Creed knew that he wasn't really looking at them because most of the fugitives were probably a pile of ashes back in Whiskey Lick. Seconds passed before a tight, humorless smile wavered in the corners of the sheriff's thin lips. He leaned over an open drawer and pulled out a money bag, then tossed it across the desk. Chance cleared his throat and growled, "Go on, count it. It's all there."

Creed grabbed the bag and nodded warily. "Nice doing business with you sheriff, but I reckon I'll be on my way now."

"Not so fast, Goodnight," Chance barked sharply, "We have another matter to discuss."

Creed rested his hand on the Colt, snarling, "Unless you aim to explain that empty noose outside, you and I have nothing more to talk about."

The sheriff looked momentarily puzzled before regaining his composure. "That noose is none of your concern, gunslinger. It's not for you and that's all you need to know."

Creed backed away slowly toward the door. His expression

was unreadable as he tilted his head and forced the issue. "Humor me."

Sheriff Chance snorted and shrugged his beefy shoulders. "Well. it's not entirely related to your usual field of expertise, but I suppose there could be some reward money in it for you." He finally had Creed's full attention. The gunslinger slid his hand off the Colt, slumped into a chair and propped his boots up on the battered desk.

Sheriff Chance placed his fingertips together. Resting both elbows on the desk, he began without preamble, "The lawbreaker intended for that noose was a local woman, Rebecca Surette. She turned herself in of her own volition. I'll admit that her story was compelling at first. Here, I'll read it to you." Chance shuffled through the papers on his desk. When he found the one he was looking for, he put his glasses on and read, "Merciful sirs, I fear my wits have been bedeviled by evil influence. Though I have no clear memory of the heinous act committed, I now must throw myself upon your justice, and that of this fine city. At this very moment, my dear husband grows cold in our bed, my carving knife plunged deep into his heart. Upon my word, I left him where he lay and came directly here. I fear my poor bones will never find rest until I have a shroud to wrap his body in."

The sheriff shook his head in disgust. "At that point, she started bawling uncontrollably and collapsed to her knees. As you can imagine, we were all visibly shaken by this disclosure, but doggedly continued to press her for details, as is procedure." The two surly deputies interrupted, weighing in on the story by grunting in agreement. Chance adjusted his glasses and glanced up at Creed. "Rebecca wrapped her arms tightly around her knees, rocking silently back and forth as if absorbed in thought. Her pale, withered face was devoid of emotion when she finally looked up."

He raised the paper and began reading from the confession again. "My husband, Albin, returned home from the Civil War early last evening, a scarred and broken man, recounting events so heavy with pain and horror it would take a saint to bear them. The night fell and as was custom, I took him to bed. Before he could touch me, I put a hand to his chest, pushing him back. I held a secret that it was vital he hear. You see, I have a demon who desires me with a powerful intensity that keeps him waiting nearby. Should my husband try to make carnal love to me, the fiend would surely kill us both in the act. My husband was outraged. If he were to believe me, he demanded to confront this demon straight away. Not to be dissuaded, he vowed that if it was another man that I loved, then and there would he kill me himself." Then, that woman looked me straight in the eyes and swore that the next thing she remembered was waking up next to her husband with her knife in his chest.

When the boys and I searched the house, we found the corpse of Albin Surette twisted in the bloody sheets, just as she had stated. Tragically, further inspection revealed the bodies of her two small children as well, huddled together in bed, left to die in a spreading puddle of congealed blood from multiple stab wounds.

We arrested her on the spot and dragged her down to the courthouse to stand before Judge Stockwell. His honor was so overcome with shock and revulsion, it required several minutes for the shaking in his voice to subside before he could pass sentence. When he finally spoke, his judgment was swift and final. He says, "Rebecca Surette, as it seems that you and this demon you speak of are not so far apart, I hereby sentence you to be hanged by the neck this very evening, until you are dead. Once this is done, you may plead your case with Satan himself. Do you have any last words?"

Well, when Rebecca rose from her seat, she literally drained the light around her. Those evil, black eyes narrowed with fury and hatred and a wicked leer kind of spread across her distorted face. She says, "As the day of my death has been decided, I may as well make a full confession. It's true that my husband asked nothing of me but to guard my honor and keep a fire burning in the hearth. Had I been widowed, I might have remarried and all this could have been avoided. Albin was a stingy man, tight with his purse. As you well know, women desire pretty things. Even witches like me," The bitch stopped right there, grinning at the impact of her disclosure. When she was sure we'd all been sufficiently shocked, she glared at the judge and said, "Mark my words, Judge Ethan Stockwell, you are my enemy now, all of you, and I will escape the noose."

When the hour of execution arrived, a group of four formidable guards from the prison were sent to fetch her from the cell and escort her to the gallows. With all attention focused on the two scheduled executions and the hangman, there was no way to tell how it happened, but the four guards were soon discovered, vacant eye sockets gaping obscenely and tongues torn out at the root. The judge was found hours later in a similar state. As for the witch, she had vanished with no trace left behind."

Creed tossed the moneybag into the air and caught it with an overhand catch, grinning at the sheriff. "That was quite a yarn, Chance. Hell yes, that witch is mine. Start counting out the cash." He pushed back in his chair to leave and caught the sober expression on the sheriff's face.

Thunder rattled the windows. The blue skies outside blackened rapidly with low-rolling storm clouds. Chance didn't seem to notice. He clenched his jaws and leaned forward across the desk, breathing evenly. "Sit down, Goodnight. It's time we talked about the real matter at hand."

Something in the sheriff's tone of voice set Creed's teeth on edge. He'd be damned if he was gonna wait around to find what it was. He shifted in his seat, smiling just wide enough to expose his fangs. "If it's all the same to you, sheriff, I think we'll save that for another day." Before Chance could reply, the heavy door banged open with a grieving moan, revealing a gaunt, menacing figure shadowed in the half-light. The towering man would have radiated an intimidating presence even without the long, black frock, neatly buttoned up from his grizzled cowboy boots to a starched white collar around his neck. A heavy, silver crucifix resting on a fascia sash at his waist left no room for doubt.

Needles of unease honed in on the echoing silence when the anxious deputies went for their pistols and braced for a gunfight. Creed lunged from his chair. His hand flew to the shotgun under his duster and he snarled as the barrel jerked upward, "Step wide, boys. You don't want to be making enemies."

Sheriff Chance slammed a fist on the desk, demanding attention. Wiping the sweat from his upper lip with the sleeve of his shirt, he glared at Creed, "Lower that shotgun, fool. This man has a lucrative proposition for you."

Creed gave him the side-eye and sneered, " I'd love to, sheriff, but those two bastards are gonna shoot me."

Chance threw his arms in the air and barked at the deputies, "For chrissakes! Dub! Shanks! Holster those weapons, boys. We talked about this."

Spirals of dust muddied the air as the intruder resolutely closed the door behind him. Creed didn't take his eyes off him, or let his expression change as the man strode across the room with an air of stony indifference. If this self-righteous zealot figured to get under his skin, he needed to think again.

The man pulled up a chair beside the sheriff's desk, then extended a gnarled hand, motioning for the gunslinger to do the same. Creed slumped back into his seat and they briefly sized each other up before he spoke, "If I may introduce myself."

Creed impatiently raked back the matted hair stuck to his forehead and interrupted him before he could finish, "I know who you are, Archbishop Declan Mcquade. Or, maybe I should just call you the Texas Torquemada. The only man who can claim a body count that comes close to matching mine. What do you want, holy man?"

The Archbishop's eyes glinted with amusement. He replied in a deep, gravelly voice, "We all have our jobs to do, Mister Goodnight. Like shards of a broken mirror, constantly in motion, yet they all seem to fit together somehow, don't they? I kill monsters. You kill monsters. We have countless vicious beasts to slay. Still, if you had to pick a rooster for the henhouse, there's only one true contender...demons. " He let the word stretch out and hang in the air.

You were brought to our attention by Father Perez, village priest to the poor unfortunates of Acuna. He found your name and contact information scratched into the bar at Julio's Cantina. Your trail led to Whiskey Lick and I must say, we were quite impressed with your results."

Creed's expression darkened like a thundercloud. "See, here's your problem, holy man, some imbecile working with the almighty Catholic Church let the Gates Of Hell swing wide open. Those demons I killed? Well, they'll be waltzing back through, pretty as you please, before we're done talking. You've most likely figured that I'm not a religious man. I won't be going to Heaven any time soon, so I take my rewards in the here and now. Due to the grief you've caused me, and the fact that I don't like you, it would need to be something I can sink my fangs into."

The Archbishop regarded him with the deliberate arch of an eyebrow. "Yes, of course, I suppose I should have opened with that." He picked a pen up from the sheriff's desk and wrote a number on the back of a wanted poster. Folding the paper neatly, he slid it across the desk and paused, waiting for a reaction.

Creed remained stone-faced, leaning back into his chair to look at the number. He pulled a cigar from his shirt pocket, then struck a match on the heel of his boot and lit it before replying, "So, what is it I can do for you, holy man?"

The irony of this agreement wasn't lost on either of them. The Archbishop rolled his shoulders back and spoke in a low voice, "Before we begin, Mister Goodnight, tell me everything you know about the Zona De Silencio."

Creed shuddered, his lips twisting into a tight grin. "Damn, guess I knew this wasn't gonna be easy. Okay, McQuade, let's dance. On a good day, the Mexican desert is an adversary that pleads for mercy, yet offers none. She knows her own, holding no tolerance for weakness of mind or spirit.

The Zona De Silencio is a good stretch south from El Paso as the crow flies. Let me tell you, holy man, it's a whole new breed of fearsome. Those crazy enough to cross into the Zona had best do so with fresh horses and plenty of water. Compasses spin like dervishes. Fluctuation between the 26th and 28th parallels mirrors the Devil's Triangle and the pyramids of Egypt, whipping up a magnetic vortex strong enough to pull down meteorites, which some believe to be falling angels. But I guess you already know all about that.

On a more mundane level, blistering sun bakes the brain at one hundred twenty degrees, plummeting below zero when night falls and the moon spreads her shadow, inviting all manner of flesh-eating predators to slither from every darkened crevice. Aberrations three times normal size, scorpions, snakes, swarms of centipedes with purple heads and tails, hunt anything they can catch. Flesh is flesh, be it vampire or human.

Purgatorio is the last human settlement skirting the Zona. Residents there report a constant state of unease and distorted perception, riddled with visual and auditory hallucinations. If you ask them for directions to the Zona, you always get the same answer, *nunca van a llegar*, you are never going to get there. Chances are, they're right. Now that I know where I'm headed, what's the job?"

Now confident with the decision he'd made to hire the vampire, The Archbishop rasped, "Rumors of smugglers and bandits terrorizing the border and far reaching areas on either side flourished during the war. Even worse, some of these same marauders have taken to cannibalizing victims. One week prior, two of these cannibals, known to attack and murder travelers, were caught and left to hang. Their hearts were removed to serve as warning to any contemplating similar acts of savagery.

To further complicate matters, a rash of bodies and missing

persons has led to widespread belief that the witch, Rebecca Surette, has since abandoned El Paso for remote regions in the Sonoran Desert.

The church believed cannibalism and witchcraft to be the worst of it. Upon hearing your account of the diabolical abominations that haunt these forsaken regions, I am convinced that you might be the only one capable of completing the mission. Three Dominican nuns and the priest traveling with them must be delivered to the Monasterio De Los Angeles, a Catholic stronghold situated in the very heart of the Zona De Silencio. It is imperative that they arrive there safely."

Creed laughed to himself. Apparently, prayer hadn't been enough and the church needed a vampire to guarantee transport. He dropped the cigar and ground it out with the toe of his boot, grinning smugly, "I'm your vampire, holy man, When do we leave?"

The Archbishop brought the cross to his lips, then fixed Creed in an unrelenting stare. "Tomorrow morning."

## 3

HEATWAVES SHIMMERED up from the arid soil in an early morning haze. It was gonna be another damn scorcher. Needy masses populating that wide sweep of scrub terrain hugging the Mexican border, were already pitching makeshift camps outside the revival tent in anticipation of the evening show. More often than not, they kept a distance from strangers, holding their eyes and heads down, avoiding trouble, but even desert dogs can dream. It was hard to ignore the flood of colorful posters blanketing the region, MORNINGSTAR REVIVAL - Expect A Miracle! With not much else to ease the boredom, apart from christenings and funerals, they were prepared to do just that.

The Fallen called Hadriel slapped at an annoying fly on his cheek, then settled back into the office chair with a creak of battered leather. He let his eyes squeeze shut, picking at the grime under his talons with a Bowie knife. There was a change in the wind. He could sense it, but couldn't put a finger on exactly what it was. Maybe a new player, maybe not, but it was stifling and deadly, like consecrated blood. The point was, he couldn't just rot away in this hole and let some holy bastard seal the Gates back up.

Hadriel spun the cylinder on his pistol, muttering a vulgar curse. Clearly, he needed to size up the threat and squeeze out a resolution damn quick, before things got really bad. The heavy canvas tent was muggy and stifling, hot enough to singe the hair of your arms. Heedless of the swelter, sweaty, unwashed peasants worked tirelessly, preparing for the evening sermon. All that fawning and praying sparked an appetite. A broad grin cracked his face. He aimed the pistol through a slit in the office flaps and targeted a frail, hispanic woman down the gunsight. His finger tightened on the trigger, but he didn't fire. It would have been easy to feed his growling belly, just like it was easy to corrupt that simple-minded nun at the Monasterio after detecting the pungent odor of early onset dementia.

The Fallen grimaced and spat in the dust. The fiercest of his legion had struck swiftly, reducing the hated fortress to rubble while the cursed Gates were still smoking from the breach. It had been foolish to think the Book would be sequestered in the monastery. Doubtless, another team of emissaries, in possession of the book, had already been dispatched by the church to rectify the rupture. Little solace could be gained in knowing the Gates were open, when the ritual inscribed in the loathsome tome would be sealing it any day now.

Hadriel checked the bullets in his pistol, shook the cylinder closed and spun it back into the holster with a furious twitch. He must be crazy or ignorant. Retaining an angelic link to the opposition amounted to squat if you lost sight of your immediate surroundings. Those cross-monkeys were within a day's ride when the twister hit, he was sure of it. How long had the gunfighter been lying low, circling the swarm like a mangy cur? Long enough to plant enough explosives to blow his whole legion back to Hell. Such arrogance, the bloodsucker would have been dead in the dirt if not for his own dogged obsession with the Book. By result, he may have escaped fiery annihilation in Whiskey Lick, but he was the only hellspawn who did.

Crossing paths with the fancy faith healer shortly thereafter was a stroke of blind luck. A growing contingent of his legion had already clawed their way back through the breach, thirsting to rejoin the search. Conversely, not a night went by that the revival tent wasn't full to overflowing with enthusiastic victims, providing a convenient stockpile of bodies. This had been a bad spell, but as things stood now, more than twenty demons were keeping an ear to the ground, closing in on the trail.

The revival proved to be a perfect symphony of carnival, Catholicism and hellfire. Obvious benefits aside, the shady healer had a mouth full of moon and a soul full of midnight. It was a definite step up from the loutish brute he'd been stuck inside of for almost a year. The new body was sexual dynamite, lean and muscular with a chiseled jaw and broad angular cheekbones. Women and men alike found him indecently mesmerizing. He kept his thick red-blonde hair tightly cinched into a short ponytail at the back of his head, leaving a blunted fringe to hang loose across the shoulders of an austere, black frock coat. There was a fluidity to his movements now, like a dancer, straight but not stiff, confidence tailored by success. Deep-set mahogany eyes twinkled with humor when he smiled like you were a long lost brother, shaking your hand with just the right amount of squeeze. Hadriel shifted his weight, flipped a smoke in his mouth and lit it with the tip of an index finger. He would have to thank the vampire next time they met, before he ripped him into small chunks and fed his body to the crows.

The breeze was brisk and clean, deep reds and oranges streaked the sky hinting at sundown. The desert air was cooler now, but not by much. Sunburned and sweaty, the rabble began to pour in beneath a mud-splattered banner reading, MORNINGSTAR REVIVAL - Portents! Wonders! Miracles! True believers sang the praises of Brother Hadriel's good works. Piously insisting that beauty is only skin deep, they flocked to him in droves, privately magnetized by lust, like praying in a closet with the door shut. Hadriel's lips parted in a wide, fearsome smile. Greedy humans, they might have had a chance at salvation by looking a little deeper, but they never did. After all, why would ignorant peasants like these suspect a galvanizing Adonis, spitting fire and brimstone, to be the host body for a fallen angel? Upkeep on the preachy puppet grew tiresome at times, but he truly detested having to chase bodies. Why should he? No one has to advertise a fire, just strike a blaze and they all come running.

Flimsy metal poles swayed, curving slightly from the weight of the cavernous tent. Stained canvas flaps served as window covers to block out all vestiges of outside light, leaving the interior dimly illuminated by strings of bare bulbs. There were plenty of musty hymnals stacked at the entrance to a wide aisle, left open in dead center. The room filled quickly with frantic disciples, pushing and shoving to grab a seat in one of the crowded rows of wooden chairs before they were all taken. More than two hundred of the faithful, bone-weary from affliction and the burdens of life, swirled around the room weeping and praying. Subdued by a heavy fever brought on by guilt and organ music, they eventually settled into chairs or squatted on the floor, hypnotized by a continuous stream of familiar hymns. The overcrowded space smelled of smoke and sweat, more befitting a brothel than a house of God. The scene had been set and the outcome was inescapable.

Hadriel waited behind an extended wooden platform constructed along the front, timing his entrance. Several of the elderly passed out cold when he leapt onto the stage like a panther, chest heaving, nostrils flaring, igniting a deafening ovation of cheers and applause. Rigidly extending his right arm, he waved an accusatory finger back and forth across the delirious crowd and wailed, "If the devil is in your house it's because you let him in! Oh, but take heart, children! Brother Hadriel has heard your cries for help and I join with you here tonight to cast out the wicked and harvest men of faith. Can I get a Hallelujah?!" A responding Hallelujah shook the rafters.

The Fallen sliced into his congregation with the momentum

of a raging fire in a tinder-dry forest, praying and swaying until not a soul among them remained unconvinced. His fiery words kept them hanging from a slender thread, blistering in flames from that great furnace of sin, gaping and bottomless. Each held certain that Brother Hadriel had been sent to fly them away from the torments of Hell and back to salvation on the wings of angels. Relentlessly, he held the heat to their feet until he'd baked the true faith right out of them.

Muscles twitched in the corners of his mouth. Hadriel wrinkled his expression into a look of pained sincerity and braced for the finale, his favorite part of the show. He methodically prowled center aisle, pumping hands and flashing a white, toothy smile while evaluating the decaying wall of flesh. His beady eyes didn't miss a thing. A bodiless devil, recently returned from the bowels of Hell, hovered in the shadows. The Fallen exchanged glances with the newcomer, indicating a brawny shirt-sleeves rancher with a scar running the length of his coarse, leathery face. The hellion gave a short nod of compliance and latched onto the man with the lethal speed of a rattlesnake.

One last matter remained to be dealt with before the faceless worshippers would be released back into a multitude of pointless, shabby lives. The Fallen paused and tilted his head, red sparks glinting in his pupils. His stomach grumbled as a thick, greasy aroma wafted up from the back of the tent, smothering his senses in the deliciously human aroma of heavy fats and sugars.

In an instant, he traced the scent to a husky, drunken ruffian, smeared with filth and sweat. Flies buzzed around the empty chairs on either side of him, suggesting that others avoided him like a contagion. Fighting back an urge to slap the sobbing drunkard, he sidled up to stand beside him. Resting a hand on the wretch's shaking shoulders, he coaxed in low, soothing tones, "Let it all out son, it wouldn't be a revival without a few tears."

The congregation moaned and wailed in empathy, "Preach it Brother Hadriel!"

Hadriel grandly waved an arm across the crowd then turned his full attention back to the target. "Blessed be! There is a crying need right here in this tent tonight for men just like you."

Tears of rapture streamed down the man's face. He grasped the Fallen's hand and shouted, "Hallelujah, Brother, Hallelujah!"

Hadriel stroked his head lovingly. "There, there," he cooed, "Less praying and more obeying! I must insist that you remain after services this evening. We can work on your burdens together."

The drunkard gasped and choked, "Hallelujah..hallelujah...hallelujah!"

When the show was over, a plodding congregation dragged their feet, reluctant to abandon the intoxicating bliss of the revival tent. Scarcely able to contain his annoyance, Hadriel abruptly ushered them outside with promises to meet again tomorrow. Once the tent was empty, he leered at the intended victim, motioning for him to follow.

The newcomer was given orders to lay low after possessing the oafish rancher. A flinty intensity gleamed in his eyes when the Fallen stalked into his office, leading the lamb to slaughter. Before the hellion could stop himself, he snatched the Stetson from his head and jerked to his feet. Clearly agitated, the brute ran thick, clumsy fingers through an unfamiliar tangle of greasy hair, rubbing at deep creases in his swarthy neck. "Hadriel, I have news!"

Slowly raising a talon to his lips, the Fallen jerked his chin toward the trusting disciple. Without warning, he spun the man around in front of him and pulled the Bowie knife from his belt, pressing its tip against the victim's jugular Hadriel lowered his gaze and leaned in until he could taste the drunkard's sour breath, then let his eyes snap open, pinning his prey in a smoldering red stare.

The horrified man quivered spasmodically, struggling to

process the shock. Overwhelmed with panic, he shoved hard against the Fallen's chest. Blasphemous curses poured from his mouth like the last words of a lost and broken soul. Weak with fear, he crumpled to his knees, screeching, "What are you? You're not human! HELP ME! Oh God, PLEASE, someone help me!"

It was increasingly hard to concentrate with all the screaming. Hadriel preferred to let a victim bleed out slowly, adrenaline added spice to the meat, but the newcomer had spouted something about news. Curiosity boiled in his veins, what news? He tilted his head thoughtfully, stuck the knife back in his belt and hauled a bloody ax out of the weapons chest. Lightly tracing an index finger along the sharp steel blade, he mimicked the traumatized man's pleas, "Help me! Help me! Do I look like your savior, foolish sheep?" When there was no response, he raised the ax and swung it down hard at the base of the victim's skull, spraying the office with a red, sticky mist. Hadriel drew down before the meat hit the ground, fanning three bullets into the severed head as it rolled across the floor.

The damn drunkard tasted bitter, riddled with disease. Hadriel had suspected as much. He ate quickly, swallowing most of the body without chewing. At least, servile peasants had left a pitcher of water and a basin for him on a wobbly table in the corner. He tipped the pitcher, rinsing gore from his bloody hands, then poured the rest into the basin, splashing handfuls into his face and mouth.

Flies were already collecting on the kill, attracted by the stench. Hadriel spat and kicked at the reeking husk hard enough to send it flying out the office entry panels. Irritation still prickling like needles on his skin, he hooked a boot under the dead man's back and slung the body under the stage. Ripping several window flaps open finally offered some relief from the stagnant confinement. The night air was fresh with the faint but pleasant smell of an approaching storm.

Feeling much better, Hadriel slumped into his chair, propping both boots up on the desk. Apart from a droning hum of flies, the air fell silent as he sized up the newcomer. He knew this one, part human, part Fallen, raised by hellhounds. His fleshy mother named him Reverend Jim, after her father, before leaving him to die at the Gates Of Hell. Ignored for the most part, he ran with the hounds. Damn if that little halfbreed didn't turn out to be the best tracker in the legion. Hadriel grinned amiably and fixed the boy with an intense stare. "Welcome back to paradise, halfbreed. What news do you bring?"

Rev shifted his weight and cautiously got to his feet. He made a wide sweeping gesture with his right arm and tried to speak, but his new tongue was still thick and uncoordinated and the words came out garbled. For a moment, hesitation flickered in his flat, resentful eyes, then he tried again and nailed it. "Hear me out, Hadriel. I confess to receiving the mandate to rejoin you and claim a new body, but if you know my name, you know that I'm driven by instinct. It's my nature to track prey and I don't rest until the job is done. Which is exactly what I did.

I drifted in the desert for days after my escape, until I spotted a sloppy trail of wagon ruts. I tracked it to a Catholic transport coach carrying a priest and three nuns. Sound familiar? The coach was headed south toward the Zona. When I left, they were a hundred miles or so from a desolate village called Almas Perdidas, a necessary stop to water horses and restock supplies. It doesn't amount to much, just a church, a jailhouse, a sundries store and three cantinas. If you hurry, you can easily overtake the town and be waiting when the coach arrives."

Rev shuddered, then shook it off. "The body incinerated in Whiskey Lick was my own, not some disposable skin sack. I was itching to whistle for the hellhounds, skin that crusading priest and grind his bones to dust. Instead, I backtrack here to bring you the news and get stuck in this lumbering waste of flesh." His defiant face twisted into a grimace, showing almost all of the rancher's decaying, yellowed teeth. "I'm thinking I deserve better than that."

Hadriel's deadpan expression turned savage with a curl of his lip. "Well, I guess you got lucky then, boy. If that pious slut got ahold of the Book, it's gonna take a lot more than you and a few mutts to bring him down. Henceforward, you would be wise to remember that I pull all the strings, including yours. You'll ride that body until I say otherwise." He side-eyed the rotgut tequila teetering at the edge of his desk, took a long pull, then tossed the bottle to Rev. "Now, get out here, halfbreed. Give me a little space to summon the legion. Tomorrow, we ride."

4

---

LATE MORNING SONORAN sun burned down, cruel and unyielding,
setting fire to a colorless, barren sprawl of sky. Raul Lopez
squatted atop a craggy boulder at the mesa's edge, urgently scanning the sweeping miles of wasteland encircling him.The glare
was so bright it stung his eyes, driving salty beads of sweat down
the creases in his face. Flustered, he nervously shoved the
sombrero to the back of his head and cupped a shaking hand to
his forehead, shielding his unflagging gaze.

A wisp of mist drifted across the cloudless sky, casting elongated shadows like an omen. Brief gusts of hot, sandpaper wind
dried the sweat from his face, then the shadows were gone and
the sun was higher, hotter than before, blistering the ground
under his feet. Raul was no coward. He'd fought shoulder to
shoulder with the others many times, beating back the roving
bands of cannibals that carried off small children in the night. A
shudder passed through him. This was different, much worse.

He'd found himself in a state of restless dread since sunrise. It
was almost uncanny. Still, heat madness can play tricks in the
desert. He first saw the truth of his misgivings when the goats he
was tending banded together, circling in the center with female

alphas to the outside, protecting the kids and weaker animals. When the mist passed over them, resistance turned to helpless screams of fear.

Raul shouldered his rifle and rose to his feet, squinting defiantly into the blazing sun. Far in the distance, an indistinct blur broke through the watery waves of heat rising off the desert. An undulating wall of dust swallowed the horizon, as a legion of steely hooves thundered toward Almas Perdidas.

A horrifying image forced its way into his thoughts, striking a chill to his marrow. Raul faltered in spite of his resolve. In this vision, the ravagers stared into his face without speaking a word, all sharing the same startling pallor as that of a corpse. Certainly, none of these riders was a living man. His heart skipped a beat, then pounded harder realizing that they'd been inside his mind.

Vivid sunlight pushed back the darkened edges of consciousness. Raul's eyes flew open, saliva hardening to a thick knot in his throat. Salty blood flooded his mouth as he bit his bottom lip, picking up first one foot and then another in a shaky, unbalanced stagger to his horse. He spurred the terrified animal, ripping rocks and scrub from the ground in an uncontrolled slide down the mesa, then rode hard for the village, shrouded in a cloak of dust.

Eager dogs nipped at the heels of shoeless children playing games in the sun-baked street, gusts of heat at their back. Red chili ristras were slung over rafters, yellowed tongues clicking in the breeze as laughing women draped the village of Almas Perdidas in brightly colored paper flags and banners in preparation for the harvest fiestas. The thick aroma of boiling coffee and grilled meat hung in the air. Rosa Ruiz set a long wooden table for the evening meal while crows and finches squawked over scraps. Her hands and face were rosy from the steam of fresh tortillas when she waved to the farmers spilling in from the fields, favoring her with grateful, sunburned smiles. After everyone had been served, she carried a basket of vine ripened tomatoes and fresh sweet corn to Pastor Mateo, in case he'd forgotten to eat again, as he often did.

Though somewhat solitary and sober, Pastor Mateo was no man's Sunday morning sermonizer. He'd traded a comfortable life in Mexico City to bring guidance and salvation to the people of Almas Perdidas, armed with the unshakeable faith of a man who has seen the worst of sin and survived. In his waning years, he was compelled to impart this faith and fighting spirit to others.

The pastor was rehearsing his speech for the fiestas when a rifle shot pierced the calm. Raul Lopez charged into the plaza, with Hell not far behind him. Raul fired twice more, shrieking maniacally, "Diablos!! Diablos!! Sound the alarm! RUN! Madre de Dios!! DIABLOS!!" Shock gave way to panic as the muffled ringing of hurtling hooves reverberated in the distance.

Without hesitation, Pastor Mateo shot to his feet and rushed to the bell tower. The old preacher wasted no time, climbing the stairs two at a time. His ragged, shallow breath was lost in the creaking of the wobbling staircase as it slapped against the ancient adobe. He wrapped the heavy rope around his forearm and heaved, again and again. An ominous clanging of bells resounded in the plaza, weak at first, then deafening, calling the villagers to arms.

Chaos erupted and the icy paralysis of horror rapidly turned into an hysterical stampede for safety. Frantic mothers gathered terrified children and the infirm, pressing them to make haste and seek shelter in the home of Rosa Ruiz. Doors and windows were shuttered and bolted, barricading them inside.

No strangers to sudden attack from flesh-eaters and roving zombie hordes, the younger men and women carried rifles, machetes and pitchforks, taking up familiar posts in doorways and on rooftops. Raul tethered his horse and joined with five of the strongest men, charged with protecting the church. When the defenders were inside, the pastor threw a heavy wooden beam across the doors, then knelt before the altar to pray.

For the space of a heartbeat, time stood still. Confused dogs began to whine and bark, then slunk away at a resounding pound of hurtling hooves that echoed from the walls like a raging river. Savage shrieks shook the ground as Hadriel's legion closed in from every direction, ripping and clawing in a mindless, surging swarm of bloody carnage. Screeching in hollow, inhuman wails, a ravening torrent of teeth and talons swept the village until not a soul in the street was left alive.

Huddled in Rosa's home, women wrapped terrified children in their arms and wept silently, knowing the crumbling adobe walls offered no protection against the monsters outside. Bored with the mutilated meat on the ground, the hellions pounded on Rosa's barricaded door, hungry for the mind-numbing fear that glazed the ragged edges of every exquisite moment of their terror and suffering.

Hadriel buried his disgust with the witless hellions. Lips pressed tightly together, he snapped impatiently, "Not yet, imbeciles. Until the Book is in our hands, these people may prove useful in negotiations. For now, we leave the buildings be." Facial muscles twitched involuntarily as his eyes flickered to a gold cross perched over the church doors. "All except for one."

Flanked by three of the most ferocious Fallen, Hadriel took his time, advancing slowly. Pastor Mateo joined hands with the six defenders, leading them loudly in prayer, "Our father who art in Heaven..."

Issuing a shrieking torrent of howling and curses, the riders circled the church. Old nails ripped from the frame with a fearful screech when the church doors tore from their hinges in an ear splitting explosion of splintered wood. Massive stained glass windows rattled, then exploded inward in a raining shrapnel of jagged glass as frenzied horses leapt into the church, frothing at the mouth. Heartbreaking screams of anguish rent the air. Sharp, steely hooves crashed down again and again, trampling the men to death in a whirlwind of shredding flesh and bone. Loved ones, trapped behind the barricades, covered their ears but could not shut out the tortured wails.

Pastor Mateo showed no fear, never ceasing his prayers for the dead. Hadriel dismounted, releasing an incensed roar that reverberated like a thunderclap. Long, sharp talons tore at the preacher's flesh, rolling him over on his back. The frustrated Fallen raised a heavy boot and brought it down hard on Pastor Mateo's fragile chest, snapping his scapula and most of his ribs with a sickening crunch. Wedging the old man's head between powerful hands, he flung him viciously about the room amid hoarse howls of rage until the head finally snapped from the body, spraying blood across the pews.

A reedy piping of wind echoed off bloodied walls like the fragile songs of martyred saints. Hadriel clutched a long pike, holding Pastor Mateo's head in a bloody-knuckled grip. He reined his horse to a stop, pausing in the shattered, wooden doorway. A second Fallen moved into step beside him, bearing a pike with the head of Raul Lopez, his sightless eyes staring vacantly.

Villagers cowered as the Fallen paraded through the village, two severed heads shimmering wetly in waves of heat rising off the bloodied street. Sundown haloed battered edges of the desolated church. If Rev had been accurate in his assessment, the Catholic Transport coach would be arriving soon.

A vulture soared overhead breaking an otherwise oppressive silence. Sharp shadows lengthened, shrinking back into the walls until the final glare of blistering sun wavered and dipped below the horizon. Bright threads of tangerine and crimson mingled with heavy overcast and black wisps of sulfur, rolled in as the night deepened. What remained of the village settled into a desolate emptiness that slumped across a rubble of corpses and destruction.

Out on the mesas, the hours crawled by slowly, with no sign of the transport coach. Unblinking and full of unsated bloodlust, the better part of Hadriel's legion prowled the perimeters of

Almas Perdidas. A persistent whine of coyote song was occasion-
ally broken by high-pitched, terrified screams when a stray dog,
or one of the miserable cowards who had fled the massacre, was
ferreted out and devoured.

The Diablo Rojo Cantina served as the last watering hole for
stagecoaches heading south into a vast, unbroken expanse of
desert. As such, liquor shelves were kept well-stocked and
larders were brimming with food staples like beans and dried
jerky. It was regrettable that all the fancy girls had been eaten,
but tequila was plentiful.

Hadriel slouched onto a wobbly stool and propped his elbows
on the bar. His bloodshot eyes bulged with frustration. He was
not accustomed to waiting and it was starting to bring out the
bad side of his ugly nature. To make matters worse, there had
been a composed resolve on the preacher man's face, even as the
head snapped from his body. The Fallen couldn't shake the
feeling that, somehow, the old bastard had beat him and it left an
empty space that throbbed like an open wound.

By the third bottle of tequila, Hadriel grew increasingly
belligerent and agitated. He stretched an arm across the bar,
gesturing at a nervous skin boy to toss him a fourth bottle.
Snatching the tequila, he jerked his head back and siphoned the
last drop, then slung the empty bottle at Rev and snarled
viciously, "What do you think, boy? Starting to look like that
transport coach might not be coming? Don't screw with me,
halfbreed. I'm a lot more Fallen than you'll ever be, with a lot
more muscle than you'll ever have."

Rev's stony eyes flashed crimson. He choked back the resentment rising in his throat and answered impassively, "I'm never
wrong about these things, Hadriel."

Just after midnight, the oppressive overcast lifted some. Visi-
bility sharpened rapidly and anemic streams of moonlight broke
through the heavy cloud cover in fits and starts. A churlish
hellion squatted atop the mesa, wolfing down the last of Raul
Lopez's goats. Satisfied with himself, he wiped his bloody hands

on the knees of his pants and resumed his lookout position, grumbling to himself, "Damn right, I ate every last one of them and if you have a problem with that, you can kiss my unholy ass." Skin boy, that's what the Fallen had called him. Arrogant bastard, thinking he was better than the demons who served him.

The rambling tirade died in his throat as a faint rustle of hoofbeats sounded in the distance. The jittery hellion screwed his bloated face into a squint, anxiously scanning the skyline, quite certain he'd spotted two wavering pinpoints of light in the dust. His teeth clamped shut when he heard the distant, thundering clatter of a transport coach fast approaching from the north. Seconds later, he cried out as it broke through the clouds of dust, pulled by six steaming, black horses wrapped in a fiery haze of light from the coach lamps. The air vibrated with the ringing of hooves burning into the road, ripping rocks and vegetation from the ground and flinging them wildly into the air.

The coach closed the distance at an alarming pace and fear spread through his body like an infection. Spurred to action, he howled a warning signal to the others and stumbled to his horse, waving his sombrero and shouting like a lunatic. His yowling wails were amplified by a chorus of demonic howling rolling in from the outposts. Unabated, the hellish clamor intensified, rising in pitch and timbre until it echoed from the walls of Diablo Rojo Cantina.

The horrified coach driver cringed, his pale, craggy face pouring with sweat. Stories of bloodthirsty bandits, and worse, that haunted these remote regions slithered under his skin, setting off a surge of adrenaline that exploded in his brain. His only hope would be to outrun them and seek help in Almas Perdidas.

Faltering and nauseous, the determined driver stood from his bench and snapped the whip over his head with a sharp, resounding crack, urging the terrified horses forward at a full gallop. The violent screeching sounds of wooden wheels slamming and shaking on rutted terrain were muffled by a loud pounding of hooves as the travelers rushed from the darkness, plunging into Almas Perdidas.

Startled, the trembling driver tilted his head, filling his nostrils with the foul, pungent odor of sulfur and rotting meat. His mouth flew open in a silent scream. The horror stretched out in front of him sunk to the marrow of his bones. Grappling to keep his balance while the shuddering carriage rocked back and forth on a tangle of corpses, he bellowed at the top of his lungs, "Hee-Yaw", and cracked the whip once more. The coach picked up speed, hurtling recklessly over the carnage at a breathless pace.

Muzzle flash from a shotgun blast briefly illuminated a host of demons waiting in the shadows. A second shot shattered the harness linking the horses and pitched the carriage off its wheels, slamming it down hard on the suspension. Frantic, the driver struggled to untwist the reins from his grasp. He released a strangled scream, the kind of scream of those not long for this world, as the panicked animals charged into the desert in a furor of galloping hooves, dragging his crushed and bloodied body behind them.

The driverless coach careened out of control. Crashing into a water trough it flipped into the air and plummeted to its side in a battered chaos of splintered wood and flying wheels.

Hungry hellions quickly ran the horses to ground, dragging them back to the wreckage. One of the fallen peered into the ragged gash where a door had been. He cocked his head with mild interest and sniffed the air, relishing the tart, bitter sting of fear. He supposed it was better that the priest and nuns were still alive. Hadriel would be pleased. After a moment, he whistled at a couple of skin boys, instructing them to bind the hands and feet behind their backs, then drag the unconscious bodies over to the Diablo Rojo.

Once the holy baggage disappeared inside the cantina, the quiet street shocked to life. Hellions swarmed the carriage, their eager faces glistening and greedy as they scavenged through wreckage in a feverish attempt to locate the Book. Mounting frustration smoldered in their slitted eyes when the search came up empty.

For a fleeting moment things seemed smooth and glazed over like the remnants of a dream, then Father Amantino's eyes rolled open, every thought snapping into high definition. The blurring faded and his surroundings snapped crisply into focus. His shoulder sockets screamed and he realized that he and the Sisters were tied up, face down on what smelled like the floor of a saloon.

At least two ribs had been broken and his chest strained when he fought to fill his lungs. A foul, pungent smell of sulfur and dust filled his nostrils. The priest gagged back his queasiness and raised his head to get a good look at his captors. He locked eyes with the Fallen, Hadriel. Mentally crossing himself, he thanked God that he had only been called upon to assist and was not in possession of the Book.

Hadriel rocked back and forth on the rickety bar stool, tapping his foot impatiently. His temples pulsed as fragments of the day rattled and coiled in his mind. When the priest raised his head, Hadriel sat erect and grew deadly calm. He snorted and grinned enthusiastically, "Padre! I was hoping you weren't dead! See, I have a proposition for you that I think you're gonna like. Because I'm feeling generous tonight, I'm gonna let you rescue all those helpless women and children cowering behind flimsy doors, just waiting for someone to save them. I already know you don't have the book, so you won't be giving anything up. It's simple, tell me who has the Book and you and the girls walk out of here alive. What do you say? Do we have a deal?"

Father Amantino gripped the Fallen in a steely gaze and found his voice, "Exorcizamus te...omnis immunde spiritus..."

Hadriel shrieked and lunged at him, kicking viciously at his head and body until the priest fell silent. Faltering between bargaining power and the instinctive compulsion to pull the priest's intestines out through his nose, he decided that nothing short of an act of Grace could save the bastard now. Still seething, he gagged the four hostages and slung them into a small, cramped food pantry.

The Fallen swiveled abruptly to face Rev, flinging a dangling strand of saliva into the boy's face. The tracker swiped at the spittle, his expression devoid of emotion. Angered by the lack of response, Hadriel hissed, "Call your hellhounds, halfbreed. I need a message delivered to Archbishop Declan McQuade at the El Paso Diocese. NOW, you cretin!" Rev studied his fingernails impassively and shrugged in solemn agreement.

SILENCE SWAMPED OVER ALMAS PERDIDAS LIKE A SLOW-ACTING poison.

# 5

DULL, leaden moonglow left a brassy glare on the highly polished marble floors, draining the room of color. The office was expansive, high and narrow, charged with a compelling current of mysticism and knowledge. Ornate wooden bookcases committed to weighty tomes and religious artifacts lined the walls, floor to ceiling, an oppressive quality offset by windows that were always left open when weather permitted. Tonight, the air was fresh with the faint but pleasant smell of rain.

A slow turning ceiling fan filled the office with the bitter smell of boiling hot coffee. Archbishop McQuade would not be getting much sleep until the Gates Of Hell were sealed.

He clenched his jaw, breathing evenly as he thumbed through the notes on his desk, impassively dissecting the details of his meeting with the vampire, Goodnight. He dug deep to picture a chain of events where a blasphemer could be the only hope for Christianity. His higher mind refused to accept the continuity, throwing it back at him in esoteric questions.

Common sense told him to stake the bloodsucker and escort the coach himself. His lips hardened, then melted into a smile, a sort of dead smile. Despite his disquiet, it was hard to ignore the extraordinary smitings in Acuna and Whiskey Lick. The gunslinger had an extensive knowledge of the Zona De Silencio and every abomination it contained, yet he'd accepted the task without regard to the gravity of danger. The Archbishop steeled his resolve, now firmly convinced that this flexible truce with the vampire was the only practical option to put an end to the scourge.

At once, he heard the metallic clank of a lever and a muted whisper of cylinders turning. The heavy office door swung silently open on its well oiled hinges. Though filled with foreboding, the Archbishop did not once consider calling out for help, reaching for the shotgun under his desk instead. A cursory scan of darkness beyond the door frame yielded no results. Not a man or animal could be seen, nothing but a deep, pervasive silence which he broke with a threatening shout, "Who's out there? Show yourself coward!" Only the echoes of his own voice in the void replied. When it became apparent that his efforts to communicate were futile, he pulled a rosary from beneath his robe and began to pray.

A pack of what appeared to be mutant wolves or coyotes snarled and grunted, cackling like hyenas as they emerged from the darkness, slinking around the perimeters of the room in an almost ritual dance of tightening circles.

The Archbishop counted thirteen, then shouldered the shotgun. They were enormous, with exaggerated muscling. Some looked to stand at least five feet tall or more at the shoulder. All had extended claw-like talons and missing patches of fur that exposed greenish gray skin, leathery and reptilian. A stiff ridge of hair ran from back to hindquarters and several had thin, transparent bat-like wings protruding from the shoulder blades.

They turned to face him with a precision of movement that made his spine tingle. Sunken eyes, red and smoldering, met his challenge with a stony, piercing stare. Long, writhing tongues smeared with blood and saliva darted in and out between the razor sharp teeth of a stubby, wrinkled muzzle.

Unshaken, the Archbishop lightly squeezed the trigger sending a shining silver bullet whizzing inches from their heads into the wall behind them with a loud bang that echoed through the room. Furious howls were drowned to silence by the second roar of the shotgun. He rapidly reloaded and stood his ground. He had their attention.

A sibilant whispering filtered through the air. The largest of the pack held a folded paper between its jagged yellow teeth. The brute padded slowly up beside him and released the letter on his desk. Then, as quickly as they'd appeared, they bounded through the open windows and vanished into the deep, black Texas night.

The Archbishop held the shotgun to his shoulder for a good fifteen minutes, until he was sure the dust had settled and they wouldn't be coming back. Then he picked up the letter. The paper was dark crimson, embossed with what looked like dried blood mixed with bits of flesh. It was hot to the touch so he scooped it up with the sleeve of his robe and held it under the lamp for a better look.

He read the letter twice, then let out a deep sigh and slumped back into his plush office chair, shaking his head. It was going to be a long night. The letter was from a Fallen named Hadriel. He idly wondered if, when angels take the plunge, God makes sure they land on their head. The message opened with, "The rabbit can declare sanctity, but it's a wash unless the hawk signs off on it. Don't you agree, Padre?" It was pretty much downhill from there.

The Fallen, Hadriel, had intercepted a coach transporting the support team to the Monasterio. Now he wanted to trade his hostages for the Book. As maintained by twisted demon logic, it made perfect sense as one was useless without the other. It was generously added that, perhaps, the church could steal the Book again in the future.

Mercifully, the demonic legion was unaware that there were two priests sanctioned to complete the ritual. After Goodnight delivered the primary team and the Gates were sealed, he supposed he would have to hire the vampire a second time to rescue the hostages. Mysterious ways, indeed.

The Archbishop grimaced. There had been no response from the monasterio since the breach was discovered. This could be due to the remote location, so he had continued messaging the nuns to keep them updated. He wasted no time in sending a wire explaining the hostage situation. With some reluctance, he requested that the vampire escorting the primary team contact him immediately upon arrival.

It was late morning when Creed rode up to the Catedral Del Espiritu Santo. A sturdy, private coach, glossy black with silver crosses nailed to either side, was hitched to six anxious black horses. They snorted and pawed at the ground, waiting obediently for their passengers.

His face cracked into a wide grin. Could be the silver crosses were for ballast because they meant nothing to him, never had. Still, seeing as half the fee went to settling debts, he sure as hell wasn't gonna be the one to tell them that. He checked straps securing gear and extra provisions on top, then tethered Cuchillo to the luggage boot in back.

Creed shuddered with a deep sigh, dreading the four solemn figures waiting on the steps, sober black vestments starkly contrasted against a vivid white. The priest stepped forward. A clear, measured cadence resonating in his voice, he identified himself as Father Candido Fantoni. His demeanor was unexpectedly powerful and driven, more than his soulful smile would suggest. Even more disturbing was the thin metal case handcuffed to the man's right wrist. That made the hair on Creed's arms stand up and dance.

Lips pulled tight, the priest introduced his charges, Sister Celeste, Sister Mary Agnes and Sister Constance, not much more than a child. It's always best to let folks know who's calling the shots at the onset, so the gunslinger moved in to shake Father Fantoni's hand and was immediately taken aback by the firm, almost painful strength of the priest's grip. Eyes narrowed with suspicion, he nodded to each nun in turn, hesitating at Sister Constance to comment, "We'll, aren't you just the sweetest little ray of sunshine, sugar?" Sister Constance blushed crimson and a faint giggle escaped her lips.

Father Fantoni's steely eyes emanated a fierce intensity. He answered for the girl in a controlled timbre, "We are moved by your efforts to put us at ease, Mister Goodnight, however the Sisters of the Monasterio De Los Angeles have sworn a vow of silence, complete silence. They listen for the word of God, contemplate the mysteries of salvation..." The priest's eyes squeezed shut. He cleared his throat and continued, "And stand as a bulwark against heresy and evil. I am permitted to speak on their behalf, but please do not address them directly as they might be tempted to reply, breaking that vow."

Creed was not inclined to wait around for the word of God. He was perched on the driver's bench, studying his fingernails, before instinct forced him to cut and run. When the passengers were seated, he howled defiantly, snapping the whip with a sharp crack. The horses powered forward and soon they were hurtling into Mexico at bone-jarring speed.

Seats and windows squealed, vibrating with each bounce of the suspension as the desolate scrublands coursed past them. Just outside of Purgatorio, Creed was startled from reverie when a coach window slammed down with a loud clang. A quick glance over his shoulder showed Sister Constance forcing her body through the small opening. She got as far as her waist and stopped, staring at something out in the desert, pointing at it as if calling it to her.

He muttered a low, threatening snarl and clutched the shotgun at his side. His feral eyes blazed, scouring the scorched wastelands for zombie stragglers, or maybe bandidos looking to cash in on that fancy metal case handcuffed to the priest's wrist.

A simpering giggle filtered through the clouds of dust. Most times, nobody played him for a fool and lived. He let his gaze shift sharply back over his shoulder, fully intending to give that crazy nun a piece of his mind.

Sister Constance's spine cracked as she twisted to face him. Her face was bulbous and distorted, barely recognizable. She swayed silently back and forth, mocking his shocked scowl and grinning maniacally. Blood trickled from the corners of her mouth, soaking her vestments. There was a ferocity in her eyes that seemed to reflect every evil ever witnessed. Those eyes had ceased to be a part of this world, entirely. He caught a noxious whiff of rotten eggs that told him everything else he needed to know. Damn demons never knew when to give it a rest. The barrel of the shotgun jerked upward. A single bullet through the forehead launched the little hellion back to whatever cesspit had spawned it.

Purgatorio appeared from the darkness. A thin scattering of lights grew larger on either side as they careened into the town square. The incessant thumping of Sister Constance's lifeless body, dangling from the coach window, was lost in the screeching spark of iron-rimmed brakes scraping hard against the wheels. The sweaty horses reared up, nostrils flaring from exertion, and the coach stuttered to a stop in a pounding wave of rubble.

Shrill wails ripped the air, shattering the silence. Father Fantoni forced the coach door open and lurched forward incoherently, head teetering at an unnatural angle. Bloody spittle drooled thickly from a swollen tongue. His bloodshot eyes bulged insanely, then rolled back into his head. The frantic priest dug sweaty fists into the folds of his garments and began shredding the vestments to tatters, exposing himself while confessing all manner of blasphemous sins.

Locals started gathering to see what all the fuss was about. They cleared a path to let the priest pass while he thrashed disjointedly, dancing back and forth like a marionette, oblivious to the vile obscenities spewing from his mouth. There was an enthusiastic smattering of cheers and applause when Creed cocked the shotgun and sent him back to Jesus.

The coach door creaked and swung wide. Creed spat disgustedly, it was a sure cinch what he'd find waiting inside. He pinched his nostrils to lessen the stench of body fluids and sulfur. Sister Celeste and Sister Mary Agnes were leaning together on the seat in a spreading puddle of blood dripping from wounds where the bodies had been gnawed. Shreds of flesh still clung to the bone. Their vacant eye sockets gaped obscenely, trapped in a final moment of terror.

A dark thrill of rage coursed through him. Creed bristled and slammed his fist against the door. What had he expected with demons in the mix? They'd fucked him again. His glare intensified with animal cunning. Those Catholic zealots had coughed up a serious payday to deliver a priest and three nuns to the Monasterio De Los Angeles. Damn if he didn't intend on doing just that. Nothing in the arrangement said they had to be breathing.

Creed clenched his teeth, then dragged the priest's body back to the coach and heaved it in, leaving a bloody trail on the rutted cobblestones. The younger nun's upper torso was still wedged in the window, sagging from the dead weight. He tipped his hat, propped a bootheel against the wheel and shoved hard, adding her to the pile.

Abruptly, he pushed away from the wheel and leveled the shotgun in a single, fluid motion, startling a collective gasp from nervous onlookers. He fanned it across them and hissed with a croaking bray, "Now, here's what's going to happen. What you have witnessed here is an unfortunate accident. I'll be transporting the last remains of these holy folks to the Monasterio De Los Angeles, under protection of the Catholic church. Any man fool enough to follow me is fool enough to join the pile." His eyes swept the crowd. If he read their expression correctly, this was one thing they could all agree on.

Creed was growing impatient with the whole alliance. While it would make an entertaining story to share back at the blood bordello in El Paso, all this church business had nothing to do with him. Far too much time had been wasted already and he was eager to collect his purse and head back. Though disquieting, he dismissed the urgency in the villager's eyes. It's not like he was the witless fool that opened the floodgates in the first place. If they had a bone to pick regarding the demonic infestation, let them take it up with the Archbishop. Oh that's right, His Grace was probably catching a nap back in El Paso.

The thought of sleep reminded him that Cuchillo had been tied to the back of a speeding coach since early morning, forced to keep up at an unwavering pace. Most likely he was in need of food and water to boot. Creed didn't need to sleep often but the other horses could probably use a good rest as well before they headed into the Zona. He walked to the back of the coach and untied the exhausted horse, gently stroking his mane. " Don't worry boy, we'll take it nice and slow. You can run alongside the coach while we find a place to hole up."

He lowered the shotgun and turned to face the crowd, attempting a friendly grin which still looked a lot like a disturbing grimace. "Say, would any of you upstanding citizens happen to know of a place this side of the Zona where I can rest the horses and pass the night?"

It seemed they had anticipated his question. An elderly man removed his sweaty sombrero and stepped forward. He reached his gnarled fingers into a pocket and produced a tattered map that had yellowed with age. Reluctantly, he admitted that, if Creed was so keen to find death, there might be a place, but he must first listen to the warnings. Were he to follow the trail due west for a few miles or so, he would come upon a crossroads. There would be an isolated swing station there that once provided food and shelter for travelers headed into the Zona. Moreover, it was possible he might find supplies there to carry him through the journey, but he must take only what he could carry, then leave at once.

Should he chance to fall into company with creatures venturing out into the Zona, it would end badly for him. However, the diabolical abominations that haunted that deserted station were to be feared doubly so.

No doubt, the villagers would have kept him there all night had he not clapped the old man on the shoulder, thanked him for the map and headed out. Creed continued at a brisk pace until he could no longer hear the man's protestations, then turned to look. He was still waving and pointing in the opposite direction, indicating Creed should head back to El Paso.

## 6

THE WASHED out trail was a testimony to the raw horror awaiting misguided fools headed into the Zona. Creed squinted to avoid heaps of emptied suitcases and carpetbags piled in the road. The luggage had been rifled through, robbed of valuables and hastily discarded. Swarms of flies were stuck to grinning skulls and scattered bones, bleached white by the merciless sun. The work of bandits, most likely, cannibals from the looks of things.

Common sense told him to remain focused, but Cuchillo, no longer restrained, had other ideas. Creed's weathered face cracked into a broad smile, watching him whinny and prance, keeping pace with the coach at a high-stepping gallop. The stallion's powerful hooves pressed hard into the sandy soil, raising clouds of dust that masked all traces of their passing.

Deep ruts carved into the road from years of travel, meant the trail was still discernible for the most part, though obscured on occasion by thick scrub and massive chunks of Saguaro cactus uprooted by storms, likely teeming with all manner of poisonous snakes. The trail frequently crossed through ominous patches of dark, brackish sludge, which kept him on his guard.

Such stagnant, murky pools, afforded refuge to countless predators that would make even the bravest heart tremble.

He soon lost track of time, all evidence of life outside the desert had vanished entirely, swallowed up by a heavy overcast with only a few small fragments of gray sky showing through. The cloying odor of rotting vegetation was stifling. He had to swallow hard to choke back the nausea. Braced by thoughts of the Archbishop's generous offer, he ran a sweaty hand down the stock of his shotgun and forged ahead.

At last, as the final traces of light were fading from the sky, he pulled into a clearing overhung with sticky fungus and ancient mesquite trees. From the moment Creed caught sight of the swing station, he was filled with unease. Wisps of dirty fog creeping along the foundations, muttered in sere, rasping whispers. There was no welcoming smoke curling from the chimneys, no livestock or dogs barking, nothing but a profound desolation. His dry tongue swiped at a thin line of sweat on his upper lip, and he advanced cautiously.

A twisted tangle of roots enveloped most of the exterior. It was apparent that the windows had been shuttered and boarded over for quite some time. Splintered wood, blackened with mold, framed the entry where the door had been kicked in and now hung limply from its hinges. Creed concluded that this must be the station that the old man warned him about.

No sooner had he crossed the threshold than he found a faded note, hastily scribbled in what could only have been dried blood, nailed to the inside of the door. It confirmed his suspicions. "Traveler, I entreat you, pray for the soul of Cedric Vincent, keeper of this station. Take leave of this foul place at once. Above all else, do not pass the night here or it will be your last."

It wasn't that Creed didn't believe the old man's warnings. It was more about the fact that he was a vampire and most likely more dangerous than anything that might be inhabiting this station. Heavy fatigue now threatened to overwhelm the horses and they would need rest if he intended to make the monasterio by tomorrow. Besides, these walls and the stables next to them had to be safer than what lay in wait outside them.

First things first. He stabled the horses, leaving plenty of food and water from provisions packed atop the coach. Cuchillo was left free to decide where he wanted to sleep. Creed was glad when he stayed behind with the others to rest. He didn't expect to see his weary companion again until morning. Things would be different tomorrow. He could dump the coach at the monasterio and he and Cuchillo would ride back to El Paso together.

The sun had just set. He put to use the last vestiges of light to inspect his surroundings. He had already decided to get a little shut-eye himself and settled on a chamber directly adjacent to the main room to spend the night in. This was mostly because it contained the only bed in the station as well as a small night table with the remnants of a candle stuck fast to the surface in a puddle of hardened wax. Further exploration turned up a lantern which he used to investigate a second, empty bedchamber, a kitchen and a storeroom with a rickety ladder leading down to the cellar.

Most travelers probably searched the station to reassure themselves that the premises were free of devils, but in truth, Creed was more intent on finding something with a little blood in its veins. It had been quite some time since he'd last eaten. For this reason, he suppressed his misgivings and descended the shaky ladder.

The moldering cellar appeared to be a hub of some sort, connected to a series of passages burrowed into the earthen walls, each of which tapered into darkness. He found nothing to ease his hunger, not so much as a rat, merely dust and decay. He tried not to think of who had used these tunnels, or to what purpose, and climbed back up into the storeroom.

As the night grew darker, the oil in his lantern dwindled and began to sputter. At that point, he decided to call it a day and hit the sack. Instinct told him to ditch this funhouse at the first light of dawn, after the horses were rested up.

The bed was a filthy, rumpled mess. It crossed his mind that he might find something to snack on hiding in the bedcovers. He gave the blankets a hard shake and damn if a bottle of red wine didn't just roll right out. Not what he'd expected, but gratifying just the same. After placing his prize on the night table, within arm's reach, he extinguished the lantern and crawled into bed. An anemic smudge of moon, magnified by the greasy window, offered scant illumination. He would have preferred a brighter light, but thought it best to preserve what little oil remained in the lantern, in case he needed to torch his way out.

The hunger, which still tormented him, kept him from sleep. A slow, evil grin played around the corners of his mouth, seems it was true what folks said, no rest for the wicked. Twisting in the sweat-soaked sheets, dark thoughts pulsed in his brain. The hellspawn attack on the transport coach happened real damn quick, almost like it was planned. Hell, they could be tracking him right now. Oh yeah, the sinister tunnels down in that cellar were ripe for an ambush. Still, the sad, fearsome warning nailed to the door indicated that those tunnels belonged to something else, maybe something waiting for him to close his eyes. Creed sneered, "Fuck that. Let 'em come." He opened the wine and drained the bottle.

His hand flew to the Colt at an unexpected rustling in a far corner of the room. Instantly sober, he snarled and lit the candle on the bedside table. Just as suddenly it went out. He felt a transient shiver which made his blood run cold.

There was a slight tug at the blanket, then he heard a melodic, feminine voice, "I too am lost in this wretched desert. I have been so very frightened, dear soldier, let me join you under your blankets." She spoke these last words in such a cruel, impish way, Creed slapped his forehead, realizing that the fugitive witch, Rebecca Surette, had totally slipped his mind. He'd lay money that the murderous bitch had left the cursed wine for him to find.

At once dazed and feverish, he felt a great heaviness wash

over him. A loud rushing filled his ears. He blinked repeatedly as the veins at his temples began to swell. All his muscles ached, growing weaker with an unbearable numbness. Beads of sweat stung his eyes, blurring his vision, and the room began to spin.

The witch inched closer, shadowed in the half-light. Malice undulated from her body in waves, like a rattlesnake, sending tremors deep into his bones. Frustrated by the heaviness in his limbs, he lunged at her and fell back on the bed. He found himself unable to move as the dreadful creature crept slowly onto the bed. A vague, unfamiliar panic seized him as she slid her half-naked body over his, pressing her lips inches from his face, close enough that he could taste her foul breath when she simpered, "How dare you darken this door, piteous miser. You would have done better to die in your petty, little war."

Creed caught the glint of a carving knife clutched in her right fist and thought, *"Oh come on, bitch! Dead man's blood? Whose was it, your husband's or your children's?"* Swift, paralytic shock swept his body. Rebecca twisted to her knees, towering over him, and pointed the dagger at his heart. At that instant, the bedroom door cracked inward on its hinges, diverting her attention. "Thank God!" burst involuntarily from his lips.

His religious epiphany was short-lived. Hideous, bulky silhouettes emerged from the darkness, long, yellowed talons clawing at the air, all the while drawing nearer at great speed. Helpless to resist, he felt one of the obscenities seize his right ankle, dragging him from the bed. He tried desperately to move, to shake himself free, but another brute loomed up beside the first, staring at him with terrible, hollow eyes and poking out a long, gruesome tongue, dripping with gore. With one hand, the beast lifted Creed over his shoulder, as one would a child. His pace was rapid and insistent, lurching apishly through the station with an unsavory shuffle.

His captors met up with several others of their kind in the kitchen. The pain intensified, making Creed groan horribly as they descended the ladder into the cellar, but that wasn't the worst of it. Anger engulfed him, pushing all other thoughts aside, when he realized he was just another piece of meat to these bastards and they were headed down one of the nightmarish tunnels he'd seen earlier in the evening. His muddled senses, inflamed by the poisoned wine, conspired to make it feel as if every fiber of his body were on fire. Blood drained sluggishly from his face, all sensation escaping his body until, finally, everything spun to black.

Watery waves of consciousness rippled through darkness, and Creed's eyes rolled slowly open. He choked back the soured taste of saliva, thickened in his throat, and curled both hands into tight fists, digging his talons deep into the palms. The blurring had faded but his body was still sluggish and heavy from the effects of the dead man's blood. While he was not totally incapacitated, neither was he at full strength.

He was in the open air and could make out what looked to be the crumbling ruts of the Zona trail in close proximity on his right. A brief assessment of his circumstances made it clear that they had surfaced from the tunnel through an open grave. The rank odor of death and decay clung to his skin. He steeled himself against waves of vertigo threatening to force him back under. Tensing against the shaking in his limbs, he inhaled deeply to counteract the drowsiness overwhelming him.

As the faintness gradually eased, he was revolted to find himself atop a mound of decomposing corpses, tangled in a rotted mass of fragmented bone and human remains. Winding rows of wooden crosses and crumbling stone marked graves, desecrated in like manner, stretched out to either side of him. Things were starting to make sense. The blistering desert heat cooks up the perfect breeding ground for every creeping disease in Mexico. Remote locations, like Purgatorio and surrounding villages, would need to bury their dead in a cemetery far removed from the living.

Slivers of moonlight yawned out between the shadows, exposing countless more of the vile creatures slinking out from dark holes, merciless and bloated with malice. It was damn disgusting. He would have spit if his mouth wasn't so dry. Creed Goodnight, the Big Bad, gets put down by some crazy witch, only to be captured by ghouls. At full strength, he would have sliced the whole sorry lot of them up for kindling. Fucking ghouls, of all things, lowest scumbags on the food chain!

As a rule, he didn't traffic with ghouls, but seeing as how he was still partially paralyzed, he mentally made a short list of what he did know. They were repulsive aberrations that haunt isolated graveyards, feeding from flesh of both the living and the dead. A lack of immediate interest made clear they had mistaken him for the latter.

Scant seconds later, dust choked the air, mingled with the putrid stench of decaying meat. A grave, not fifty feet away, bulged and collapsed. Grasping arms breached the contaminated ground, dragging the witch, Rebecca Surette, with them. Wild, incoherent pleas for help burst from her lips as ruptured flesh peeled away from the bone, flapping from the effort like tattered parchment. Creed bared his fangs and whispered, "Tough break, bitch."

The largest of the ghouls grasped her by the throat and plucked out her eye, then darted his wormy tongue into the bloody socket. She bellowed from the pain as if all hell shrieked with her. The ghouls turned as one, unleashing a menacing growl of mewling throats, building slowly in a feverish clamor. They shambled toward her, moldy, blackened tongues lolling and twisting between snapping yellowed teeth. Enraged at having to fight for his kill, the monster ripped her screaming head from the body and flung it. It rolled to a shaky stop, nose to nose with Creed. He smiled wickedly. "Well, hello beautiful, looks like you might be worth something after all."

Cuchillo slipped silently in from the shadows, unnoticed in the tumultuous clash over Rebecca's corpse. He dropped to his knees directly beside his friend and lowered his head. Creed grabbed a fistful of thick mane and struggled up onto the stallion's bare back, clutching the bloody head of Rebecca Surette in the crook of his left arm.

The trail was slippery, riddled with potholes and spiny cactus. Cuchillo's hooves slapped and shifted on the loose rocks, echoing sharply against the emptiness of night. Creed licked his dry, cracked lips and closed his eyes, mindful to catch any sound of pursuit. He heard nothing more than sloppy sounds of rending flesh and crunch of snapping bone.

The getaway remained undetected so far, but there was still a score to settle. Creed was starting to feel cocky and seriously pissed off. He was healing rapidly now, itching to rain payback on the whole bloated infestation. Suddenly, Cuchillo snorted, ears cocked back in concentration, then broke into a full run. All racket pouring from the ghoulish feast ceased abruptly. The seething fester of grunts and moans was replaced by frightened, ringing silence.

Albeit faintly, a piercing cascade of keening bellows in the distance soared into a salvo of baying howls that resounded from every direction. Creed leaned down and whispered in Cuchillo's ear, "Right as usual, boy. We need to shelve ghoul-smiting for the present and get that holy meat wagon back on the road."

# 7

STATIC GLARE RICOCHETED off the heat thermals, punching back into a gunmetal sky. Parting shots from a grueling sun as it plummeted below horizon, yielding to a sallow, sinister moon rising over the Zona De Silencio. Scathing night winds swept a festering infection of desert, punctured by illusive, shadowy carnivores and the gutted carcasses of slower species. Creed was in the habit of being the predator, never the prey. He didn't much care for the feeling and crossed the distance at an unflagging pace.

An arid burst of wind whipped up dust devils, briefly limiting his line of sight. The racing coach cracked against a boulder, spinning it up into the air. It wobbled erratically, then slammed back down, jolting his decomposing passengers who'd been fermenting in back since the unfortunate standoff in Purgatorio. Creed flinched at the horrible odor and let the rising desert wind in his face wipe the ripe stench of death from his nose and mouth. The taste lingered, but the gnawing creep in his gut, telling him someone was out there and closing in, was persistent.

There was no doubt that he was being followed. Nothing to

really put a finger on, just rustling movement and the slightest jingle of spurs in the distance. The bastards picked up his trail early in the morning, back at the swing station. They'd kept just out of sight all day, making no effort to conceal their presence. Hell, they wanted him to know he was being tracked. Raising up a little dust somewhere in front of him, then doubling back behind, just to make it clear that they could take him any time. Well, they could try anyway.

Might be something, maybe nothing, but he could smell them. No way of telling how many. They were bestial for the most part, musky and stinking of sulfur. Hellhounds circling their prey, if he had to guess. What he found puzzling was the scantest scent of a lone rider mingled in with the pack, definitely human, wisps of sulfur, and something else, a hell of a lot scarier than he was.

It was making his skin itch, and that was making him cranky. Creed dragged some life into his cigar and snarled viciously into the darkness through gritted teeth, "Fuck this game, you spineless stalker. I'll deal with you directly, if and when you decide to show your face, hellhounds be damned."

Cracks of heat lightning forked across a dead flat of desert, broken only by the sporadic swell of an occasional mesa. Darkness buckled and brilliant streaks of moon sliced through the heavy cloud cover, exposing a writhing nest of centipedes, each with savage, snapping jaws. The monsters spasmed then clenched tightly, twitching and clicking in a feeble attempt to stem the voracious attack of a hungry scorpion the size of a coyote. Greedy mandibles shoved chunks of meat into the scorpion's gaping maw as it shook its venomous, upraised tail, striking again and again.

The fearful horses reared and whinnied, straining at the harness. Creed pulled back on the reins, wresting control in low, soothing tones, "Whoa! Easy now, that's it!" The lathered team slowed to stop, pawing the ground nervously. Creed shook his head and shrugged, whistling with a sharp intake of breath. He might have let the monsters have at it, but they were blocking the road. There were four coach lamps, one would do the job. He grabbed the closest lantern and hurled it into the pile. The undulating mass ruptured and burst into flames. It was quiet and efficient, nothing but a putrid stench of melting flesh as the heap liquified and sank into a viscous, black pool of ichor staining the dust.

He thumbed a match and lit a fresh cigar, rolling it to the corner of his mouth. Attending to the local wildlife had burned up a good bit of time, but Creed wasn't worried about his pursuers catching up to him. The sons of bitches were clustered atop a mesa a few hundred feet down the rutted trail. That was a damn good thing because he was done with being tracked.

From where he slumped on the driver's bench, he could make out a dozen or more hellhounds positioned along the ridge, with probably a dozen more circling behind him. Well damn, he was outnumbered and out-fanged. He thought better of making the first move and slid the Colt from its holster and waved it over his head, bellowing ferociously, "I've got six in the chamber, you mangy bastards. If you're feeling froggy, come on and jump, but know this, the first bullet is gonna send your master shrieking straight back to Hell."

The menacing beasts padded silently back, clearing a path. There was a clink of stirrups and a loutish brute rode past the hellhounds and galloped down from the mesa in a plume of dust. The man reined to a halt at the bottom, sizing Creed up. There was a short pause, then he urged his horse forward with a slow, plodding clop, keeping his hands in the air, palms raised to show he meant no harm.

Creed scratched his head, choking back a laugh. He didn't know who or what his adversary was under the skin, but his baggy clothing and sweat-stained hat made him look like a farmer. What the hell, maybe he'd dodged a bullet here after all. He whistled for Cuchillo and leapt onto the stallion's back, spinning the pistol back into his holster. If this character was up for a parlay, he might as well meet him halfway.

They closed the distance, leaving less than a foot between them. The stranger relaxed back into his weathered saddle, his tone sober and contemplative, "Creed Goodnight, I see you still like to play with fire, same as you did when you torched my body back in Whiskey Lick. Yeah, I took that real personal. I liked that body, I was born with it. See, now I'm stuck inside this rotting flesh until that sumbitch Hadriel feels like giving me a new one and that really pisses me off. As you can imagine, I was all hopped up for you to die bad and bloody, harder than any blood-sucker had done before. I planned to be there when you did, laughing my ass off. But then, gears started clicking in my head. When one vampire smites an entire town of rotters and skin boys, then rides away, you need to sit up and take notice. I'm a practical man and I figure there is more to gain from a brilliant enemy than an ego-driven ally. The only true allegiance I owe is to the hellhounds."

Creed was unimpressed. He rested a hand on the Colt and thought about giving this joker a look at that little hole that sudden death comes out. A glance back at the fierce beasts cutting off his escape said it might be best to hear the stranger out. He gently slid his hand from the pistol and leaned forward. "Fire cuts to the heart of a matter, quick and clean. If it ain't broke don't fix it. You demons know how this plays out in the end but you keep on coming. No hard feelings, but it puts cash in my pocket and it's not my job to turn you away. I take it this isn't a social call." Creed's laugh was lazy and relaxed. "And you aren't here to lock horns, so make it quick. Something I can help you with, son?"

The stranger locked eyes with Creed, holding his stare a few seconds longer than necessary while his steely gaze slid across the vampire's face. Hesitation flickered in his smoldering eyes, then he grinned wide, like they were old friends. "I'm no demon, Goodnight. The name's Reverend Jim, throwback from a human mother, but you can call me Rev. My father was a Fallen, same as Hadriel, something our swaggering legion commander tends to forget. Now, the difference between me and my brimstone sire is that he chose to take the fall. I never have, so I'm not entirely sure what that makes me. Being as I was raised by hellhounds, there's one thing you can lay money on, I'm the best damn tracker that ever was."

Rev went silent, staring past Creed at the hellhounds poised behind him. Suddenly, his tongue clicked against the roof of his mouth and a calculated sneer jerked up the corners of his mouth. "I'll give it to you straight. I know you have the Book, vampire, I can smell it. The point is, I could have taken it from you back in Purgatorio and left your meat for the hounds. But I suppose there's always time for that later, if we can't come to an accord."

Creed's eyes narrowed suspiciously, bulging with dispute. This Reverend Jim was a cocky bastard, but not entirely unjustified given the beasts at his back. He couldn't say what book the kid was rambling on about, but from the sound of it there might be a hefty reward. He'd look into it once the coach had been delivered to the monasterio. Creed shifted the cigar to the other corner of his mouth and growled, low and slow, "Maybe I could send you and those mutts of your back to daddy. Maybe not. We'll agree that's still on the table. I'm going to do you a favor and listen to what you have in mind. Well speak up, son, I haven't got all night."

Something changed in Rev's expression. He tilted his head, the vicious pools of red in his eyes deepened. When he spoke again, his words gleamed with a flinty edge, smooth as silk and soft as ashes, "I only recently returned from the last time you sent me to Hell. You should know, vampire, that there are multitudes of hungry specters, withered souls of the damned, waiting on Hadriel's word to fuck up this lucrative little deal you've got working up here. Yeah, you can bitch about how things come about, or why, but a more direct question is, what are you gonna do about it? Now I can give Hadriel the Book and make that nightmare happen before you reach the monasterio, or you can agree to three demands and I let you ride out of here.

First off, I want those Gates slammed shut bad as you do. Chasing renegade specters is a pain in my ass. I just want to be on THIS side of the seal when they do. I need a guarantee that you'll have my back when Archbishop Torquemada brings the fire down from Heaven. Secondly, you stole my skin. You need to rectify that mistake. I'm thinking the snake oil preacher that Hadriel's been riding around in would make us even. When you take the bastard down, make damn sure not to damage the body." Rev's lips tightened into a grimace and he stared at the ground.

There was an awkward silence and Creed arched an eyebrow, prompting the kid to continue, "Sounds reasonable, shouldn't pose a problem. What's the third demand?"

Rev's head jerked up and he snarled with a savage glint in his eyes, "Don't EVER call me halfbreed."

It may have been the oafish farmer that the kid was stuck in, but Creed felt almost sorry for him. The gunslinger cleared his throat and managed a straight face. His eyebrows knitted into a sober frown and he nodded in somber agreement, "On my word, Reverend Jim, we have a deal."

Rev grinned and tipped his battered hat, then spurred his horse, vanishing into the darkness. When he was safely out of sight, the hellhounds turned as one and bounded off behind him.

Somewhere in the distance, the piercing screech of a crow echoed into infinity.

# 8

---

A DUSTY HAZE furrowed the sky, bathing the moon in an ominous red hue that spilled over the open desert, tangling in a web of abstract shadows. Flies swarmed the coach, inside and out, drawn by the stench of rotting corpses. Most likely, it was attracting more treacherous predators as well, things with sharp, pointed teeth and scraping claws. The terrified horses sustained an unremitting gallop, rock and debris popping under their pounding hooves like collapsing stars.

Creed's lips were cracked and bleeding and his tongue had swollen to the roof of his mouth. A stilted, electric rush of wind permeated the air, drawing out a cold sweat across his skin like frogs after a hard rain. He had no way to judge the distance, but he was pretty damn sure they were closing in on the monasterio.

Dust filtered into his eyes and he blinked in an effort to adjust his vision. He listened intently for the crack of doom, or maybe the songs of angels. Try as he might, he couldn't get Reverend Jim and the hellhounds out of his mind. If he wasn't Fallen, what was he? A bonafide angel with an arsenal full of mojo, or just some stray nephilim barking at the Gates Of Hell?

Either way, he got the impression that the kid didn't make friends easily.

Maybe that book he mentioned was somewhere in the meat wagon he was dragging behind him. If some big shot Fallen was so fired up to lay hands on it, how much would the almighty Archbishop McQuade offer up to get it first? He was still deliberating on how to spend the money when the Monasterio De Los Angeles welled up from the dregs of darkness, rising like a fortress in front of him. Pristine white, it radiated an angelic luster against the grim and fevered sky.

Creed stiffened, his hand flying to the Colt. The gunslinger's teeth clamped shut and a warning piped up at the back of his skull. The damn gates had been left wide open and the whole place reeked of massacre. Sensing bloodshed, the horses started to panic, their frothing heads whipping back and forth in raw terror. Loud, pounding hooves jarred to a violent stop, knocking the coach into a veering slide. Ears pinned back, the horror-stricken animals reared and pawed at the ground, refusing to go any further. Creed stood in the driver's bench and whistled, then cracked the whip, bellowing in a strident voice, "YAW! GIT ON NOW!" Holding firmly on the reins with an iron grip, he urged the reluctant team forward, past the gates.

The gunslinger braced himself against thick, noxious air spiraling around him and threw his weight into it, heaving the enormous iron gates closed with a resounding clang. His fingertips were inches from the trigger, poised for a challenge. When there was none, he slid the heavy bolt, locking them in place, then unhitched the shivering horses.

Once the exhausted animals had been fed and watered, he checked the chamber on his pistol then spun the cylinder shut and slipped it back into the holster. Sun-scorched trees huddled and moaned in the ancient courtyard, protesting this violent disruption of their isolation. Scathing desert winds whipped across his face as he licked his parched lips, taking in his surroundings.

The untended monasterio sprawled eerily quiet and still.
Things didn't add up. A fancy church like this should have come
with a welcoming committee, or at least a few trigger-happy
crusaders. He snarled through his fangs and shouted menacingly,
"Hey all you cross kissers! Vampire in the courtyard! Coach full
of corpses!" There were no signs of life at all, only a deep pervasive quiet with his scathing taunts lingering in the echo.

Creed forced back a mounting hunger tightening into an
insistent knot in his stomach. Any more time wasted on this job
meant he'd be drinking from the horses soon to fuel his edge.
The way he saw it, his obligation ended just past those gates and
he was fully justified to saddle Cuchillo and ride off into the
sunset. He could collect his pay at the diocese in El Paso and
wash his hands of the whole damn trainwreck. On further
reflection, the long history between vampires and the Catholic
Church said maybe he should investigate further.

Signs pointed to an ambush and he damn sure wanted to be
holding all the cards. Carefully extracting the priest's rigid
corpse from the coach, he stretched it out on the ground.
Without a key, there was only one way to remove the handcuffs
and it's not like the man was gonna feel it anyway. Creed
removed his hat, leveled the shotgun, and blew the padre's dessi-
cated hand off. The metal case was heavy. He gave it a vigorous
shake and was rewarded by a loud "thunk".

When there was no reaction to the shotgun blast, he tossed
his prize onto the driver's bench and strode aggressively across
the courtyard, pausing at the threshold. He let his eyes squeeze
shut, ears tuned for the slightest movement. Massive oak doors,
now loose from their hinges, banged repeatedly against the
crumbling adobe facade, groaning with each sway, nothing
more.

Cautiously, Creed stepped inside, senses heightened. His foot-
steps echoed on the cold stone floors. It was difficult to make out
much in the dim lighting, but he could see enough to figure why
the gates were untended. Broken moonlight shimmering

through cracks in a stained glass window depicting the crucifix-ion. It cast a murky amber glow on dark, frozen blood stains smeared along the walls and curdled in icy puddles on the rough, wooden pews. A rustling sound in the dark recesses behind the altar made him flinch involuntarily. There was something in here with him. At once, he heard a faint heartbeat, something warm and alive.

The gunslinger rested a hand on the Colt in that fragile second before the stranger stood erect. A timid crunch of foot-steps emerged from the darkness. He blinked to make sure he wasn't dealing with an uneasy spirit, then she spoke, "Well, I knew God would send help, but truly, I was not expecting a vampire. I suppose in every sentient creature there is a hunger for justice and truth. I am Sister Anjelica Mansour, the last of three sworn to this citadel, charged to stand guardian between Man and the forces of Hell." She studied his face, genuine amuse-ment radiating from her quick smile. "No offense."

She was slight of frame and soaked to the bone. Strands of ginger hair tumbled recklessly from her wimple and matted to a delicate, heart-shaped face. What struck him most was the right-eous fire dancing in her clear green eyes. He decided he liked her and flashed a toothy grin. "None taken, but forgive me, Sister, aren't you a bit chatty for one who has sworn a vow of silence?"

Before she could reply, a mangy, brown rat scurried over the toe of his boot and into a hole in the thick adobe. His stomach rumbled and Sister Anjelica laughed dryly, shaking her head. "Yes, just so, but that's a bit like closing the stable door after the horse has bolted. Now, first things first. You'll need your strength if you're going to help me tend to Father Fantino and the Sisters." The petite nun walked briskly, stopping directly in front of him, then pushed up the sleeve of her robe and extended an arm.

Creed threw his palms up and backpedaled nervously. His feral green eyes widening in shock, he stammered, "We need to be clear here, ma'am. I'm an evil blood drinker, the Big Bad. Well, maybe not THE Big Bad, but I'm sure as hell on the list! You're not the least bit scared of me?"

Her chin jutted outward and she thrust her arm closer to his face. "Even the Big Bad requires an act of mercy on occasion, mister vampire. If he believes he is doing good, he becomes a part of God's divine plan. Unless, of course, you believe that you are doing bad. Then you would be a monster. Do you believe that you are doing bad?"

Creed wavered, giving the question his full attention. He'd dealt his fair share of death, never once killing an honest man. Not that he'd given it much thought, but truth be told, he'd probably saved a heap of innocents in the process. He removed his hat, looked her square in the eye and shook his head, "No ma'am." Arms spread to his sides, he dropped to his knees and bared his fangs, gently piercing the skin of her wrist. He tasted her blood on his tongue then cringed back, staring wildly around the chapel.

Sister Anjelica broke into a fit of girlish laughter. She caught her breath and smiled, "I assure you, I am neither an angel nor a saint. Now, hurry up, you aren't going to burst into flames."

The lingering taste of blood in his mouth roused a powerful thirst. He clutched her frail arm in both hands and sank his fangs deep into her wrist, letting the sweet warmth fill his veins. The rush of blood made him dizzy, it took everything he had to push back. Feeling suddenly clumsy, Creed swallowed hard and got himself upright, unsure of what to say to a nun he'd just fed on. Nothing came to mind so he dusted off his hat, and nodded solemnly. "Much obliged, your holy sisterness. Now what can I do for you?"

Sister Anjelica's eyebrows arched wryly and she shot back quickly, " For starters, we need to burn those bodies in the coach and salt the earth so they can never return. After this has been done, we have a situation to settle in Almas Perdidas." The shine in her eyes sparked and she clapped her hands sharply, several times. " Let's shake it mister vampire, we don't have much time!"

Creed heaved a sigh of relief to hear the nun needed a bit of time to collect a few personal items for the ride before she could assist him. The situation was already awkward and it saved going into sordid details about the tangled heap of decomposing corpses. He waited until she disappeared up the stairs before walking back to the coach for a blacksmith's hammer and hauling the bloody pews out into the courtyard with vampiric speed. Cuchillo trotted over with a puzzled expression, watching calmly while he smashed the pews to kindling in a frenzied blur.

By the time that Sister Anjelica joined him, Father Fantoni and the three nuns were laid out atop a towering pyre, arms respectfully crossed. She remained silent and motionless while he doused the bodies with oil from the remaining three coach lights and struck a match on his bootheel. Crackling flames caught fire and bloomed out with a wilding hiss. The dried corpses instantly ignited, spewing twisting tendrils of fire and smoke into a starless sky.

Creed snorted and shook his head. A raging bonfire that size would alert every slithering predator or rabid hellspawn for miles. It was an amateur move he'd likely never live down. That is, if he lived. Even so, it was a damn sight better than facing off with that feisty nun.

Sister Anjelica knelt beside the pyre, reciting the rosary until the bodies were reduced to embers and buried in salt. Rising, she brushed the dust and ashes from her vestments and pointed at the metal case on the driver's bench. Creed cursed under his breath, "Well, hell!" He reluctantly retrieved the case, grumbling while she secured it inside her saddlebag.

The breeze was stale and feverish. Pale oranges streaked the sky, hinting at sunrise. It was gonna be another sizzler, but he didn't mind. It was one day closer to El Paso. He fetched provisions from the coach, then saddled Cuchillo and the lead stallion. When the saddle bags were full, he left the remaining food and water for the other five horses. She could contact the church from Purgatotio and have someone sent to collect them. By his reckoning, this damn job was done and dusted. The ground trembled under his boots as he muscled the gates open and stared out at the desert. What was it that the kid said? Something about hellbound souls waiting on their marching orders?

He startled guiltily when she walked softly up behind him. "No, time to waste," she chided sternly, "There will be no mercy if we fail and our souls are consigned to Hell." Her eyes twisted into a squint. "At the very least, mine will be. No offense."

His lips curled into a smug grin and he fired back, "None taken, and the name is Creed Goodnight. Look, sis, you're okay for a nun, but this was never a part of the deal. I'm just a paid delivery man. I'm sure as hell not the hammer of God. I'll ride with you until you're clear of the Zona. After that, it's gonna require a bit more grease on the wheel. I'm not in the habit... no offense...of jumping into things with my eyes closed. So, start talking now and make me believe it or I'm afraid you're on your own."

9

THE DISTURBANCES BEGAN with a low rumble in the ground. A rank, evil wind blew around his bedroll as night bled slowly into daybreak. Rev swatted at the flies stirred up by the commotion. His eyelids fluttered open and he filled his lungs with reflexive gasps of putrid air. The stench of rotten eggs hung in the air, leaving a residual pall that clung to his skin like a death mask. He felt a cold shiver at the base of his spine and a bead of sweat kind of rolled off his scalp and splashed on his upper lip.

Of course, he knew what had happened. As master of the hellhounds it was his job to know. When the condemned got lucky and slipped the leash, the call to damnation cut straight to his soul and hit him in the head like a hammer. Muscles twitched at the corners of his mouth. He'd been camped out next to the breach, keeping vigil for that very reason. Now, it seemed that was a good move.

An insatiable greed for power prompted all of Hadriel's decisions. There was an empty hole where his grace should have been and he was cold inside. Not the kind that comes with fresh air, but a stale cold that left him tight and listless, wiped clean of every emotion but his obsession. As long as the Book remained lost to him, he would have no interest in releasing his army of souls.

It was clear that the insurgents must have acted on their own. A blatant disregard of orders, coupled with the threat of impending torture, meant that something drastic had incited them to riot. The question was, what riled them up and how many were there?

Rev crouched down low and moved swiftly to the edge of the mesa to survey the damage. The Gates Of Hell stretched empty under a searing Mexican sun. The peripheral vicinity was rutted and desolate, not a man for miles to flinch at that crack of thunder when a soul went south. He took a measure of the specter signatures and counted Twenty-seven. It would be an easy containment.

He drew in a deep breath and paused briefly, growing reflective. It was a Friday morning that his mother dragged him down to the Pecos River so her father, Reverend Jim, could baptize him, but the son of a bitch swore it didn't take. Early Saturday morning, she put on her Sunday dress and left him at the Gates with a note to his father who art in hell. He'd tracked his mother down once, but left without confronting her. Maybe he could have loved her, she was soft and smelled like rose water, but there are some wounds you just don't bounce back from.

Nothing was gonna make him human, but he wasn't a damn demon either. The rock bottom truth being that Hell was a tedious, painful heap of repetitive brimstone and he didn't belong there. Once the gates were sealed, he'd save up some cash so that he and the hounds could disappear into the Sangre De Cristo Mountains. Maybe he'd take up painting.

Rev's jaw stiffened, the situation wasn't going to fix itself. He'd best whistle for the pack and get to it. Instinct told him the insurgents were chasing the Book. It was a short ride over to the Monasterio De Los Angeles and he could pick up the trail from there. He didn't look back, but could hear the horrible shrieks and the rending of flesh just behind the Gates.

Vultures circled the monasterio, hovering in heat thermals from a waning funeral pyre. Rev drew his pistol and signaled the pack to stay back, nudging his horse into the courtyard with a slow clop of hooves. Cast iron bells, stirred to life by a sudden rush of wind, clanged erratically with a hollow dissonance, sending a swarm of squawking vultures flapping out through the shattered stained glass windows of the chapel. The monasterio was deserted now, but the mob had been through here alright, less than two hours behind the Book.

Rev worked his jaw and spat into the dust. A dark flush of rage coursed through him, bitter with the aftertaste of resentment. Billowing spirals of yellowish gray smoke spiraled high over the imposing adobe walls, shrouding the desert for miles. In all his time as a soul tracker, playing off every half-brained mistake ever devised, never once was he called on to contain an agitated mob.

Veins pulsing at his temples, Rev screamed at the empty walls, "Creed Goodnight!" He flung the gunslinger's name like a curse. What was it with that demented vampire and fire? Stunned by the unfamiliar loss of control, Rev's cheek muscles stiffened with determination and he drew a deep breath, running thick, stubby fingers through a shock of sweaty hair. Like it or not, he had unfinished business with the dim-witted bloodsucker.

HE SHIFTED IN THE SADDLE AND TOOK A LONG PULL OF ROTGUT whiskey from the thin, metal flask in his pocket. Anger boiled in his eyes, churning through his system, then dissipating slowly as he shut out the world and weighed his situation. It was a given that the appetites driving Hadriel's compulsive obsession with power were non-negotiable. If the mercenary bastard got his claws into the Book, he'd be trapped in this clumsy rancher while the body decomposed. After that, he and the pack would be forgotten in the bowels of Hell until needed again, not that it mattered. The legion would ravage everything beautiful or inspiring in this world, then burn it down.

He didn't know, or care to know, how a vampire came to be thick as thieves with an inquisitor like the Archbishop. All he needed to know was that he and the hellhounds would be safe from the line of fire when the holy smite went down. Rev tended to take things personally and he was stuck to the idea of jacking Hadriel's ride like a dog to a bone. That should clear up any hard feelings over the mess stirred up by the pig-headed funeral pyre.

The kid slapped reins against the horse's flanks and charged after the insurgents as if Satan himself were biting at his heels. The hellhounds bristled and lowered their massive heads, sniffing out the scent of their prey, then did what they were born to do.

RAW, BLISTERING SUN BEAT DOWN UNSPARINGLY, WAVERING IN A swelter surging off the Zona floor. Creed paced the horses at an easy gallop, slowing every few miles for them to catch a breath, then resuming momentum. The sun rose by degrees. By the time noon rolled around, Sister Anjelica would be roasting inside her heavy black vestments. Rather than suggest she remove a few garments until they reached Purgatorio, he stayed alert, ready to catch her when she fainted and dropped from the stallion.

Twelve-thirty found her perfectly erect in the saddle, spine stiff and eyes rigidly fixed on the trail ahead. The ringing silence was unnerving, nothing but the creak of leather and a rhythmic clop of hooves slapping on the rugged terrain. Every so often, one of the horses grunted, but the nun hadn't spoken for hours, not since his parting shot back at the monasterio.

Torrid heat spiked with boredom can play tricks on an idle mind. He raised an ear and caught her heartbeat. Satisfied, he leaned back in the saddle. At least she hadn't just up and died in the saddle, setting up in some sort of holy rigor. Not that he would care much if she did, but it would serve him best to keep in her good graces. There were valid reasons why his passengers were dead on delivery. No need for her to get the Archbishop all worked up over the gray areas.

Creed slapped at the flies stuck to his coat and grumbled to himself, "I'll never make sense of women, with all that frilly lingerie and twisted logic. Flesh-eating monsters are a damn sight less complicated than a creature that can't just come out and tell you what's on their mind. He turned in the saddle and gave her a critical once over, frowning with bemused curiosity. Even more devious, this was no woman. No, this was one pissed off nun.

Dead certain there must be rules of conduct for situations like this, he smiled politely and took a crack at small talk, "Hot enough for you, sis?" He might as well have been hollering down an empty well. She pursed her lips into a reproving frown and glared straight ahead, refusing to meet his eyes.

Creed raked back the sweaty hair stuck to his forehead and steadied himself to confront her on the nature of her problem. By his reckoning, only bad men and money left that kind of ice in a woman and he'd damn sure done nothing to justify this childish tantrum. He cleared his throat to speak and caught movement in his peripheral vision. A wall of dust was building in the desert behind them.

Clumsy attempts to make nice seized up. Adrenaline pumped in his veins, sharpening his senses. Finally, something to smite, now that was one thing he was scary good at. He gave a short whistle and Cuchillo spun to face the onrush. Within seconds, hulking forms erupted from the dense shroud of dust with a grinding stomp, closing the distance at supernatural speed. A sustained barrage of mewling wails slicing through the air, grew in volume with unbroken fury, making clear their intent. They chanted in unison, shaking the ground like rolling thunder, BOOK! BOOK! BOOK!

Creed scratched his jaw, shifting his narrowed gaze left to

right. It was hard to make out what kind of nasty they were just yet, but there weren't that many of them, less than fifty of the sumbitches. He was outnumbered, but the dynamite packed in his saddlebag would turn the odds in his favor. His grim countenance left no room for argument when he pushed an open palm toward the wide-eyed nun, indicating that she should wait. She brushed the dust from her face and threw a worried glance up at the sky.

Creed charged the assailants at a full run, holding a stick of dynamite in each hand, clutched in an iron grip. He covered half the distance then leaned in, lighting both with the cigar clenched firmly between his teeth. When he was close enough to see the malice in their eyes, he hurled the explosives into the mob. Cuchillo reared and pivoted, hurtling away at a breakneck pace.

Shockwaves from the blast shattered the ground, lingering in tremors. A blinding, white-hot ball of fiery light swallowed the sky, launching rocks and debris in every direction. Creed ducked and shoved the nun down against the saddle, covering her body with his.

The blue-sparked odor of smoke and gunpowder choked the air, stinging brutally at his eyes. Waving the smoke away with both arms, he squinted and searched the settling dust. The explosion had bought him less than a minute. The chant resumed, louder and more ferocious, BOOK! BOOK! BOOK! Now, they were pissed off and almost within striking distance.

Creed shook his head disgustedly and cursed, "Well, hellfire!" He should have seen it before. He was up against specters, souls of the damned. Mortal weapons would have no effect. Outrunning them was off the table with Sister Anjelica in the mix. She knew it too and when he stood his ground, she shrugged and smiled gratefully. "God be with you Creed Goodnight." He slid a rugged hand over hers, squeezing tightly. "Close your eyes, Sister." She crossed herself and laid a protective hand over the saddlebag holding the Book, then did as instructed, praying fervently.

Creed leveled the shotgun in his right hand and spun the Colt from his holster with the left. This was as good a place as any to die, but he'd damn sure go out guns blazing. His lips pulled back in a fierce snarl and he charged forward with a menacing bellow, "Come on you rotten-ass bastards, let's wrap this up!" Just as suddenly, he jerked back on the reins, screaming, "EASY BOY! WHOA! WHOA!" Cuchillo whinnied shrilly and skidded to a faltering stop. The scent of hellhounds was the kind of thing you never forget. A guttural serenade of yips and howls keened distantly, swelling into sharp screeching bays that froze his blood.

The mob sniffed the air and recoiled, bleating in terror as a horse and rider thundered from the mesa, tearing up the ground with the fever of an avenging angel. He was swiftly joined by sixty-six hellhounds, bearing down on the paralyzed revenants in a merciless torrent of ruthless devastation that sent them stampeding to all sides. In a short time, the clamor of slobbering snarls and snapping jaws faded away, replaced by a violent thrashing and scraping as broken, tortured souls were dragged back to the fires of Hell.

A dead calm, wreathed in dust and gunpowder, pulsed under the burn of a setting sun. Skeletal shadows settled in as daylight drained slowly away. Visibly shaken, Sister Anjelica fought back the unshed tears welling her bloodshot eyes and quickly composed herself. Clasping her rosary in a firm grip, she dabbed at the sweat on her pallid face with the sleeve of her robe and prayed for the damned between measured breaths.

Creed had hardened his heart to acts of savagery, but never once had he come across the raw brutality of hellhounds on the hunt. It was damn sure a thing he'd never want to taste first-hand. The rider drifting toward them at an easy trot still wore the same shabby farmer's getup he'd been wearing when they'd first met up. It was dirtier now, stinking of sweat, and the skin on his face showed further signs of decay. Creed struck a match and lit a fresh cigar, blowing a steady stream of smoke to cover any reaction that might have slipped out. He leaned forward in the saddle and grinned, "That you, Reverend Jim?"

The kid fired back, "Damn right it's me, you son of a bitch! You nearly killed me with that explosion...again! How many times do you plan on pulling that little trick? Until you put me down for the last time?"

Creed wrinkled his face into a look of pained sincerity and nodded solemnly. "Yeah, damn good thing I didn't, you saved my ass out there. Much obliged. So, tell me, Rev, how did you just happen to be riding by?"

A loud rushing filled his ears and the kid bristled. He felt volatile, crazy enough to do anything, but he kept it to himself. If he pulled that thread too soon, the whole deal would unravel. He chose his next words carefully, "Can't rightly say. Must be divine providence."

Sister Anjelica gasped, and raised the large silver cross around her neck, holding it out in front of her. "Blasphemy! Be still, demon!" When he didn't vanish in a pillar of fire, she aggressively extended it to arm's length, catching the final rays of sun and bathing him in a blinding white light.

He sighed heavily and pulled his hat brim low across his forehead, shielding his eyes from the glare. His clipped response was polite and to the point. "If you don't mind shifting that a couple of inches to the left, Sister, I'll clear things up. First off, you can call me Reverend Jim or just Rev, but PLEASE stop calling me demon. I know it's a bit much to take in, but this vampire here can explain it all to you later. What is crucial that you understand is that we're all after the same thing. See, that book you've got in your saddlebag needs to find its way into the proper hands before all hell breaks loose, literally.

With all due respect ma'am, had I not chanced by, those condemned souls you're praying so hard for would have sucked the marrow from your bones and delivered your head on a platter to the commander of Hell's elite, along with the Book." He read the look of shock and confusion on her face and figured it

best to move along. When it came time for the vampire to negotiate his terms with the Archbishop, her take on things might tip
the scales one way or the other.

He locked eyes with Creed and snarled with a steely glint in
his eyes, "Vampire, I'll be seeing you by and by." His expression
softened and he tipped his hat respectfully. "Sister, It's been a
real pleasure. Seeing as how you folks are in no real danger, I'll
be taking my leave."

Creed caught something in the kid's attitude that made his
skin itch. It was probably nothing but he wasn't inclined to let
sleeping dogs lie. His eyes narrowed with suspicion, and he
repeated his earlier question, "Hey, Rev, it's a big desert out
there, plenty of places to pass the time. How is it you ended up
here?"

Rev laughed and dug his boots into the stirrups, spurring his
horse into a brisk canter. When he was almost out of range, he
shouted back over his shoulder, "Some fire-loving jackass held a
holy cremation at the Gates Of Hell!"

## 10

NIGHT FELL and the bleak breath of pestilence settled into a raw-boned landscape.

Grueling as the torturous days might be, the Zona was a hungry, haunted wasteland once the sun went down. Carnivorous scavengers circled in the inky blackness, just beyond the ghastly glow of an anemic moon. Creed rested a hand on the Colt, alert for any shift in the pattern that might spell trouble. If he held the horses to a steady, measured gallop, they'd make Purgatorio by daybreak and he could wash his hands of this hornet's nest. He'd damn sure rain fire on any bottomfeeder fool enough to put a hitch in that plan.

A wavering howl sang out in the shadows. Creed flushed crimson, cursing that smart-ass Rev and his mangy mutts. Just let the kid run up against a bossy nun and see how fast he built a funeral pyre. Maybe all nuns carried themselves with that kind of backbone, but he truly doubted it. Her fragile human bones and muscles were sure to be aching by now and she still showed no signs of slowing down. It took a strong heart to sustain conviction in the face of horror.

A firm voice piped up behind him, breaking his chain of

thought. "Mister Goodnight, you are a dangerous man, but it is a dark time and many lives are at risk. Perhaps the church needs dangerous men to banish a greater evil. As a guardian of the Monasterio De Los Angeles, I am well versed on the subject of hellhounds." She pursed her lips and arched a stern eyebrow, fixing him in an unflinching stare. "No excuses! We both know that those were hellhounds. Yet, had I not witnessed them with my own eyes, I would still have trouble believing it. How is it that you are connected to a man who controls these beasts and why do you call him "kid" when he is quite obviously a full grown man? More to the point, how did he gain knowledge of the Book? I must insist you tell me everything you know about this Reverend Jim!"

Blindsided by her rapid-fire questioning, Creed skirted the issue, needing time to come up with answers that would keep him and Rev on the right side of the exorcist. His chin jutted out doggedly and he slowly shook his head side to side, "NO!" When her mouth snapped shut, he worked his jaw and met her rigid gaze. "No ma'am, not until you tell me what got that wimple of yours all up in a twist last morning. Maybe it was when I told you to start talking or you'd be on your own? Cause if it was, I hold to that request. It's my unholy butt on the line out here and if you can't see clear to fill in a few holes, you'll need to start looking for another 'dangerous man' to pull your fat from the fire. Well, what was it, sis? Spit it out!"

Sister Anjelica stiffened and lowered her head, quietly staring at her hands. Creed flushed again and shifted guiltily in the saddle. Seeing her haloed in the moonlight, all pale and delicate, he cursed himself for being so rough on the poor nun. It figured that a woman who faced rampaging monsters and the hounds of Hell without screaming, would be up for dealing with a few harsh words. He palm-slapped his forehead and buried his frustration with a grunt. Even staring down the damn barrel of eternity, women would forever confound him.

He raggedly cleared his throat, composing himself to render

an apology, when she spun to face him with the quickness of a scorpion strike, pinning him in the glowering glare of an inquisitor. Red-faced and startled, both eyebrows shot toward his scalp line and Creed cringed back, holding his open palms out in front of him. There she was, that scrappy nun he'd grown to admire.

Deepening shadows flitted anxiously in the rasping rattle scathing desert winds. Creed was regretting his decision to rile her up when her chest heaved and she finally spoke. "As you wish, Mister Goodnight. Seeing how you have made it your mission to determine what got my 'wimple all up in a twist', let's discuss it, shall we?"

She tilted her head, her eyes glittering feverishly. "God may suffer fools and children, but there are no margins for error open to a woman traversing treacherous territory like the Zona with a vampire. One should never mistake compassion for naivete. As you busied yourself constructing the pyre that Reverend Jim found so amusing, I seized the opportunity to search through your saddlebags for indications of malintent. Shall I tell you what I found, Mister Goodnight, or would you prefer to do that yourself?"

Creed scowled, scratching his head in confusion. In an instant, he caught on to what had set the nun off and laughed out loud. His face relaxed into a wide apologetic grin. "Oh, yes ma'am, I can rightly see that might be cause for concern." Annoyed by her disdainful expression, his lips hardened and the laughter was gone. He bristled and defiantly ransacked the saddle bag, pulling out a decomposing head with a segment of spine dangling from the severed neck. Still irritated that she'd been digging through his personals, he scowled and thrust it toward her. "Get a good look, sis. You're damn right I'm a dangerous man! I hunt the hunters and this head you're all steamed up about is a prime example of that "greater evil" you're going up against.

Good sense told him to take it down a notch, but he didn't

care. A man's saddlebags are sacred. She was gonna hear him out, every bloody detail. "Sister Anjelica, meet the witch, Rebecca Surette. This young lady here, viciously butchered her husband and two small children in their beds as they slept. Matter of fact, she kept on stabbing, even after all breath had left the bodies. When the honorable Judge Stockwell sentenced her to hang for these heinous crimes, she slaughtered him, and the four guards sent to escort her to the gallows, in unspeakable ways. As it calls for the darkest kind of black conjure to escape the noose, I was offered a good amount to bring the witch to justice and that's precisely what I intend on doing."

Sister Angelica crossed herself and swallowed back the nausea rising in her throat. Having learned the value of second thoughts, she was silent for several minutes, methodically considering the details of his story without bias. If she were being completely honest, it had been her duty to confront him on the spot and demand an explanation for the atrocity. At the same time, a few gray areas remained, demanding clarity.

She took a deep breath, softening the creases in her face. "As you can imagine, Mister Goodnight, I am not familiar with the reasons for taking a life, though I understand that killing is a serious business. Even so, there are factors to your actions that I cannot condone. I won't contest the fact that she had to be undone before inflicting further grievous harm to others. Despite this, we are all God's creations, even one vile as Rebecca Surette. Was it truly necessary to end her life in such a savage manner? How will she find her way back to God now, and what does that say about you? Oh, and please put that nasty thing away."

Creed grabbed a fistful of grisly hair and shook off a nest of flies stuck to the head, then stuffed it back into his saddlebag, grumbling curses. As usual, it was the craziest damn logic he'd ever heard, but he was in no mood to argue with a contrary nun. He caught her staring at him and squinted sideways. "So, you got no problem with me killing a bloodthirsty ripper? I'll drink to that! You can say a few words over my saddle bag to try and put her straight with God, but watch your backside. If we don't close that breach, she'll come knocking and you can ask her yourself."

A twinge of conscience tugged at the edge of his skin. She had him dead to rights on the savagery. Hesitation flickered in his eyes before he spoke, "Look, sis, when I claim a head, it's quick and clean. Since you're book smart on hellhounds, tell me what you've read about ghouls."

Her eyebrows knitted into a frown and she shrugged. "Ghouls are obscene creatures that linger in cemeteries, feeding off the dead."

Creed grew deadly serious. "Well, you're half right. The dead will do unless the bastards catch something livelier." He gritted his teeth and lowered his voice to a low growl, "If you breathe a word of this to anyone, I won't be taking you to the dance, got it?"

Fascinated, the corner of her mouth twitched into a half-smile and she nodded.

He leaned in close and kept going in hushed whispers, "I swear to you, sis, this never happens to me, but that demon-infested witch got the drop on me. Poisoned wine, that's how the harlot did it, paralysis due to dead man's blood. There I was, stretched out like a Christmas turkey, enduring a rambling string of psychotic babble while she worked her way up to plunging that big, bloody knife in my chest.

But that wasn't the end of it. A smelly, slobbering posse of ghouls busted in and dragged us both down a dark tunnel, forcing me to suffer further humiliation. Seeing as how I don't have a heartbeat, they tossed me on the dead pile and went to work on Surette. By that time, the paralysis was wearing off, so when her head rolled up next to me, I figured I could haul it back to El Paso and make some cash. It's not like I didn't earn it. Cuchillo here, tracked me down and we both hit the trail before a bad spell got any worse."

Her tired eyes crinkled at the corners and she giggled,

breaking the sullen mood. God must be laughing too. This vampire was a deadly gunslinger, but he was also an ally, one she now trusted to do the right thing. Despite his better intentions, it remained to be seen if his assumptions were clouded. If Reverend Jim posed a threat to the mission, he must be dealt with sooner than later.

Her bottom lip tucked between her teeth and she raised an eyebrow. "I'm onto you, Mister Goodnight! You're a bit slow on the uptake if you think I can't recognize an attempt to deflect a direct question. Your reluctance is understandable. Consorting with devils is a blasphemous affront to God and The Holy Catholic Church." She sank back in the saddle, arms folded reprovingly across her chest. "Given the time constraints, either convince me this demon, Reverend Jim, can be relied on or see him banished to perdition with the rest."

Creed's wolfish green eyes narrowed, a cynical grin burrowing into the sides of his face. "Uh huh. You pious folks NEVER rub shoulders with devils. Is that about right?" Her saddle creaked as she shifted uneasily. He sparked a match on his thumbnail and lit a cigar, pointing it at her like an accusatory finger. "And yet, here we are, me with my pitchfork and you with your Book. Here's a little something else you don't know. I crossed paths with Rev and the whole pack before ever reaching the monasterio. Take my word for it, sis, if he was after the book, that thing would be long gone. He has reasons to want that breach snapped shut bad as you do. All the kid is asking in return is absolution from the holy fireworks.

Oh, and seeing how you opened this Pandora's Box, we should probably talk about how you'd be dirt nap dead right now if he were so inclined. I'd have ponied up a miser's bankroll to smite that horde myself, but it was Rev that pulled the trigger. To my way of thinking, that's cause for gratitude, not threats. Or don't they teach you about gratitude in Sunday School?" He knew he'd struck a nerve. The blood was pulsing in her pale cheeks, he could smell it.

"Mister Goodnight," she was trembling slightly in discomfort, "You can't expect me to trust a demon merely from an act of mercy. Demons are deceivers." She slowly raised her right hand, closing her fingers protectively around the Book. Her pulse quickened. "But you raise a good point. Please, continue."

Creed drew deep on his cigar, suppressing a hunger kindled by her rapid heartbeat. He blew a cloud of smoke to mask the gleam in his eyes and regarded her soberly. "Well alright, sis, now that we're on the same page, let's say I feel like talking and you feel holding back a rush to judgment a while longer. Get it straight, Rev is no shiftless demon, sidewinding in the shadows. His father was a Fallen, but to the best of my reckoning, the kid is clean. I'm not sure what that makes him, thought maybe you could tell me.

Now, those hellhounds don't love you or hate you. It's not like they go trolling for God-fearing folks warming the pews on Sunday. They have a job to do, tracking dumbass humans when they've plowed through ten good years of a demon deal. The fools know damn well what's coming for them when their card comes up. When Rev's human mother dropped a newborn infant at the Gates Of Hell and washed her hands of him, the beasts weren't rightly sure what to do with the baby. No one stepped up to claim him, so they raised him as one of their own. The hell-boys got wind of a human hound with Fallen powers and decided to keep him around. Those mutts aren't his minions, they're his family."

A sarcastic leer twitched in the corners of Creed's mouth. "Not that I would presume to weigh his suffering against his sins, he has a bad bone for sure, but most closets in this neck of the woods keep a stockpile of shovels and rope that ain't never washing clean. There are two sides to this story, sis, the one where you save him, and the one where you condemn the poor kid to the bowels of perdition. What's it gonna be?"

Sister Anjelica nodded, grinning sheepishly, "Ah, very well, you win, Mister Goodnight. God knows no child deserves that dreadful sort of treatment. I'd be risking the fires of Hell, myself, if I didn't try to help him. Ironic that a vampire was prepared to show mercy when a nun was not."

A pale husk of moon clung to the sky, ghosting toward sunrise. Creed hadn't thought much past confronting Sister Anjelica about Rev and now hours had passed. Cupping one hand against a blustery shift in the stinging wind, he sparked a fresh cigar and killed a few minutes sounding out the terrain. By his reckoning, they were within fifty miles of Purgatorio. He grinned evilly and laughed to himself. If memory served there was a blood brothel there, so he wouldn't have to eat the mouthy nun.

The trail wound through a dense copse of saguaro cactus and sister Angelica suddenly yelled over the loud clop of hooves, "Whoa!" She tugged on the reins and the stallion reared to a full stop. When Cuchillo halted abruptly, the nun dismounted and began walking briskly into the desert.

Creed clenched his teeth and growled plaintively, "Aww, come on sis, you made like you and me were square! That's the Zona out there, not some church picnic. Haul your holy butt back here, NOW! Don't make me chase after you, cause I will if need be!"

She spun to face him, both hands on her hips, "We are indeed "square", Mister Goodnight. Regardless, it seems to have slipped your attention that we've been riding since daybreak. Not to be indelicate, but I AM human!"

He shrugged his shoulders, giving her a pained look. "All due respect, ma'am, you're not my first human and it's nothing I haven't seen before. On my word, I'll keep my eyes squeezed tight and we'll never speak of this again."

Without waiting for him to protest further, she shook her head emphatically and waved a dismissive hand over her shoulder. "Five minutes, Mister Goodnight, and we'll be on our way again."

Creed snarled in frustration, "Aw hell, WOMAN!" A real bad

feeling washed over him as she disappeared behind a thicket of cactus. Five minutes went by, then ten. The silence was deafening. Her time was up and it was too damn bad if she had had a problem with that. He called out warily, his voice rising an octave with each repetition in the rising wind, "Sis!...Sister!...SISTER ANJELICA!" His shouts made the silence deeper.

He spun the Colt from his holster and vaulted from the saddle, charging into the darkness. Whipping winds chased a murk of stagnant dust across the empty expanse of moon-blanched desert. Sister Anjelica was gone.

---

LEADEN clouds of dust pulled down a waning moon. Creed hunkered down low to the ground, guilt pooling in his mind like venom. He was slipping, letting a little snippet of a girl call the shots. Any fool can tell you that the Zona is a blighted stain on the earth, infested with hellish predators. She was gone. It was his fault and he damn well knew it. He meant to save her scrawny ass, or slice her from the belly of the scavenger that ate her. Either way, he was bringing her home.

Whatever bottomfeeder snatched her was sure as hell moving fast, too fast by his reckoning. How long had he hung back, ten minutes? Might be something, maybe nothing, but not a damn thing he knew of dropped from sight like that in the desert. There was always some kind of sign to mark the passing. But there was nothing, not so much as a trail of dust.

He rubbed a thumb along his rigid jawline, scouring the perimeter again. A fierce gust of wind whipped up the sour stench of open graves. Vague images of his first skirmish with ghouls scratched at his skull, lighting a slow burn in his bones. He'd missed it in the first scan. Most likely foggy recall due to

CHAPTER 11 | 91

residue from the dead man's blood. It was a wide sweep of desert, but she had to go and pick this hellish place.

He'd been meaning to pay these scumbags a visit, anyway. Some things just begged for a smiting. Gasping in hot, bitter breaths, he inhaled rancid plumes of grave rot and chased the scent up a plateau directly ahead of him. He shouldered the shotgun and topped the rise, hovering above the serpentine rows of crumbling headstones and splintered crosses like a fearsome harpy. Dust devils danced like ghosts, spitting and whirling between the desecrated graves. Apart from that, the ruined cemetery simmered in empty silence. There was no sound of a heartbeat, human or otherwise.

Trickles of fading moonlight filtered through the gloom, washing the markers in a pale, shimmering glow. Creed trudged down the winding rows with slow, deliberate steps, studying each open hole with an exacting gaze until he picked up both her scent and one other. Soil heaped up to either side of the grave was freshly dug and there was no indication of blood or struggle. Creed balled his sweaty hand into a fist and smashed it against the headstone in frustration. It looked to be almost an hour since she'd been dragged alive, but unconscious down into those filthy, vermin infested tunnels and he damn sure needed to find her before she came to.

He snarled and spat into the grave, cursing humans and their frailties. From what he could piece together, some worm-ridden ghoul had straggled off on its own, sniffing around for scraps, and by pure dumb luck got its greedy talons on a live one. While he wallowed in guilt, wasting precious time in this empty bone-yard, the slimy bastard was heading back to the litter with its catch.

In truth, Creed never wanted to set eyes on the heinous swing station again, or anything that lay within its tainted walls, but it added up that the ghouls would be holed up there. Best he could remember, the station was a short ride from the cemetery. He'd best get the lead out.

A close, stagnant pall hung in the air, shadowed sickish purple by a colorless moon. When a place reeks of abomination, it made good sense not to stir things up without a real good reason. The swing station was one of those places, even so, he reckoned that Sister Anjelica was reason enough. Creed wasn't much for waiting when there was killing to be done, but as long as there was a slim chance she might be alive, he couldn't risk charging in, guns blazing.

Warily skirting the derelict buildings, he led the stallion down into a deep ravine beside the abandoned stable and dismounted. The panicky horse strained against the reins, snorting and rearing, its bulging eyes white with terror. He pulled hard on the reins, securing them around a sturdy mesquite tree, then whispered in low coaxing tones, "Easy boy! Whoa! Whoa!" Cuchillo flanked the stallion, gently bumping noses and whinnying softly. After things calmed down a bit, he pulled several sticks of dynamite and extra ammo from the saddle bag, then signaled Cuchillo to stay put.

Creed clambered up the slippery ravine, dislodging pieces of loose rock and scrub that scudded to the bottom in a noisy clatter. Quickly pulling himself over the edge, he pushed his body back up against the stable wall and rested a hand on his pistol. Apart from the usual creaks and moans of a swing station, it was utterly silent. Seeing as the ruckus hadn't set off a rampage, he'd lay bets on catching the scum all clustered together in the station.

The gunslinger crouched low and ran past the stable doors to the edge of the corral. The rusted, metal gates were open, flattened to the fence by gusting desert winds. They lifted on their hinges then crashed against the posts in swollen waves. He choked back disgust as the sour, metallic smell of blood and urine assailed his nostrils. Flies swarmed the mangled remains of three horses piled up against the fence in a thick, sticky pool of gore. Creed winced at the mindless slaughter. The poor horses were ripped open at the underbelly, organs spilling out across the dirt, then hastily cast aside for something that must have smelled a whole lot better.

The animal kills were fresh. With luck, one or more of the ill-fated travelers might still be breathing. Creed kept low, closing the distance in seconds. He pressed up close to the building to get a feel for the odds through a missing slat in one of the shutters. Walls in the main room dripped crimson with splattered blood and ragged shreds of flesh. The mutilated corpses of an older man and woman hung from a rafter, swaying back and forth in shrill desert winds whistling in through the shattered door frame. The ribcages were cracked open, exposing gaping cavities smeared with gore. Half-eaten arms and legs, ripped from the torsos, lay scattered on the floor in dark red puddles.

A sallow-faced boy of eighteen or so, naked except for his tattered boots, was strung up to the left of the butchered couple. His cadaverous body was damp and sticky with clotted blood from weeping wounds where strips of skin had been peeled away. Tremors in his hands and feet showed that he was still alive, but his vacant eyes were glazed over in a glassy stare, indicating he suffered from severe shock.

Creed growled deep in his throat and reached for the Colt, then froze in horror. A sodden, gore-soaked ghoul shuffled out from the dark recesses of the station in stops and starts like a rabid beast. Shocks of bushy gray hair scabbed to its face in greasy clumps, knotting into tangles of beard that protruded from the chin like steel wool. Sister Anjelica's veil was stuck to the top of its distorted head, pulled to one side by bloodied edges buried deep into the beast's massive haunches.

Before Creed could react, the monster jerked upright, slobbery threads of spittle drooling from its slack, yawning mouth. One knobby, swollen hand hooked claw-like around the boy's throat, holding him steady while it plucked his eye from the socket with a long blood-caked talon. It spewed a pleased, gravelly whine, licking pieces of eyeball and brain from its filthy fingers, then shambled from the room. The taunting whine warped and twisted in Creed's ears, stabbing at his brain like an ice pick.

Dim lantern light bled out from the kitchen storage area. Hoarse brays of laughter and the cracking crunch of bone gave him a rotten feeling in his gut. Moving stealthily, he drew his pistol and worked his way through slippery carnage to the open doorway. Flies buzzed and swarmed, wings sticking to the weathered wood, wet and shiny with blood. He counted nineteen ghouls, eyes black as ashes, howling in celebration over a grisly feast. Consumed by gluttony, they rocked back and forth to a tuneless hum, devouring jagged chunks of human meat and flesh until broken bones were gnawed to the marrow.

Red cinders sparked in Creed's eyes, tracing a trail of ripped and shredded vestments to a frail, naked body hanging by the wrists. Sister Anjelica showed no fear, moving her lips in a silent litany of prayer. Her close-cropped red hair was matted to her head with sweat and she was covered in greenish purple bruises, but otherwise unharmed. He figured that was due to an instinctive fear of the heavy silver cross still dangling from her neck. He got lucky this time, hunger would have ended that standoff in short order.

He quickly raised an index finger to his lips for silence when her bloodshot eyes fluttered open, wild with hope. Sensing immediate danger, the savage brutes turned to glare at the intruder, fistfuls of bloody meat splattering to the floor. Outraged, they shrieked a challenge and crouched to attack.

Creed was so damn mad his breath made a furious hissing sound. The barrel of the shotgun jerked upward. A hail of rapid-fire blazed from the muzzles of both his weapons, resounding from the close walls in deafening echoes. He emptied the chambers and reloaded with vampiric speed, firing again and again. Each blast was a dead shot, punching gaping holes into the bloody faces and glutting the room with the acrid smell of fear and gunpowder. The beasts roared and screamed in blinding agony. Vicious talons slashed at the air until they finally fell still and dropped dead to the floor.

When it looked like he was going to reload and shoot them again, a weak voice broke through the frenzy, "Excuse me, Mister Goodnight, is this a rescue or not?" Creed flinched, and pivoted on a bootheel to face Sister Anjelica. His head tilted at an odd angle and both smoking guns sagged to his sides. Completely stunned, he continued staring at her with that look kids save for birthday cake. He'd been too damn concerned about whether or not she'd been chewed on to notice how perfect she was, easily the most beautiful woman he'd ever laid eyes on. Her lips pursed into a firm line and she demanded sternly, "WELL, are you going to cut me down or do I have to chew through the ropes?"

Creed flushed and shook it off. Uneasy at having impure thoughts about Sister Anjelica, he nodded politely. "Uh huh. Yes Ma'am," and spun the colt back into its holster. He grabbed the Bowie knife stashed in his boot and sliced the ropes, leaning forward to catch her in his outstretched hands. She whimpered softly and collapsed into his muscular arms, resting her head on his shoulder. That same curious emotion he'd felt when staring at her the first time flooded his senses, but he choked it back, knowing damn well she deserved better than that after the grim horror she'd just been through.

Unsure of what he should say to comfort her, he brushed the sweaty strands of hair from her eyes and grinned confidently. "Easy, sis, the monsters are gone and they won't be coming back tonight." He didn't know if that was true or not. Another hunting party could show up at any minute, but the smell of her skin was making him crazy. All the more reason to wrap this mess up and run like hell.

Creed dumped the dynamite from his pockets and eased her awkwardly to the floor, gently covering her shivering body with his duster. The bleary-eyed nun hugged his coat tight to her chest and struggled to sit upright. Nodding emphatically at the explosives, she laced her fingertips together and rested both hands on her knees. She drew a deep breath and raised her head, looking squarely into his eyes. Her voice was clear and controlled, "Do you take me for a fool, Mr. Goodnight? Playing with your fireworks at a time like this is like setting the table when the kitchen's on fire. We both know there are more monsters where these came from and I insist we leave this vile nest at once, before they return to eat us both."

Creed cracked his knuckles, then armed up with a fistful of dynamite and one of the lanterns. He was halfway down the rickety cellar ladder by the time her words tapered off.

Muttering distractedly, he shouted back over his shoulder, "Yes ma'am, we'll be doing just that, directly." It sounded like boss nun was back in the saddle and he'd best speed things up.

He pushed away from the ladder and dropped to the dusty floor. One stick of dynamite placed strategically at the opening of each tunnel should effectively seal them off. Satisfied, he doused the cellar floor in kerosene and vaulted back up the ladder.

Sister Anjelica crossed herself, still shaky but relieved to see him return so quickly. She stepped forward and tripped over yards of fabric, puddled around her feet. Creed eyed her with a critical squint, then burst into a fit of shoulder shaking laughter. You could've squeezed two of her into the massive coat with room left for supplies. A look of pure misery darkened her expression, but the laugh lines around her mouth quickened to a weak smile. He shook his head, regarding her with a broad grin. "Make yourself useful, sis! Fasten the top five buttons and roll those sleeves while I finish up here."

After planting the remainder of the dynamite where it would do the most damage, he hoisted a bullet-ridden ghoul off the floor and slung it through the kitchen window, smashing the glass. There was only one lantern left, but one was all he needed. The curtains flapped and twisted in the lashing winds blowing in through the shattered glass. He soaked them in kerosene, then snaked a thin trail of the fuel to the dynamite.

Ghoul gore and gunpowder crusted to the dirt on his hands. He wiped what he could on his pants and crouched down in front of Sister Anjelica, pawing through the duster piled at her feet. When he found the front corner of the hem, he pinched it between a thumb and forefinger, then thrust his other arm between her legs. She released a sharp, squeaking gasp and her knees clamped shut, trapping his arm in a vise-like grip. Creed heaved an irritated sigh and barked, "Spread your legs!"

Refusing to release his arm, her eyes widened in shock and she sputtered, "MISTER GOODNIGHT!"

His tilted eyes narrowed slightly at her reaction, then he grasped the reason for her mounting apprehension. He reckoned he couldn't blame her, seeing as how she was a naked nun, stuck with a vampire in a room full of dead ghouls. He grinned broadly, exposing an ominous set of striking white fangs. "DO you want to ride out of this place?" She nodded suspiciously, still gripping his arm between her knees. Shaking his head with what seemed to be genuine amusement, he casually remarked, "Uh huh, well okay then, SPREAD your legs!"

Fidgeting nervously, she studied his infectious grin as it stretched easily across a wide, angular jawline, dimpling all the way back to the sides of his face. After a minute, she scooted a foot to one side, widening the space between her legs. Creed nodded politely, "Thank you, ma'am."

Quickly matching the material pinched in his fingers to a similar corner on the black flap, he rolled the duster up to her thighs and knotted the ends tightly together. When it held, he did the same on the other side and stood, raising his hands in the air, palms out, "See, sis, just being helpful. Take a few steps and see if you can walk." She waddled forward in an awkward shuffle like a barrel cactus in clownish pantaloons, forcing him to stifle another burst of laughter.

Suddenly, coyote song rang out in the distance, sobering the mood. Creed fired up a cigar, his face deadly seriously in the match glare. "Time to move. Can't stay around here waiting to get eaten." Without further discussion, he threw her across his shoulder and headed back to the stables.

The coyotes had smelled out the bloody slaughter congealing in the corral. They circled the stable, yipping and moaning hungrily. Ears pinned back, Cuchillo flanked the stallion facing the darkness, braced for attack. Creed figured those coyotes were damn lucky he'd shown up when he did. He skittered down the steep ravine, teasing, "Hey boy! Miss me?" Cuchillo reared and pawed the ground, nuzzling his shoulder excitedly. Creed stroked his sweaty mane and grinned. "Yeah, I missed you too."

Sister Anjelica grabbed the saddle horn and he swung her up onto the stallion's back. He adjusted the stirrups to her bare feet, then passed her the reins and mounted up. Creed kept a cautious pace, weapons close at hand, but there were no sounds above the steady clop of hooves. When they passed the perimeter's edge, where he'd first scouted the swing station, the path widened to a downgrade that spilled out onto the trail. The road stretched empty and there were no signs of pursuit.

Creed reined Cuchillo around and blocked the stallion from going any further. He held a hand up and frowned. "Wait for me here! Be ready to ride when I get back!"

His eyes were hard and she knew it would be useless to argue. Killing was a dangerous business and she supposed that was the reason he'd been chosen by the Archbishop.

Bent upon settling the score, Creed cut straight across the station grounds and reined to a stop next to the kitchen window in seconds. Shards of glass clung to the busted frame, clacking like a death rattle in the gusting wind as he sparked a cigar and drew deep until the tip glinted red as hellfire. A fierce growl rumbled in his throat, "Kiss my undead ass, suckers!" then he flicked it into the station.

Tendrils of fire slithered up the curtains, coiling up across the rafters. Dry, weathered wood whined and sputtered, blossoming into spitting plumes of flame that engulfed the low ceilings.

Creed leaned into the saddle and galloped hard for the trail, shouting at the top of his lungs, "HOLD ON!"

Sister Anjelica crossed herself and clenched her teeth, digging her knees into the horse's flanks. Shadows heightened his fixed features as he barreled toward her in the billowing dust. He slowed without stopping, giving the stallion a hard smack on the rump, hollering, "HEE-YAW!" The horse bolted and they thundered away from the station at a full run.

A wicked smile creased the nun's battered face. It would require many trips to the confessional to atone for the intense satisfaction that swelled in her heart when the first in a series of resonating explosions shook the desert floor, ricocheting from the mesas in thunderous echoes.

## 12

SUNRISE LEAKED around edges of the time-weathered village of Purgatorio, casting early morning shade, but blustering swirls of wind were already hot as a furnace. Rugged and sometimes unruly, the notorious village rested in a dusty basin, sprawled up against a ridge marking the only passage leading in or out of the Zona De Silencio. Due to its unusual location, days from El Paso, miles from the next shot at water and a hard day's ride to the doorstep of Hell, it was known as a hotbed of outlaws, missionaries and monsters.

Purgatorio boasted one church, twenty Bibles, three saloons and one brothel. A few still scratched out a meager living tending the fields, but most were open for business, servicing the steady flow of pilgrims and fugitives. When asked about the strange anomalies plaguing the Zona, local residents of Purgatorio shrugged their shoulders and insisted there are no strange phenomena, only strange people.

The weary pair rode side by side down a drowsy, cobblestone street, with a slow, dragging clop of hooves. Creed tipped his hat brim to shade his face, and risked a glance at his companion. A twinge of conscience stirred in his gut. Hours of saddle time in the blazing heat without food or sleep had only served to strengthen the fiery nun's resolve. No getting past the fact that she had grit and smarts, but riling up a nest of skin boys for no good reason was a sucker's move. That much was for damn sure. He leaned back in the saddle and sighed patiently, "Look, I get it, sis, you figure church business is sacred, or some such nonsense. Can't say it hasn't been a pleasure riding with you, but either spin a good story for that big hole in Hell, or we'll be parting ways here shortly."

Sweaty leather creaked as she lowered her head and shifted miserably in the saddle. "It is as you say, Mister Goodnight, you deserve an explanation. I owe you that. The truth is, I was deeply ashamed. When the Gates were breached, I cowered in fear, hidden while my dear sisters were slaughtered in unspeakable ways." Her eyes rose to meet his with a fierce intensity. Swiping roughly at the crusted dirt on her face with both hands, she snarled, "Disgusting layers of grime and gore will wash clean, but the torture Father Amantino and the three sisters must be enduring at the hands of these very same demons cannot be tolerated. You shall have your story, Mister Goodnight. If you still feel it's not your problem, I'll do whatever it takes to save these people without you."

He squinched his face into a pained grin and drawled slowly, "Uh huh. Well, hell. Looks like I'm headed to Almas Perdidas, after all. Good talk, guess we'll pick up the conversation tomorrow, after you've rested up some."

Creed was done talking. It was too damn hot to sleep, so he ran a lazy eye along the local establishments, scouting out a place to wash up and kill some time. The ancient adobe walls of Rosario's Cantina, crumbling and veined with greasy cracks, were wedged in between the stables and a Chinese laundry. He had it figured that the filthy bar wasn't good for much more than watered down liquor and free stabbing, when a sultry, loose-limbed fancy girl leaned in against the door frame and caught his eye. He stared openly as delicate, red-stained fingers pushed sweaty strands of hair behind her ears. She leered back at him, sinking her teeth into the cleft of a ripe plum until the thick, red juices trickled down her chin. Slowly licking an index finger, she invited him closer, her colorful petticoats lifting and twirling in the torrid winds. Yeah, it might not be the best place he'd ever passed a night, but it was damn sure convenient.

Dazzling waves of sunlight radiated from a tall silver cross rising above the austere, sun-bleached facade of La Iglesia De La Santa Cruz. The well-tended, whitewashed church skirted the edge of town, providing stark contrast to the sin and immorality surrounding it. Padre Ignacio Torres sat calmly on the steps, resting his hands on his knees in silent prayer. The haggard priest caught sight of them approaching through a hazy film of dust and leapt to his feet. He crossed himself and called out to them, enthusiastically waving both arms over his head.

Sister Anjelica's face broke into a wide smile and she pushed up in the saddle, returning his greeting. Neither she nor Creed noticed the withered figure, dressed in the loose-fitting, white clothing of a field worker, trotting briskly toward them on horseback. The old man pushed the sombrero back on his head and squinted into the sun to make certain, then kept riding as if he'd seen nothing. It was the gunslinger, he was sure of it, the same vampire who'd shot a priest and fled into the Zona in a coach stacked with the dead.

Creed dropped from his horse and tethered the stallion to a hitching rail, then gently lifted Sister Anjelica from the saddle. He took a quick step back to clear a path as Padre Torres rushed excitedly down the steps, clasping both of her hands firmly in his. Seeing how she was buck naked under his duster, Creed studied his fingernails, waiting for the priest to spew something preachy. Curiously, the holy man expressed nothing more than relief and gratitude at finding the nun safe and alive.

The old man returned on foot with a rifle slung across his shaking shoulder. Six more grizzled field hands, armed with pistols and pitchforks, appeared from darkened doorways, sending a cluster of rangy chickens clucking and squawking off in all directions. Creed spun to face the angry villagers, aiming the Colt before anyone could draw another breath.

The terrified challenger took a step forward, letting the rifle slide into his hands. His sunburned face furrowed with resolve. "We don't want trouble, gunslinger, but we must insist you step away from the church before more blood is spilled."

Creed scratched his jaw and growled, "Uh huh. Well, you know what they say, amigos, don't start trouble and there won't BE trouble." He fanned his pistol across the trembling mob to drive the point home, then waited for the first move.

Creed flinched when Padre Torres moved up quickly next to him. Calmly resting a hand on the pistol, he pushed the weapon down to the gunslinger's side, then spread both arms wide in a welcoming gesture, standing between the adversaries. Confused, the field workers respectfully dropped their weapons, shuffling restlessly. The priest smiled, speaking in low, reassuring tones, " You have done well, my sons, standing ready at the first sign of danger. I know this must be difficult for you to understand, but Mister Goodnight is doing God's work. We are facing a peril far greater than any you've encountered before. Men like him are necessary if we are to stand a chance at defeating this evil. You must treat him with courtesy and respect while he is a visitor in our village. Meanwhile, stay alert in case you are needed again."

The field hands nodded contritely, walking away from the church. The old man glanced back over his shoulder with a threatening squint. Creed released the trigger and twirled the pistol around his index finger, letting it fall back into the holster. His chin jerked up and he gave the old codger a firm thumbs up.

Heavy wooden doors swung open and two solicitous nuns scurried down the stairs. They carefully wrapped Sister Anjelica in a long cloak and herded her inside, muttering in hushed whispers about food and rest. Padre Torres grabbed Creed's hand and shook it earnestly. "Thank you, my son. God be with you." When

Creed nodded, the priest followed the others into the church and let the doors close behind him.

Creed shook his head at Cuchillo and shrugged, then swung into the saddle. Seconds later, Sister Anjelica pulled the cloak tightly around her and yelled out the door, "Tomorrow, Mister Goodnight!"

In his mind, he saw her as she'd looked under all that prudish, religious get-up. He regarded her with a wistful grin and tipped his hat. "Yes Ma'am!" Without another word, he reined Cuchillo around and galloped off toward the stable.

The stable was clean and well-organized. Creed spotted a curry comb resting on the bottom rung of a ladder leading up into the hayloft. The stable boy looked on with mild interest while he gave Cuchillo a good brushing and stocked the stall with fresh hay. When he was finished, he tossed the kid a twenty for extra oats and water, ordering him to leave the stall gate open. The kid spat and shook his head indifferently. Tilting his head, the gunslinger casually bit down on a fresh cigar, and shoved the kid against the wall, striking a match on his left fang. He blew a stream of smoke and barked, "We on the same page, BOY?" The stable boy's jaw dropped and he squeaked, "Yes sir! Extra oats and water, leave the stall gate unlatched!" Creed growled, "Good, thought we might be. You look like a smart kid."

Brutal late afternoon sun beat at the cobblestones, forging molten heat thermals in the shifting dust. Creed stretched and ambled lazily over to Rosario's. The hooker was gone, but he reckoned he knew where to find her. It was shaping up to be a long wait. Hours remained until sundown and the noisy cantina already boomed with raucous laughter and the sound of shattering glass. At least he would be near Cuchillo if things went south.

His lips peeled back over his fangs and he shoved the door open. Resting a hand on his pistol, he cautiously stepped inside, tensed for signs of trouble. Exhausted prostitutes hovered over a small clutter of sloppy drunks. He felt somewhat relieved when the plum girl was not among them. Chipped adobe walls were scarred with bullet holes and years of chronic neglect. Layers of dust mingled with the scent of sex and cheap whiskey, engulfing the sweltering pall of claustrophobia. Beyond that, it looked like business as usual. He supposed he could spend one night anywhere, even Hell if he had to.

His spurs jangled sharply on the rough-hewn wooden planks with a hollow, clinking
noise as he made his way across the room, hell-bent on at least two deadly sins. Leaning into the bar, he slapped a sweaty wad of bills on the counter and barked, "Mezcal!" The barkeep wiped a film of dust off the bottle and set it on the bar, twisting his gnarled face into a smug look of recognition. Grinning lewdly, the geezer jerked his craggy chin toward a staircase in the corner. Creed arched an eyebrow and side-eyed the stairs suspiciously. When the barkeep nodded slowly, he grabbed the bottle and tipped his hat.

He climbed carefully while the shabby staircase wobbled against rusty nails holding it in place as it slammed against the rotten adobe. A bare bulb dangling from the ceiling on the second floor exposed a long, narrow hallway, crowded with doors. Room fifteen was cracked open. He damn well knew it was an ambush. A nest of slimy skin boys were probably crouched behind the door, looking to make a name for themselves. First, he'd send the bastards screaming down to Hell, then he'd go back for the smart-ass bartender.

Creed leveled the Colt, silently working his way through the trash and broken bottles. He wiped the sweat from his eyes with a shirt sleeve and kicked hard at the door, mostly because he felt like kicking something. Grinning like a lunatic when the door banged hard against the wall, he snarled and launched in, gun first.

He hadn't known exactly what to expect, but it wasn't this. Plum girl was curled against a pile of cushions stacked up on an ornate red velvet sofa, naked as the day she was born. Her pale breasts heaved slightly with shallow staggered breaths. She giggled impishly, twirling a long, shiny strand of golden hair around her finger, then pursed her lush lips into a pout. "Hard day, gunslinger?" She had a low, seductive purr, like some silky Satan, so he let her talk. Lightly dragging long, red fingernails along the inside of her arm, she grinned wickedly. "Clean yourself up and let me make it all better."

Moves like that didn't happen overnight, they matured with practice. What kind of fool was he to have missed the clawfoot tub sitting smack in the middle of the room? The sweet scent of rosewater drifted in waves from hot, steamy water. Maybe the little vixen had a gun stuck under those cushions, maybe not, but it didn't matter either way. Creed pulled off his boots, eyeing her skeptically. When she laughed again, he unbuckled his gun belt and let it drop to the floor, fumbling with the buttons on his shirt.

Plum girl slid from the cushions like a snake, restless fire simmering in her eyes. Her pale, slender legs melted seamlessly into sensually rolling hips as she cat-crawled toward him in a silken slide. Glistened with sweat, she threw his dusty boots across the room and tugged his pants off with a skilled precision, sliding her trembling hands slowly up his muscular body. She pressed a cool palm to his chest and shoved him roughly into the fragrant water. Every nerve in his body tingled when she slipped sensuously into the tub, offering her arm with a wanton moan. Plum girl wasn't a beauty like the nun, but she was damn pretty. At that moment, he wanted to build her a temple and sacrifice a goat.

Come morning, a timid shuffle of bare feet rustled outside the door of room fifteen. The latch clicked, and the aging door creaked slowly open. Creed grunted blearily and vaulted from the bed. He instinctively reached for his pistol, stupefied to find that he was stark naked. A small boy of no more than six years old held out a stack of clothing, neatly cleaned and pressed. The gunslinger raised his hands to show that he meant no harm and quickly counted out five dollars from the night table. Keeping at arm's length, he swapped the money for his clothes and instructed the boy to deliver a message to the church, informing the padre where he could be found. The kid stared at the money and his eyes grew round as saucers. Amazed at his good fortune, he beamed, "Si Senor" and scampered off to find the priest.

Plum girl laughed, patting the rumpled pillow beside her. "Aww, tell the truth and shame the devil, gunslinger. Wanna come back to bed?" It was easy to say that he liked the hooker, a lot in fact, but not so easy to say why. Then he got it, she was straight up, making no bones about who she was or what she wanted.

The fresh clothing felt good on his skin. When he was finished getting dressed, he buckled the gun belt low on his hip and knotted the rawhide thongs around his thigh. He flipped the cylinder on the Colt and spun the chamber to make sure it was loaded, then snapped it shut, dropping it back into the holster.

Plum girl made a pouty face and he countered with a devilish grin, tipping his hat, "Much obliged ma'am, can't rightly recall the last time I had this much fun."

It was verging on noon when Creed eased behind a table with an open view of the door. The barkeep leered like a cat waiting to pounce on a mouse and scuffed over with a bottle of Mezcal and two glasses. His rheumy eyes glinting with amusement, he hacked and spit, then cocked his head toward the back, rasping, "You got company, gunslinger."

Creed nodded, pressing a crumpled ten into his outstretched palm, "Yeah, saw that when I walked in. Guess I must be a popular guy." The geezer stuffed the bill in his pants, grinning through snaggy yellowed teeth as he slowly backed away.

Distracted, as if fevered by ghosts, a hulking oaf pushed away from his table. Oblivious to the flies stuck to rotting patches on his face and arms, he clomped heavily across the room, slumping into an empty chair across from the gunslinger. The brute cracked his knuckles, pinching the sweaty shirt away from his chest to create an airflow. The two exchanged slow, laconic glances.

Creed clenched his jaw and spoke up first, "Rev! You aren't lookin' so good, kid. Thought you liked to stick to the shadows when the heat was on. Must be damned

important to risk showing that pretty face in Purgatorio."

Rev snarled violently, pulling several stiffened cheek muscles, "Laugh it up, jackass! Get a real good look at this flimsy skin I'm riding and tell me that nun of yours, with her big, bad Book, signed off on the deal we made. Or maybe you're no different from Hadriel and I should just whistle for the pack and handle this myself!"

Creed squinted pensively, taking a measure of Rev's odd agitation. Here was a soul catcher who ran with hellhounds and right now you could read heat thermals rising from the sweat in his voice. He took a hard pull off the Mezcal bottle and kept his mouth shut, waiting for the kid to brass up.

Rev's eyes darted tensely around the room, then he swallowed hard and spilled the rest, "Okay, vampire, maybe I should have mentioned this right at first, but you tend to piss me off. Can't say for sure if I was followed, but Hadriel will be releasing the first wave of specters tomorrow and I thought you should know what you're riding up against."

Creed dragged some life into the remains of his cigar and stubbed it out, then poured the kid a healthy shot. "Thanks kid, I owe you one. Have a drink on me."

Rev threw his head back and drained the Mezcal, slamming the empty glass on the table. "More like a bottle by my count, jackass. Start pumping holes into my fancy faith healer and we'll see how you like Hell."

Both Creed and Rev went for their pistols when the door swung open. Sister Anjelica paused in the door frame, letting her eyes adjust to the dim lighting. Blazing white sun burned at her back, silhouetting the severe outlines of her immaculate, crisply starched vestments. After a moment, she closed the door and joined them at the table with an air of quiet authority.

She nodded to Creed, placing his clean and freshly pressed duster on the table. Her serene face betrayed no emotion when she turned to face Rev and took his decaying hand in hers, patting it reassuringly. "Reverend Jim, let me thank you for saving our lives in the Zona by informing you that Archbishop McQuade has granted your request to be spared from the cleansing."

A barrage of high-pitched, keening howls burst from the surrounding desert, echoing from the sun-baked buildings. Rev leaned across the table and snatched a cigar from Creed's pocket, then rose to his feet. He bowed low to the nun and smiled. "It was my pleasure ma'am. Now it seems the boys grow restless. Please convey my sincere gratitude to your Archbishop." He grabbed the bottle of Mezcal off the table and nodded to Creed. "Jackass, we'll be seeing you around." Terrified patrons stared back over their shoulders with pallid, haunted faces as he walked out the door.

Seconds later, the cantina hummed back to life and plum girl flounced over to the table with a fresh bottle of Mezcal. She gave the gunslinger a crooked smile and winked, then sashayed off. Sister Anjelica stared at Creed, taken aback by how handsome he was, all cleaned up with his hair combed back. She opened her mouth to ask him why a vampire smelled like roses, then thought better of it.

Creed picked up on her peculiar expression and figured she might be trying to weasel out of her promise. He gently slid his palms across the table and fixed her in a steady gaze. "Look sis, everybody's fallen hard at least once. I don't give a damn about what you did or didn't do. I just need to know what I'm risking my cold, dead butt for. After that, we'll move on."

The nun frowned and tilted her head, then grasped his meaning. Her face reddened and she nodded curtly. "Yes, of course, Mister Goodnight, as you wish.

"Sister Maria Borkowska, Sister Katherine Raspante and I were part of a select team assigned to the Monasterio De Los Angeles. We were tasked by the Pope to stand watch over the Gates Of Hell for a period of three years. We all swore a vow of silence and assembled in the chapel.

"Your passenger, Father Fantoni, joined us shortly after. Tragically, he was one of only two priests in this country sanctified by the church to recite the Ritum Sanctum Praesidium, from the Book enclosed in the case you delivered. Once this was done, we were confident that the seal would stand fast for the duration of our watch, as it had done for previous centuries. The Father was to return in three years with our replacements, repeating the ritual.

"We found it easy to slip into a routine of silent prayer and daily maintenance. It was of great importance to ring the great brass bell, suspended in the east tower, from the first crack of dawn until the sun had fully risen. As you well know, this is a dangerous hour in the Zona De Silencio. Creatures of the night must scurry for a place to hide, lurking in the shadows until sunset. A deterrent is necessary to prevent nesting in the Monasterio.

"The latter chore was assigned to Sister Katherine, a kind and compassionate soul. Sadly, we were unaware of her deteriorating condition. Fifteen minutes early, as usual, Sister Katherine was kneeling at the east tower, reciting the rosary in a seamless pattern of silent gestures. Disturbed from prayer, she startled at a thin, reedy cry of despair lofting over the Monasterio walls, desperate and childlike, which intensified to deafening screams of fear.

"Impulsively, she stumbled to her feet and sprinted toward the monastery gates. The turbulent desert winds picked up, magnifying the cries while obscuring their source. She was torn with anguish. The urgent wails of misery overwhelmed her and the smallest whisper escaped her lips...'I hear you', breaking her vow of silence.

"At once, weeping and pleas for help dwindled to a hush, muted by a distant salvo of blood-curdling howls. The monasterio gates unlatched, swinging slowly open with a creaking titter as the unholy closed in. Somehow, Sister Katherine managed to reach the threshold just as they breached the compound in a malignant surge of unchecked rage.

"Sister Maria chanced to glance out the window when Sister Katherine ran toward the gates. Curious, she descended the stairs. Assigned to upkeep that week, I was crouched behind the altar, polishing a fresco detailing the crucifixion that rested above a fountain of holy water. I heard Sister Maria's footsteps first, followed by rabid screeching of the demonic horde. In an instant, I knew what had happened. Tears streamed down my face. I watched silently as they punched through sister Katherine's chest, ripping through muscle and bone to expose her still-beating heart. Fighting the urge to run, I forced my hollow limbs to move and inhaled deeply, submerging myself in the fountain.

"Even beneath the water I could hear Sister Maria's heartbreaking screams, shrill at first then fading out to silence. Apart from stolen gasps of air I lay there, still as a corpse, while they desecrated my beloved sanctuary, tossing ancient books and holy relics into a bonfire blazing on unsanctified ground beyond the gates.

"By God's mercy, they instinctively avoided the fountain in their frenzied hunt for survivors. My head pounded, every cell in my body screamed for more oxygen until at last I broke the surface. Fetid air rushed into my lungs, pungent with the coppery smell of blood and disembowelment.

"Maybe it was a need to show respect, maybe it was shock that enabled me to focus on the task at hand. I gently gathered what I could find of my sisters and wrapped them in crisp, clean sheets. The telegraph was damaged in the search. I could receive messages, but was unable to send for help. So, when the mortal remains were cremated and the earth consecrated with salt, I dropped to my knees and prayed for a champion. And there you were, a vampire."

Creed scowled and shifted his weight. Being a hero wasn't part of the agenda and he damn well expected to be compensated for services rendered, but chances were he'd been the one to shoot himself in the foot in the first place. What if that giggling nun nonsense back in El Paso had been the final fuse in the powder keg? He placed a firm hand on Sister Anjelica's shoulder and gave it an easy squeeze, choosing his words carefully, "Now, take it easy, sis." His spine stiffened in case she decided to break out bawling. "You seriously can't tell me that a big-time outfit like the Catholic Church, whose business it is to save souls, wouldn't forgive one tiny whisper."

Her solemn stare flickered then ignited. "Mister Goodnight, a Vow Of Silence is just that! Once the Ritum Sanctum Praesidium is invoked, no voice may speak louder than God! You bear witness to the demonic carnage suffered at the monasterio in their ferocious search for the Book. The second priest I spoke of earlier, Father Amantino, was intercepted in Almas Perdidas, along with the three nuns in his charge. He is the only living person capable of ending this abomination in time. They remain alive until such time as the Book is found. As we debate this, the very Gates Of Hell swing wider. A soulless, unblinking legion of the damned waits on the other side. Perhaps you've met some of them? They will descend without mercy, befouling the sacred, possessing most in their path and devouring the rest. I would imagine that extends to vampires as well. THAT is why we ride to Almas Perdidas."

Creed clenched his jaw, breathing evenly "Uh huh, about that, sis, Rev might have mentioned something about an order being issued to release the first wave of specters tomorrow. Now hear me out, we're riding out of here today, but we're already burning daylight as it is. We need to keep our heads down and stay one step ahead. I'm up for a good fight, that's the deal I made, but those slippery bastards walked through an explosion that would have leveled a horde of rotters."

Sister Anjelica cleared her throat, a thin mixture of conviction and courage creeping into her face. "We will indeed make Almas Perdidas and be waiting when they arrive. Father Amantino will know what to do. Once the head of the snake has been removed, the body will wither and he will deal with them at that point." She stood efficiently and straightened her skirt. "I'll wire Reverend Jim's warning to the Archbishop, then we ride."

Creed threw back a hard slug of Mezcaland pushed away from the table, grinning. "Yes ma'am, if there's one thing I know how to do, it's chop heads."

# 13

LIGHTS FROM EL PASO blurred in the distance, dully outlined by a ghostly waxen moon. Reeling from loss of blood, the desperate outlaw swayed feebly in the saddle, wheezing with a dry cackle. Despite surviving days alone in a sweltering expanse of Sonoran desert, he was probably going to die before reaching the outskirts of town. What did it matter if his saddle bags bulged with silver from the bank robbery in Piedras Negras? Money means nothing to a dead man.

His sallow skin blanched to a sickly yellow as he bled out slowly. White, jagged bone protruded from a deep gash at his upper shoulder. Numb and useless, his right arm swung tenuously from a severed tendon. To make a bad situation worse, a buzzard, drawn by the putrid stench of gangrene, circled above his head. Braver now, the parasite swooped low, ripping a meaty chunk of flesh from the wound, beating at him with nasty black wings before flapping away. Out of reflex, he jerked the pistol from his belt, aiming blindly. He squeezed the trigger six times before realizing he'd emptied the chamber back in Almas Perdidas.

Circling lower, the screeching scavenger plummeted again.

His clouded eyes twitched as the desperado flipped the pistol in his left palm, drooling with concentration. In less than a heartbeat, his grizzled fingers squeezed into a rigid fist and he smashed the butt of his gun into the buzzard's grimy skull with a brutal crack, then sagged back into the saddle, paralyzed with the heavy fatigue that follows searing pain. Bloody bubbles of spume and mucus foamed in the corners of his mouth as he spat in the dust. "Pinche bastard! If you're going to eat a man's flesh, make damn sure he is dead! Now, who is grist for the reaper? Maybe I lick my wounds and come back to eat you, huh?"

A sharp twist of scorching desert wind spawned dust devils, drenching his face in a thick mixture of sweat and blood from gashes reopened by the strain. In his delirium, he spotted two riders in the distance, wavering like a mirage in watery waves of heat. Wobbling to the pound of thunder in his head, he blinked his raw, crusted eyes. When his vision cleared up some, he could make out the uniforms. Bright moonlight glinted off the silver stars on their chests.

Indifferent to the excruciating throb of pain in his mangled right arm, he flailed his left, screaming maniacally, "Hey YOU! Lawdogs! LAWDOGS! OVER HERE! It's ME, Pascual Sanchez! That's RIGHT, amigos! A five hundred dollar bounty to any man with the guts to bring me in!"

Saliva thickened to paste in his dry mouth and the foul, pungent smell of dust and rot filled his nostrils. He gagged back waves of nausea, crumpling from the saddle in a quivering heap.

Sanchez's eyes rolled cautiously open. An agonizing surge of adrenaline washed his body in a cold sweat but he held on, keeping his head down to avoid notice. His shoulder socket screamed as his right arm dangled limply to his side, giving way to gravity. The gouge on his shoulder had been wrapped with a coarse strip of cloth. Dark blood and septic seepage oozed through the coarse fabric, scraping at the wound when he risked going for his pistol and rusty iron handcuffs bit into his left wrist, bound to the arm of a heavy wooden chair. Squinting up from under lowered eyelids, Sanchez took a measure of the room, planning his next move.

Sheriff Quinten Chance slouched back behind his desk, his weary eyes narrowed with suspicion. He hauled his hat off, swiping at the sweat trickling from his scalp with a beefy hand, and fixed the two nervous deputies in a piercing stare. "Gotta hand it to you boys, that's the wildest piece of horseshit story I've ever come across. You mean to sit there and tell me Pascual Sanchez just rode right up to you in the desert, confessed to a bank job in Piedras Negras and begged you to bring him in? Is that about right?"

Deputy Moody bristled at the cynical tone in the sheriff's words and shrugged the heavy saddle bags from his shoulder, slamming them on the desk. Shanks Hewitt pointed at the silver spilling out of them and curtly picked up the story, "Yessir sheriff, that's right. With all that's goin' on these days, we were riding the perimeter, keeping an eye out for anything peculiar in the wind. Maybe Sanchez here ain't no demon, but we can sure as hell lock him up for thievery. My gut says he figures into this mess, somehow."

Cords of muscles knotted in the sheriff's thick neck and he smiled grimly. "Sorry, boys, reckon you're right." His craggy face reddened with relief when the door creaked open and the Archbishop paced briskly across the office with a commanding click of bootheels.

Sanchez saw the heavy silver cross around the man's neck and strained at the cuffs, shooting savage spikes of pain up his arm. "Praise God, padre! Please, help me! I need a doctor, maybe a cup of water! It's been days since my last meal. PLEASE! PADRE! HELP ME!"

McQuade shoved the silver aside and clutched the wanted poster beneath it in a firm fist. Nodding to each of the lawmen, he scraped a chair across the floor and positioned himself face to face with the prisoner, speaking softly, "Do you know who I am?"

Drinking in the thick, heavy silence, the desperado recoiled with recognition, tensing painfully against the shaking in his limbs. Tears ran down his face as he nodded slowly. "You are Archbishop Declan McQuade. Until two days ago, I thought running up against you was the most terrifying thing that could happen to me, but I was wrong. What I faced in Almas Perdidas was far worse than anything you can do to me."

The archbishop pinned him in a cold, iron glare that turned the blood in his veins to ice. "Don't bet on it, son." He gave the trembling outlaw a contemptuous sneer and held the wanted poster inches from the man's face. "Take a good look, prisoner. Is this you?"

Sanchez knew it was useless to lie. He groaned wretchedly through gritted teeth, "YES, Your Grace. As you say, I am a thief, but I swear on my mother's eyes I'm no killer. My name is Pasqual Sanchez and I'll tell you whatever you want to know, but I need a doctor, or I will die before you can kill me."

McQuade wadded the poster up and hurled it against the wall, snarling, "Yes you will, son, one way or the other. Start talking. I want everything you know about Almas Perdidas. Depending on your story, I might patch you up before I hang you."

Sanchez's feral eyes gleamed with the ferocity of a man who has nothing to lose. Rattling the cuffs, he jerked his chin, gesturing at a bottle of whiskey on the sheriff's desk, then locked eyes with McQuade. "Pour it, Your Grace." He growled with the cagey arch of an eyebrow, "And I'll tell you that story."

His stoic face devoid of emotion, the Archbishop flicked a disinterested hand. "Deputy, remove Mister Sanchez's restraints and fetch him a double shot of that whiskey." The deputy hissed under his breath and twisted the key, letting the rusted cuffs drop to the floor with a clang. Thrusting a stiff shot into the prisoner's outstretched fingers, he grunted and scuffed away.

Sanchez convulsed violently, choking the liquor down his desiccated throat, then coughed. "Makes no sense, me telling you this," he rasped, licking his cracked, swollen lips, "But I'm a man of my word. See, the road knows her own and men like me grow right familiar with her rhythm. Just so you know, there's a monthly run from isolated silver mines in the desert to an assayer's setup in Saltillo. Damn fools at the mining office have it figured that moving the shipments is donkey work, not calling for much more than a pulse with a gun."

The prisoner chuckled lewdly, spasming into a fit of coughing that left him gasping for air. Irritated, Mcquade signaled impatiently for the bottle of whiskey and poured him another shot. The stinging liquid went down easier this time. Sanchez shook his head sideways and continued with a wheezing croak, "Two dimwitted guards with more scars than skin, holin' up for the night in the same village every damn time? Forgive me, Your Grace, but they were begging to be robbed.

"It was late afternoon when I rode into town, a time when practical people seek to escape the raw, blistering sun. The streets were deserted, but the cantina was loud and crowded with rowdies blowing off steam. As I had figured, the two guards were killing time, getting roostered up on a second bottle of redeye. I walked right past them and eased onto a stool at the bar. An argument over a fancy woman heated up and turned into a shoving match. When the hooker flounced up with a fresh bottle for the winner, I settled my tab and slipped quietly out the door.

As I mentioned earlier, it was a monthly run. I knew the silver was being held in the bank safe and it was edging up on closing time. It wasn't much of a village and they weren't expecting trouble, so the same teller locked up each afternoon. I had to strike fast, before that safe was locked.

Lucky for us both, the teller was unarmed. I kicked the door in and showed him my pistol, tossing the saddlebags on the counter. The old man's face went hot with fear and he backed up, raising his hands to show he didn't want trouble. Keeping the gun trained on his heaving chest, I waved a thumb toward the back. At once, he shifted his rheumy eyes to the open safe. I nodded slowly, keeping an eye on the door while he filled the bags with silver. My lips to God's ears, Your Grace, I tapped him on the back of his skull with the pistol butt, but I swear I didn't kill him."

The deputies scoffed, exchanging cynical glances. When the prisoner chuckled with them, McQuade silenced the laughter with a look that belongs in church when you're confessing, or maybe at a hanging. The two lawmen never wanted him to look at them like that again. When he had their complete attention, the Archbishop clenched his jaw, composing himself. "Mister Sanchez, we have established the fact that you are a thief. Be assured, it is now in your best interests to inform me about events in Almas Perdidas. If not, our business is concluded. Are we clear?"

Sanchez searched McQuade's face and something in the Archbishop's eyes made him shudder. Sagging muscles twitched nervously as he resumed the story in a quiet, quavering voice, "The plan was to stable the horse and escape to Guadalajara on the evening stage. Daylight was burning and there was no time to waste. I rode hard for the swing station in Almas Perdidas, but the ticket office was crowded when I arrived. Determined to be on that stage, I elbowed a path to the window and dropped a fistful of silver on the counter. The clerk rubbed at his chin stubble and looked me up and down. You know damn well the greedy weasel knew something wasn't right, but he stuffed the silver in his apron pocket and stamped my ticket just the same. Had he been an honest man, Your Grace, I wouldn't be in such dire need of a doctor now!"

McQuade's brow furrowed into a threatening scowl. "Much like the silver in your pouch, prisoner. Keep talking!"

Sanchez licked at the cold sweat pooling on his upper lip and hunched forward, clutching the weeping bandage on his arm. His bloodshot eyes went distant as he groaned through the pain, "Rifle shots rang out, again and again, muffling the sound of approaching hoofbeats. Certain that the guards had caught up to me, I slammed the door and pressed my face to the window shutters, wedging the barrel of my pistol through an open crack. One lone rider emerged from a billowing blanket of dust. He leaned into his horse, galloping at a full run against the blustering desert winds battering against him as if Hell itself were at his back. My finger tightened on the trigger, then I pulled up short when I heard what he was screaming. "DEVILS! DEVILS! RUN! HIDE!"

"A bloodthirsty torrent of screeching howls and screams closed the distance behind him. I lurched back when a savage thunder of lashing hooves shook the shutters open and the ticket office wobbled as if buckling from an earthquake. Hulking shadows of men and horses danced in the dust, slicing and clawing at struggling victims in a merciless surge of bloody savagery.

"I quickly grabbed my saddlebags and started eyeing up the room for exits, when a loutish man in the throes of panic threw himself against the door. The fool was twisting the knob, trying to get the door open when it burst from his grasp. He managed a single, strangled shriek of terror before blood spurted from a gaping slash on his throat. At first, dust and jagged splinters of wood made it impossible to see what had taken him. Then, I focused and stumbled backward. It was demons alright, skin boys, a whole damn army of 'em.

"Unsure of which way to run, a horrified wave of screaming swelled through the others. I could feel the heat and terror as the hysterical crowd rammed me from behind, breaking out into the street to be slaughtered. Shoving back, I worked my way to the rear exit. I cursed and gritted my teeth as the door squealed on its rusty hinges. When the opening was wide enough, I squeezed out into the narrow alleyway, moving fast and low in the shadows.

"Not daring to breathe, I risked a glance through a window in back of the stable. I could barely believe my luck to find it empty with the exception of my mare. I slipped silently inside, my ears ringing with keening screams and wails of the dying, caught up in the ravening madness sweeping the street. Then I understood why the stable had been passed over. Sickened to my very soul, I was compelled to witness the unholy massacre through a thin slit between the stable doors, praying for a chance to escape.

Hours passed until finally not a living man trapped in the swarm was left alive. Frenzied skin boys began pounding on the doors of those hiding inside the buildings. Figuring I was a dead man either way, I was ready to make a run for it when a ripple of silence engulfed the mob. A ghostly shimmer of moon revealed a blood-soaked Fallen clopping slowly down the street, vaguely outlined in the final rays of a setting sun. He carried a severed head impaled on a long stick. My stomach heaved and cramped, tightening my chest into a tourniquet when the monster reined to a stop across from the stable. He thrust the gory stick into the ground and turned on the skin boys in a blind rage, roaring in fury, "The Book belongs to ME! It's MINE! Saddle up and keep watch in the mesas! If I see your miscreant faces again without that transport coach, I'll burn your skins, myself! GET ON WITH IT!"

"I shoved a fist in my mouth to keep from crying out as walls warped and cracked around me when the horrified demon-spawn stampeded into the desert, spewing a head-splitting spate of shrieks and bellows. Satisfied, the Fallen tethered his horse and disappeared inside a cantina called Diablo Rojo, shadowed by a fierce band of devils who seemed unmoved by his threats.

"I huddled in the darkness for at least an hour, waiting for death to find me, but the village was completely still. Swallowing my reluctance, I heaved the stable door open with a creaking whine and froze, steadying myself to make a run. There was no reaction, so I wrapped the reins around my fist and slowly led my horse around the mangled corpses strewn in the street. At the edge of town, I hooked a boot into the stirrup and swung into the saddle, heading north at a brisk gallop.

"Coyotes yipped in the distance, reminding me that I was not alone in the desert. I stared out into the deepening darkness, anxiously scanning the horizon. A thundering rattle of wheels shattered the silence. Seconds later, the ground vibrated as a speeding, black transport coach broke through the muddled spirals of dust and flew past me. I can tell you that the passengers were alive at that point, but clouds of dust churning up along the mesas said they might not be for long.

"At the first bend in the road, I spurred my horse out into the open desert, hoping to stay clear of the skin boys. The rest happened very fast. I heard the monster circling behind me before I saw him. My heart leapt into my chest and I dug my spurs into the horse's flanks, urging her to go faster, but I could hear from the rumble of hooves that he was closing the distance fast. Soon the terrible sounds were right behind me and I could stand it no more. Eyes bulging with terror, I glanced back as the demon rode up next to me. I heard a horrible sound of meat ripping away from bone as his jagged talons sheared through my shirt and into my shoulder. Without blinking, I spun my pistol from the holster and emptied the chamber into his ghastly face, splattering brains out a big hole in the back of his skull.

"There was blood everywhere, his and mine. I fled into the desert with no way to account for events after that until the deputies found me outside of El Paso."

McQuade's lips hardened into a dead smile, the kind of smile that makes a man think twice before speaking. He laced his fingertips together and leaned forward, locking eyes with the prisoner. "Are you sure there is nothing else you can tell me, Sanchez? Nothing at all?"

Sanchez caught his meaning and nodded, a trace of fear darkening his eyes. "I've told you everything I can remember, Your Grace." Lips pulled back tight over his teeth, he regarded the Archbishop soberly. "But I can tell you this much, nobody wants to see these skin boys pay more than I do. Yes, I am a thief, a good one, and I know how to read a man. The sour smell of dread clings to this Fallen like a shroud, inspiring fear, not loyalty from the demons under his command." Sanchez moaned and collapsed to the floor, shut off from everything but the searing pain in his shoulder and the stubborn drumming of his heart.

It was clear the interrogation was over and the prisoner would die without immediate medical attention. McQuade shoved his chair back and stood abruptly, shifting his gaze to the deputies who seemed to be frozen in place. His jaw dropped and he drew a deep breath preparing to chide the men for their slow response. Taken aback by the look of pure horror on their faces, he let his mouth snap shut with a soft click of teeth, turning his attention to the sheriff. "Chance, lock this man up then fetch a doctor and a hot meal. When you're finished here, I want to see the three of you in my office." Without another word, he left them to the task.

The nervous lawmen arrived less than an hour later. The archdiocese was an imposing adobe structure with two bell towers and massive stained glass windows. A wide expanse of stairs led to a series of ornate wooden doors on the second floor. They were quickly ushered up to a meeting room and settled into chairs behind an elongated mahogany table. McQuade entered directly behind them with a brisk, ranging stride and claimed his seat at the end, letting the heavy oak door slam shut behind him. Heat streamed through the open window but he couldn't shake the clammy chill in his hands.

Dim lantern light veiled the room as the men regarded each other with a gloomy sobriety. Sheriff Chance spoke up first, not so quick to place confidence in the prisoner's story. "Tell me, Your Grace, you buy that thieving bastard's story?"

McQuade grimaced, choking back the outrage. He slid his hands over the smooth surface with a deadly calm, leaning in closer. "Every word of it! We must learn what we can from the information, regardless of what we may think of the messenger."

McQuade sensed Chance's skepticism and his flashing eyes bored into the sheriff's face. "We don't have time for this, so let me bring you boys up to speed." He clenched his jaw tight and slipped two fingers down into his boot, pulling out a crumpled piece of paper. The lawmen shifted restlessly as he stiffly shook the paper in front of them, growling, "I'll make it simple. You boys were aware that communication with the monasterio had ceased. Well, only this morning, I received a wire from La Iglesia De La Santa Cruz in Purgatorio. Sister Anjelica informed me that the monasterio had been desecrated by demons when the Gates Of Hell were breached. Somehow, she managed to survive.

"Father Fantino's team, sent to seal the Gates, were killed en route. The vampire, Goodnight, unaware that he was in possession of the Book, delivered the bodies and found the Sister hiding in the chapel. He agreed to escort her to Purgatorio for a fee."

Sheriff Chance grumbled under his breath, "Don't that just sound like Goodnight! Fucking vampires!"

McQuade scowled at the interruption. "We must thank God that he did, however a horde of damned souls sensed the Book and slipped the breach. Both Goodnight and the nun would be dead if not for the intervention of a half-breed Fallen, Reverend Jim, master of the hellhounds. You might recall that the prisoner mentioned waning loyalties within the demon ranks?

"This brings me to the Fallen that Sanchez spoke of. The monster he described is Hadriel, commander of Hell's elite legion. In fact, this letter I'm holding was delivered to me by hellhounds. The intent is clear, I either trade the Book for Father Amantino and the sisters, or they will be tortured and slaughtered in unspeakable ways. What you might not know is that Father Amantino is our last chance to seal the gates in time."

Furious, Sheriff Chance blustered with outrage, "Damn waste-of-grace Fallen's gone plum crazy if he thinks we make deals with demons. Sounds like the boys and I need to take him down a notch or two, Your Grace!"

The archbishop tensed as rising night winds whistled in through the open window, kicking up a flurry of dust in the flickering lantern light. Shadows fell across the letter clutched in his fist, adding weight to his words, "If this Fallen doesn't worry you, then you aren't listening, Chance, and I need you to listen. Don't make the mistake of thinking that madness makes him vulnerable. Ultimately, the only shot we have at sealing the breach is to rescue Father Amantino's team and let him do his job. As it stands, we're gambling on a vampire and a nun to save them from Hell's elite legion and an army of specters marching north."

McQuade kept his eyes fixed on the sheriff, giving him time to process the gravity of the situation. After a moment, the lawmen exchanged an ashen look of mutual understanding and Chance nodded calmly. "We're up against something evil, that's for damn sure. Vampire and a nun, you say? I best believe we need to do something about that. What can we do to even the odds?"

The tough-minded sheriff had never backed down in the face of danger and the Archbishop was expecting nothing less from him. McQuade lifted his chin and grinned. "Let's get to it, gentlemen. There's no provision in your training for saving the world from demons, so we need to stick together and plan ahead. Sanchez provided us with weaknesses we can use against the Fallen, his fear of the Book and the lack of respect from those under his command. We also know that there are villagers trapped in their homes that he can use against us.

"Shanks! Dub! We don't know those parts, so offer Sanchez a full pardon in return for a layout of Almas Perdidas, including that narrow alleyway, the stables and the Diablo Rojo. Chance, we need men willing to posse up by tomorrow morning, let them know what they're getting themselves into. They'll need weapons, picks and shovels. We're gonna break through the adobe walls behind those homes and free as many villagers as possible before the attack.

"Stay locked and loaded, boys. Every bullet shoots a demon straight back to Hell and that's one less skin boy in the mix. Be ready to ride if that horde of the damned turns up before we locate Father Amantino. Run as far and fast as you can, there's nothing more you can do. Are there any questions?"

No voice rose above the moaning of the wind. The archbishop crossed himself and smiled grimly. "We ride in the morning, gentlemen. God be with you."

# 14

---

Sudden, scathing winds whipped up a cloying reek of murder and decay in the lifeless streets of Almas Perdidas. Hadriel covered his nose with a handkerchief, wincing at the pungent stench snaking in through spreading cracks in the adobe walls. There was no getting away from it. Unblinking, he jerked his head back and drained the bitter dregs of tequila, then slung the bottle at flies swarming the filthy bar.

Muscles bunched in his neck with a rage that wanted to rip and shred. He'd heard the talk behind his back, voices low, but not low enough. With no response to his demand for a trade, a couple of mouthy skin boys armed themselves to the teeth and got loud about it in front of a gang gathered outside the cantina. They had it figured that if the church didn't fear him, maybe he wasn't so fearsome after all. In a blinding blur, the Fallen seized a machete and spun, slicing into both necks in a single sweep. The fools were still screaming when their heads came off and rolled into the retreating crowd.

All the same, he had to make a move soon. The insult could not go unchallenged. He took in a deep breath and let it out with a flat hissing sound. Such arrogance, this Archbishop should be more mindful of who he is dealing with. Perhaps someone should blow his holy brains out and tell God he just up and died.

No matter, if there was no word by tomorrow, he would give the order to release the first wave of damned souls, then feed the priest and his whores to the skin boys and resume operations at the Morningstar Revival. By the time another priest could be sanctified, he'd have the numbers to simply take the Book and kill anyone who stood in his path. On further reflection, he would probably do that anyway.

Fatigued with heat and boredom, he leaned over the bar and snatched another bottle. Isolated in a flat, emotionless wasteland where he passed the heavy hours, Hadriel rarely dreamed. Despite that, he found himself wondering why Rev kept coming up empty-handed on the Book's location. Maybe the kid was just angry about the new skin he'd been stuck in, but a grinding tension in his gut said that winding the surly halfbreed up before the Book was in his hands had cost him time, maybe even more than that.

A Fallen, never having tasted the betrayal of Grace, should be relentless, but Hell's primary tracker was infested with human emotions that made him weak and unpredictable. Ungrateful pup, he'd been doing the whiner a service. Angels fall and humans fail. It was best he learn his place in the scheme of things early on. Hadriel gripped the bottle, relishing the searing burn of liquor in his mouth. All true Fallen knew their place. Reflecting on events surrounding his own exile stoked the murderous fire in his brain.

Branded rebellious, his back-stabbing brothers hunted him down and severed the ties binding him to Heaven. Silenced from defending his actions, he fell hard from the world of angels into the treacherous world of man.

Acute sensation flooded his senses and instinct took over. Hot desert air stung his nose with the sweet smell of water. Sunlight radiated from the canteen of a man fishing nearby in the Pecos River. Taking possession of the human proved to be simple, almost second nature. At once, passion welled inside him like fire in dry tinder. If God loved these lowly creatures more than the angels themselves, maybe he would listen now. He knelt in the dust and prayed for redemption, but God no longer heard his voice.

Oddly, being inside the man made him feel more alive than he'd ever thought possible. Freedom to indulge his true nature, outside the censure of Heaven, made his mind tick in a way it never had. It was the last time he bothered to pray.

Fevered with excitement, he lay down at the very edge of the riverbank and whistled with a red-tailed hawk, circling in the updrafts. Silver stars sparkled in a turquoise current as one wave overlapped the next in white foamy crests, covering his legs with clear sheets of water. After a moment, his eyelids fluttered closed and he breathed in the rich, earthy air, scrunching his bare toes up in the damp, gritty soil.

Hadriel found Evangeline Hyde somewhere between his first human breath and her last. He knew she wasn't holy by the way her long, raven black hair whipped and twisted in the wind as she danced, bathing in the shadows like a wood nymph. She was clearly a white witch, a healer most likely, but he could tell she'd done her time in the darkness and survived. He released an audible sigh of regret when she scrambled up the embankment and disappeared.

Jerking upright, he thought to chase after her, when the scent of herbs and lilacs filled him with a vague sense of peace. There was a soft pressure at his back and he turned looking down at the long, slender hand on his shoulder, then up into the sultry sweetness of her face. Her pale blue eyes were innocent and curious, devoid of fear. He knew then that she saw him, the broken angel inside the man.

A bright desert moon infused her skin with an uncanny shimmer that sparkled in her widened pupils, clinging to her lashes. He drew a deep shuddering breath, letting his eyes trail down the length of her sensual body. Intense arousal triggered a hot rush of blood to his head. He shivered in a cold sweat as a swelling of veins washed through his body. Gently smoothing the tangles back from her contorted face, he pushed a knee between her legs and spun her toward him, running a firm hand along her thigh. Her naked, writhing body, slick with sweat, rose to meet him as he swayed lightly against her stomach and breasts, tracing the outline of her lips with his tongue. Blood drummed in his temples and he yielded to a surging torrent of sensation, reveling in human secrets that would never be secret again.

The longing whistle of a train echoed far away as night surrendered to a blazing desert sun. Still tingling with static, he wrapped his fierce arms around her, cradling her fragrant body against his chest. Beautiful heretic, next to her truth, everything he'd ever known was a lie.

Wildness sparkled in her eyes. She laughed and pushed him back, scampering nimbly to her feet. Turning away from him to wiggle back into her clothes, she winked over her shoulder and curtsied, "I am Evangeline Hyde, fortune-teller to those with coin in the purse. Fine spun sugar, that's what YOU are. Some men blind like lightning, others buy me pretty things, but you, I'd almost marry you. Your name, angel, what is it?"

He rose to his feet and stood naked in front of her, savoring her name as it rolled across his tongue, "Evangeline." A slow grin spread across his face as he matched her insolent gaze, "I am Hadriel."

Shadows played on her features in the bright glare, masking the fevered flush in her cheeks. "I'm not good for much more than alibis and sin, but I do know that we all need a place to run at times. When there's no way home, you make your own. One need not be a gypsy to see that your pale skin is getting redder by the minute in this blazing sun, Hadriel, so put your clothes on and follow me."

The looming fifteen foot entry arch crowned with baroque lettering, 'Doc Zion's Carnival & Medicine Show', was partially obscured by flurries of dust. The garish ticket booth just beyond it was ornately carved with cherubs and blossoming scrolls, lacquered in vivid yellow, magenta and royal blue. Hadriel watched Evangeline fumble with the clasp of a gaudy jeweled brooch, securing the shiny purple scarf twisted around her head. His face crinkled with laughter at this human vision of Heaven.

Evangeline grinned back. Stacks of gilt and copper bangles cascading down both arms jingled as she scolded him with an index finger. There was kindness in her almond-shaped eyes. Her long, wispy skirt, a chaos of silk scarves in aqua, lilac and bright yellow, swirled around her legs when she walked. The effect was mesmerizing. Heaven was more like that, or at least it should have been.

Strange and marvelous, the carnival percolated like thick black coffee. Hadriel hung suspended in the moment. His breath came in rapid, shallow bursts as a wide grin swept ear-to-ear across his face, delighted by the kite-spinners, exotic dancers from the middle east and the hot, greasy smell of meat and funnel cakes.

He melted easily into the carnival life, most particularly the compelling chant of the barkers, hawking last-chance tickets to beat the house. Evenings, when the crowd rolled in, lovers and loners gathered at Madam Evangeline's like unlicked cubs, longing for prophecies of love and luck. Gamblers and chancers stood in line for a seat at the table when Hadriel dealt the cards. Lambs don't shear the butcher, but he made sure there were just enough winners to keep them coming back.

Months tumbled by and the child now inside her grew. Riveted by love and the erotic surge of fascination, Hadriel stayed. He had an uneasy feeling about the baby they'd made, but if she loved it, he would do what he could to love it as well. He wanted nothing more from this world than to dance with Evangeline until the vineyards withered and there was nothing left but wine.

Most carnies gave Crowsworth, Texas a wide berth, but it was on the circuit and empty pockets can get pretty vocal. A mutual decision was reached to stay one night, drum up some cash and move on quickly. Hadriel pitched in with the grifters and roustabouts in an effort to get done and get gone before things could go south. They swarmed the heat-beaten ground with battered tents and creaking metal, already regretting the decision to stay.

Dogs howled, running wild into the desert on the night Evangeline died. Hadriel stiffened, needles of dread crawling up his spine as rumbling thunder cracked in the distance. The swelling stench of singed flash floated up into the air like smoke. Fire smoldered in his belly, fueling the rage until his eyes were red as embers. Without uttering a sound, he broke into a headlong run for the fortune-telling tent.

The local Crowsworth preacher and his wife, flanked by a small gathering of parishioners, waited piously outside of the tent, sweaty hands clasped in prayer. Paralyzedwith horror by Hadriel's grim visage, they cowered back as he tore through the flap, knowing that a storm had come and there would be no mercy for the men inside.

Two sallow-eyed witch hunters dressed in long black robes, hovered over Evangeline like vultures. One sadistic zealot, his grisly face framed by the flickering torch in his fist, was attempting to purge the corpse with the crackling flames, while the other rubbed his hands together, chanting in a greasy monotone. Hadriel could still taste her on his tongue when he extended his talons and clawed the butcher's face off. Blood gushed from the gaping hole as he slammed the torch deep inside it. Chanting louder, the cringing accomplice struggled to save himself and stumbled to his knees on the blood-slick ground. The man shrieked in horrible pain when razor sharp claws dug into his back, ripping out his spine before driving it through the hunter's still-beating heart. A crimson froth of blood and saliva spewed from his mouth as Hadriel tore flesh away from bone, viciously devouring pieces of meat from the shredded body parts.

The Fallen swiped at the gore on his lips and dropped to his knees beside Evangeline, gently tracing the outline of her face with his fingers. She was cold with the onset of rigor and the blood was thickening, but not completely dried on her waxy skin. Thick raven hair splayed across the pillow, tangled and stained pink with saliva, framing out her delicate face, now battered and blotched. Her abdomen and inner thighs swelled with dark purplish bruising and charred flesh where the hunters had tried to burn her. There was no Heaven sweeter than the sound of her heartbeat, no Hell more empty than a world without her in it.

Unchecked savagery boiled deep in his eyes, churning through his system, then dissipating slowly. The last traces of his Grace bled away and he let the darkness swallow him. He closed her milky eyes with the palm of his hand, indifferently shifting his gaze to the infant, laying still and silent against her right knee. It squirmed slightly when he picked the baby up, dangling it by an ankle. By a sheer miracle he didn't drop the child when its eyelids fluttered open and a high, screeching wail shattered the silence as it filled its tiny lungs with air for the first time. Callously wedging the baby under his arm, he staggered to his feet, taking an icy measure of the carnage he'd wrought. It wasn't enough, it would never be enough. He hungered to resurrect the hunters and slaughter them again and again. At once, he realized that he could do exactly that.

A dark shiver of fear coursed through the preacher's wife when he raged from the tent and slung the wailing baby at her. Her mouth dropped open in a silent scream and she snatched the wailing infant to her chest, escaping into the night.

Clouds, black as mourning, opened up, unleashing torrential sheets of rain. Hadriel threw his ferocious head back, releasing a haunting volley of soul-grinding howls that spiraled all the way to Heaven. When the barbaric hunters fell screaming down to Hell, his would be the first face they saw.

Hell turned out to be a quick study. Demonic legions shared the same festering limitations of a single-minded beast. Inherently wary of the Fallen, angels passing into Hell were seized and sequestered. Hadriel wasted no time introducing the overseer of Hell's elite legions to the darker gifts of Heaven. With a snap of his fingers, the commander burst into a pillar of sulfuric flame.

The host of hostile demons instinctively lurched toward him, then recoiled, each hesitant to attack first. After a tense silence, a menacing brute snarled defiantly and lunged forward, his slitted yellow eyes narrowed with bestial insolence. Unimpressed, Hadriel raised his hand and pinned the demon in a glacial stare, hissing, "Careful who you cross, devil." The hellion looked back over his shoulder for backup. When no one stepped up to follow his lead, the grumbling challenger melted back into the ranks.

Hadriel shrugged, tilting his head. "My name is Hadriel. I don't give a rat's ass if you want to kill me, only that you obey me." He glanced at the pile of ashes on the floor, then continued, "If you witless hellions are concerned as to my intentions or stability, bravo! You should be. Conquerors, by nature, are stark raving mad. However, small passions have no power to stir the blood. Under my command, the elite legions will rule not only souls of the damned, but the world of man as well." He jabbed an impatient index finger at the demon who'd challenged him, "YOU, release all Fallen in captivity." When the browbeaten hellion scurried off to obey his command, a slow, evil grin twitched at the corners of Hadriel's mouth. "Before we get started, escort me to where the new arrivals are caged. I have unfinished business to settle. If you have any questions, keep them to yourselves."

Soon after, when scouts patrolling the perimeter brought word that a human woman had abandoned an innocent at the Gates Of Hell, malice undulated from his body in waves like a snake. Confused by the commander's peculiar reaction, the hellions showed him a tattered note stating that the infant's name was Reverend Jim, then inquired if it should be incinerated along with the child. The Fallen's impassive stare intensified with an icy cast. "Leave him to the desert and let God sort it out."

Dusk descended, leaving a blurry sulfurous mist rippling in watery waves of heat. A shift in the wind exposed hulking forms, dimly ghosted by the rising moon. Wavering cries escalated to incinerating howls. Only one creature sang like that, hellhounds. The infant's plaintive, hungry shrieks continued unabated as the pack drew nearer and nearer. Silent and cautious, the beasts circled the child, sniffing and nudging with long, gruesome snouts.

When the infant was seized by the shirt and dragged off into the night, Hadriel assumed it would be devoured and dismissed the matter.

A series of commands summoning the missing tracker had gone unanswered, casting the shadow of betrayal. Hadriel crushed the bottle of tequila in his fist, shooting jagged shards of glass into the walls. He forced himself to breathe calmly when he wanted to rage. The connection was crystal clear. The wily tracker was a phantom, he and those hounds could be anywhere or nowhere. Calculating just how much the boy may have exposed to the church made the skin crawl up his back.

A single thought pulsed in his tumbling brain, torching every nerve in his body. He had failed to give the boy credit for his Fallen blood. Rev was furious and bitter, with enough power to act on those emotions. Hadriel's eyes glittered feverishly, the cocky little cretin clearly figured he could run his own show with those mangy hounds at his back. If the imbecile believed that, he knew nothing about his sire. To impose a singular course of action calls for no great finesse, no imagination. Total domination requires intellect, the ability to strike mortal terror into the cowering masses.

A predatory thirst swept through the Fallen, feeding his

madness. The ungrateful halfbreed, the Archbishop and the growing number of demons who opposed him would do well to ask themselves who among them was truly more fearsome. Calling shots is easy when you're hunting rabbits, but throwing a wolf into that mix changes everything. There weren't enough hounds in Hell to stop what was coming for the bastards. They all would knuckle under when every black-hearted soul condemned to perdition was free to walk the earth.

Turbulent morning winds drove in a wave of gray, ruffled clouds, obscuring sunrise in a blanket of shadow. Hadriel spread his arms in a wide sweeping gesture, intoning necromantic verses from the deepest wells of damnation. Veins and tendons stretched taut as his stiff fingers clenched into fists, summoning the damned...

# 15

RAW, swirling skies weighed heavy at the smothering spirals of
dust, clouding his line of vision. The few burning smears of sun
that managed to pierce the dismal overcast did little to dispel his
boredom. Rev slapped at an annoying fly on his cheek and
another strip of skin flew off. He raised a leathery hand over his
brow to block the glare when a patch of sizzling sunlight broke
through the pall, stretching long shadows of the riders ahead of
him out across the flat wasteland. He'd been dogging the pair
since they lit out from Purgatorio, keeping his distance. By his
reckoning, there was no further need to discuss the first
onslaught of specters that stood to be released, when there was
nothing more to talk about as yet. So far, there was still no
movement in the desert behind them with the exception of a few
coyotes squabbling over a kill.

He didn't rightly know why the coyotes had suddenly stopped
their calling some minutes back. Smelled like fear, but maybe
not. He had to admit that things had gone way too quiet for his
liking as well.

Throwing down against the legions of Hell with a vampire
and a nun was a sucker's move, but he had no regrets. Truth of

the matter is you never know what someone is capable of, so it's usually best to sit back and give it time. That being said, Whiskey Lick had already told him everything he needed to know about Creed Goodnight.

Could be that blindsiding an entire town and burning it all to the ground was a stroke of pure, dumb luck, but Rev didn't think so. The way he saw it, Goodnight was a gambler, aware of everything that stood between him and the final death. The more calculated effort he put into a gamble, the more he walked away with. Angels and demons might place their faith in prophecies, but the vampire put his money on the gamble and he knew what it felt like to win. So far, he'd never lost and his body count was horrifying to those he hunted.

Two days straight with no contact from Hadriel meant that the vindictive bastard probably knew that Rev had gone rogue. The legions would be gunning for him now, and they never missed. Not that there would be much left for them to torture. His host body was sinking fast, going through a constant mutation like wild animals were ripping at the flesh. He needed to squeeze out a resolution real damn quick, before the rest of his rotting face slid from the skull.

Rev had been on the vampire's trail for less than an hour, still within spitting distance from the Gates as the crow flies, when Hadriel's summons finally broke the stalemate, a command to unleash every thirsty soul ever condemned to hellfire. Creeping realization numbed his extremities, sending tremors deep into his bones. A fanatical maneuver like that was sheer madness, unchecked chaos with no shelter at all for those caught in the wake, demons and humans alike.

He'd reckoned dead wrong about the Fallen. This was personal, between an unrepentant angel and the God who had cast him out. Well, that suited Rev just fine. He figured where a ruthless conqueror would be wary, an entitled jackass would never see him coming. Luckily, the Gates were nearby and the hounds could run damage control before things got out of hand, but he had to strike swiftly. Most likely, Goodnight and the nun would be dodging stragglers until he could backtrack and catch up to them, but it couldn't be helped.

Rev reined around hard and dug his boots into the horse's flanks, galloping straight across the desert at a full run. The familiar, high-pitched baying of hellhounds on the hunt resounded from all sides as the pack fell into step at his heels, whipping up whirlwinds of dust.

Lit by the eerie, scarlet glow of sundown, desolate terrain skirting the perimeter looked to be deserted, showing only marginal evidence of disruption. Rev picked up maybe thirty heat signatures outside the Gates, but no sign of the crushing swarm he'd envisioned. Insurgents managing to escape had done so one or two at a time, with no pattern to their movements aside from skittering tracks spilling across the desert in all directions. It stood to reason they might hesitate, fearing retribution from the pack, but even hellhounds couldn't stand against every soul damned to perdition. Things didn't add up.

Rev pulled up the reins of his exhausted horse and dropped from the saddle to take a measure of the situation, catching a sudden movement in the corner of his eye. Instinctively, he spun the pistol from his holster, flushing an insurgent from the shadows. Drawn by the smell of meat, it sniffed the air and took a few tentative steps toward him. They faced off for a full thirty seconds, before it smelled the hound closing in from behind, the only entity capable of inflicting physical damage on it. Horrified, it tried to run, but the hound slashed out with a massive paw, gutting the specter from neck to abdomen.

He kept his finger on the trigger and crouched down low, pressing an ear to the ground. At once, he heard a roaring crescendo of furious wails vibrating deep under the earth, thundering against the walls that confined it. Rev took a brief try at figuring a chain of events that would keep the damned trapped inside like that, but it was useless. No matter, the hounds would make sure they stayed trapped until the breach could be sealed.

He almost felt sorry for the wormy sons of bitches, but not sorry enough to join them if Hadriel got his greedy hands on that Book.

The legion had taken extreme measures to conceal the fracture. Rev methodically worked his way around the Gates, step by step, until he spotted a narrow chasm in the wall, mostly obscured by massive chunks of rock and a twisted tangle of mesquite roots dangling down over the rift. The indent was tall and narrow, barely noticeable beneath a sprawling overhang that jutted out above it. No one would take notice at all, unless they were looking for it.

The powerful stench of brimstone and rotting flesh was stifling. A thick, sulfuric fog compounded the scent and veiled the rising moon. Rev stepped back to get a better look at the gap, letting his eyes adjust to the darkness. Claw marks around the entry left deep striations indicating that hellions had futilely attempted to enlarge the tight breach by burrowing into the rock. It was a simple fact that a restricted opening like this would only slow things up, not bring them to a standstill. He shifted his weight, twisting his eyes into a focused squint. The cavernous, black void inside the fissure was moving.

Curious, Rev took a few cautious steps closer. Revelation flickered in his smoldering eyes, and he grinned wide. By pulling the trigger on a sweeping exodus of every snakebit sinner condemned to fire and brimstone since the dawn of Man, the dumbass Fallen had shot himself in the foot.

Crawling and clutching, the sorry bastards were dragging themselves up from the flaming bowels of Hell in a relentless surge. A writhing, hideous mass of spectral bodies clung to the edges and walls, wedging tighter and tighter into the narrow fissure, obstructing the only means of escape. It followed that the heat signatures he'd found earlier indicated that a scattering of the recently damned were still quick enough to act on Hadriel's order before the torrent surfaced.

Rev tilted his head, relishing the tart, bitter sting of fear and defeat. Slivers of moon fell through the fog throwing light on an undulating tangle of savage snapping jaws, followed seconds later by hollow, rumbling howls as hellhounds descended on the fissure. Confused from long years of torture and decay, the specters panicked and fell back on themselves with a gurgling hiss, trampling the slow and weak in a raging crush of flailing limbs.

Mindful not to enter the breach, fifteen hounds, razor-sharp fangs bared in a gruesome grin, dug in around the perimeter, in good position to pick off the runners when they came out. The rest of the pack had already taken point in the surrounding desert, anxious to resume the hunt. Rev's lip curled into a sarcastic sneer as he ran a final check for stragglers. All things figured, defusing Hadriel's big, bad army of the damned had taken less than an hour. That left him with plenty of time to catch up with Goodnight and make sure the vampire held up his end of the deal. Soon enough, he would claim the Fallen's host body as his own.

Whistling with a forced intake of air through his rotting teeth, Rev tugged on the reins and reared his horse around, backtracking toward Almas Perdidas.

RANDOM MOTTLES OF SEARING SUNLIGHT BLISTERED THE DESERT. THE measured sound of pounding hooves rang out, echoing across the parched scrub as the pair raced toward Almas Perdidas. Creed glanced over his shoulder at the distant dust trail behind them. The damn halfbreed was shadowing their tracks, but he reckoned he was good with that. Laughter built in his throat as he scanned the desolate badlands, stretching out to either side. You couldn't see them, but they were sure as hell there alright. He could smell them. There might be all kinds of crazy in this world but nothing stood up to the fact that he was pleased to find a pack of hellhounds on his ass.

It was late afternoon when that little warning tingled up the gunslinger's spine, leaving a bad taste in his mouth. He sensed, rather than heard the one thing he'd been dreading in this whole messy goat rodeo. That crazy Fallen had actually done it. Only a raving lunatic would want the gore-stained legacy of unleashing every rotting bottom-crawler in the depths of Hell. Army of the damned or not, the gunslinger didn't let much get to him, but without Rev or the priest, he had no means of protecting the nun. When he turned in the saddle to verify his misgivings, Sister Anjelica followed his gaze. Without batting an eye, she tilted her chin at the clouds of dust retreating back into the desert and he nodded. They locked eyes, both knowing what was headed their way, and that the only chance at survival would be to outrun them.

To make matters worse, sharp veins of lightning spiked to the right of them, throwing light on a blackened bank of slow-rolling clouds moving in. If the twister in Whiskey Lick was an indication of what came next, he reckoned they'd better make Almas Perdidas before that storm grew a tail.

Creed slowed the lathered horses to a gallop, letting them rest up a bit in case they had to make a run for it. For the next few hours, they rode in silence, listening intently for any movement in the wasteland behind them.

Dried scrub and debris rattled in the rising wind as fading streaks of sunlight dwindled away. Slivers of pale, white moon flickered in and out, tangled in a mixture of storm clouds and red, sulfuric fog. Without warning, the coursing stallion spooked at a fitful burst of wind kicking up clouds of dust. Cuchillo sidled closer to the stallion, keeping the pace while the skittish animal snorted and reared, tossing its head against the bit. Sister Anjelica clung tightly to the reins, twisting side to side as erratic gusts whipped ferociously at her vestments. Determined to keep riding, the nun wobbled in the saddle, praying fervently under her breath.

Snarling impatiently, Creed stood in the stirrups and

stretched across, wrapping a strong arm around her waist to hold her steady. After she regained her balance, he leaned back into the saddle and regarded her with a cynical grin. "Look, sis, as long as you've got God's ear, tell him that we're getting there fast as we can, but we can't do the job unless we get there in one piece." A lock of sweaty, blond hair fell into his face and he spread his arms wide, staring up at the threatening skies. "You should also mention that this might be just a monsoon rolling in, but it sure as hell looks tornado-ready, which might put a serious crimp in things."

Sister Anjelica inhaled deeply and let the brisk drone of sweltering breezes dry the sweat from her face. Tensed against the shaking in her hands, she tucked her bottom lip between her teeth and regarded the gunslinger with perplexed curiosity. Her dark, green eyes flashing bright with conviction, she countered amiably, "War, Famine, Pestilence, Death, scripture tells us that the end will begin with the sound of hoofbeats. God has given us one priest sanctified to perform the ritual which will seal the Gates Of Hell and prevent this from happening. Furthermore, we've been granted one shot to save this priest in time. I believe we should keep riding, regardless of the peril. Tell me, Mister Goodnight, do you believe in anything?"

Somehow, Creed managed to keep a poker face and lit a fresh cigar like he hadn't noticed the sarcasm in her tone. He drew in the flame and blew a stream of smoke, then arched a thoughtful eyebrow, grinning lewdly. "Uh huh, after I put those jokers back in the box and collect my cash, I BELIEVE I'll pick up a few bottles of Mezcal and head over to Rosario's Cantina back in Purgatorio."

Sister Anjelica caught his meaning and nodded, a trace of regret shadowing her eyes. The muscles in her face twitched and she twisted her head to confront him again. The rebuke died in her throat. He was staring back over his shoulder, eyes darkened with foreboding. Trusting the gunslinger's instincts, she glanced behind them with a worried expression and whispered, "What is it?" She leaned back in the saddle and looked again, but there was no sign of anything behind them.

Creed's hand flew to the Colt and he growled abruptly, "We've got trouble. I'll meet up with you on the outskirts of Almas Perdidas. Get out of here, NOW!" Ignoring her protests, he slapped the stallion hard on the flanks, hollering over the clatter of racing hooves, "I'll BE there, sis! WAIT for me and don't do anything stupid!" Her answer was lost in a swelling rumble of thunder.

When she was safely out of sight he bristled, turning Cuchillo in a full circle to scan the wastelands surrounding him. Churning skies split with lightning and he caught sight of a single dust trail on the left, heading straight for him at demonic speed. Taking on one of these unkillable bastards would be tricky, but he reckoned it was better than grappling with a horde of them. He figured to dodge it for a spell while the nun put some distance between them, then make a run for it.

As the specter edged in on striking distance, he could make out the shambling form of a naked, headless female. Right about that same time, his saddlebags started to rattle and jump. Clammy chills crept up his spine, making his skin crawl. Why did it have to be HER? A tight, humorless smile pulled back over his fangs and he growled menacingly, "Well, hell, I got nothing better to do tonight. Come on you headless bitch, LET'S DANCE!"

Seconds later, she lunged for him, expelling a rancid stench of stale air from her rotting lungs. He turned right to dodge the assault and the hungry specter of Rebecca Surette turned with him. Her cadaverous muscles quivered with excitement. Gnarled hands hooked into claws, slashing blindly in the air while Cuchillo whinnied and pranced around her, easily sidestepping the futile attacks.

Confused and frustrated, the starving specter lost interest and started to shuffle off in search of weaker prey. With the speed she was capable of, Sister Anjelica wouldn't stand a chance of outrunning her. Then, it hit him. The head had reacted to her spirit at the outset.

He cursed under his breath and reached into the saddlebag, yanking his prize out by the hair. The specter froze in its tracks, then stretched both rigid arms out, frantically feeling its way back to him. Fury and hatred simmering in his eyes, he held the head out in front of him, shaking it savagely. "That's right, over here you murderous bottomfeeder! Seems I've got something you want!"

He recoiled, almost dropping the damn thing when its milky white eyes flew open, widening in recognition. Her stiff, toothless mouth opened and closed spasmodically, hoarsely spewing out the words, "Hello lover, did you miss me? Lean down here and give me a kiss."

Whistling winds picked up, swirling around them. He choked back his disgust and snarled spitefully, "Kiss an ugly face like that? There's not enough poisoned wine in the world for that, honey." A sudden, hot rush of anger pumped in his veins, making him a fraction too slow when the specter lurched forward and clutched his ankle in an iron grip. He lashed out hard with a bootheel flinging the screeching head at her in an attempt to distract the witch, but it was useless.

The specter tugged him from the saddle, dragging his thrashing body behind her. With the head held fast under an arm, she crouched over him, pinning him with her body. Cuchillo snorted, pacing nervously while the vile specter rifled through the pockets of Creed's duster until she found what she was looking for. Her desiccated lips contorted in a depraved grin as she slowly slid the Bowie knife from its sheath, running her tongue along the blade.

Furious, he pushed up on his elbows and dug his fangs deep into her hand. Only mildly irritated, she patted his cheek, throwing a bony knee between his legs. He dropped back like a sack of wet dirt, flinching from the pain. The horrible mouth opened again, croaking with amusement, "There's a good boy.

Such a shame decapitation will end you, but I simply must have your head. You understand." She oozed back with a wild cackle, poking at his chest with the knife. "You big boys are my kind of meat, but I'm really famished. After I eat you, I think I'll eat your horse."

If the situation hadn't been so serious, Creed would have laughed out loud when Cuchillo whinnied and rammed his muzzle against her hand, dislodging the knife. Ears cocked back in concentration, the massive horse snorted and reared up, pawing at the air. She cringed back, waving her arms. Muscles rippled in his hind legs as he turned, smashing his powerful back hooves into her chest.

His fingers touched cold steel and Creed grabbed the Bowie knife, sheathing it back inside his duster while the hag flew sideways about fifteen feet and rolled. The wallop hadn't done much more than boot her sorry ass off his chest, but it was a pure pleasure watching her crawl around in the dust, frantically searching for her head when it was face-down to his right. Sure, he'd be lying if he said the bitch didn't give him the jitters, but that mouthy head was worth a chunk of change, cash that was rightfully his.

Mostly he just wanted to get the hell gone, but he intended to swing down and grab the head before putting some ground behind him. Creed hooked a foot in the stirrup and slid into the saddle, idly dragging some life into a fresh cigar. Oddly, Cuchillo started straining skittishly at the reins, stomping his hooves into the ground. Creed reached for the Colt and stared out into the fog-shrouded desert. What he saw struck a chill to his marrow. He shuddered and cocked the pistol with a sharp click, brushing his fingers across Cuchillo's sweaty mane. "Right as usual, boy, we've got company."

Three sets of eyes smoldered in the darkness with a hellish crimson glint. A festering of grunts and whines rose above the screeching wind, turning his blood to ice. Creed stayed dead-still as a trio of hellhounds slunk out from the shifting sulfuric fog.

They were huge, five to six feet at the shoulder. Rev probably knew them by name, but Rev wasn't there right then.

Startled from her frenzy, the specter staggered awkwardly to her feet, faltering back with a weaving stumble. Long serpentine tongues, dripping with blood and drool, hissed in and out of snarling wrinkled muzzles as the hounds sniffed the air, circling her slowly. Sharp white fangs gleaming with menace, they identified prey and released a shrieking roar. A vicious swipe of talons across her abdomen, calculated to slow reaction time, brought the specter to her knees. They let her up, giving her a brief chance to run, then ripped her right arm away with the second strike. She smacked to the ground, clawing and twisting, fumbling to stand back up. When her will to run had been stripped away completely, the largest beast wedged her neck stump between its razor sharp teeth and dragged her off into the darkness. A second hound collected the arm and followed suit.

Creed edged Cuchillo silently toward the head, which most likely wouldn't have a lot to say at this point. Before he could reach it, the third beast backtracked and snatched the head, challenging him with a defiant stare that made his spine tingle. The gunslinger raised both hands, palms out, meeting the challenge with an uneasy smile. "Whoa, amigo, go easy with that. Appreciate you stepping in!" Satisfied, the hound loped off to join the others.

The hellhounds hadn't dragged him off along with the specter and he reckoned that was a lucky break, but he was a little raw over losing the head. Still and all, the only things to fret over now were demons and twisters. About then, he heard the clop of hoofbeats galloping toward him.

Creed Squared his jaw, a thin stream of cigar smoke snaking upward into his flaring nostrils as he shouldered the shotgun. He didn't rightly care who it was at this point. Specters didn't ride horses and there was no money in mixing it up with bandits. Lightning raked the sky and he lowered the weapon as Rev trotted up and reined to a stop beside him.

The halfbreed cocked an eyebrow, grinning smugly. "Damn, vampire, is that any way to greet the guy that pulled your fat from the fire?"

Creed's feral eyes narrowed to suspicious slits. "That right, is it? Say, Rev, about how long you been skulking around out there in the dark?"

Rev held the gunslinger's gaze and shrugged indifferently. "Long enough to see you get your dead ass kicked by a headless woman...again."

Didn't that just figure. Creed clenched his teeth, a loose, sheepish grin playing at the stubble on his face. "Uh huh. Killing a little time while she skewered me with my own knife, were you? Don't suppose you got a count on the horde. Maybe you'll get a second shot at it."

A low rumble gathered in the desert flats, growing to an echoing bellow of thunder. The storm was gonna hit any time now. They needed to wrap this up and get moving. Rev jerked forward in the saddle, tearing a patch of decayed skin from his knuckles. "Relax, Goodnight. I was gonna step in, but the horse beat me to it. Fine animal, by the way. A handful of abominations slithered out before I could contain the breach, but the hounds have rounded most of them up by now. You owe me big and until I collect, I've got your back. Are we square now?"

Truth was, Creed was relieved that Rev turned up, but he didn't want the halfbreed getting cocky. His lip curved into a snarl. "Good to know, but there's one more thing eatin' at me. What's goin' on with you, kid? You look a damn sight worse since last time I saw you. If that carcass you're riding runs out of skin, am I still "square" with the hounds?"

Rev studied his fingernails and snickered, "Damn bit of luck that would be, huh? Guess you'd find out one way or the other."

A resounding clap of thunder broke the tension and Creed sneered, "Reckon it's time to wake this fight up and make it bleed. Let's ride."

# 16

MENACING black clouds edged with crimson scudded past the window, dropping the temperature by a good ten degrees. Glimmers of dazzling white lightning faded away on the sill, followed by hollow crackles of thunder. A wise man knows to fear a night with no moon.

Pascual Sanchez stared without blinking through the rusted bars of his small cell. He'd seen it all before, but this storm felt peculiar, like that sudden shiver of someone walking on your grave. Seeing as it was out of his hands, he just sat and watched, waiting for what came next.

He had to admit that the hard-ass lawdogs made good on their promise. After the local sawbones cleaned and disinfected his wounds, he got stitched up right nicely. A sour-faced spinster dropped supper by and it wasn't half bad. It killed that gnawing burn in his gut. All things figured, the floor still shifted a bit under his feet when he tried to stand, but he could sure as hell make a run for it when that cell door swung open.

Stiff winds hammered at the door, rattling his nerves. Sanchez squatted back against the wall and tore off another meaty chunk of burrito, chewing laboriously. He licked his greasy lips with a nervous twitch as lightning crashed outside the window, magnifying flaws in the empty jailhouse walls. Crazy lawdogs had gone missing for the better part of an hour now.

A boneyard stillness settled into the sheriff's office, digging up the outlaw's earlier premonition that things were about to take a deadly turn for the worse. Maybe that shitshow in Almas Perdidas had followed him here. Maybe those damn deputies were dead and wouldn't be coming back at all. Hell, they got a kick out of telling him that he'd be locked up to rot away and die behind bars. What if they were right?

A rolling bellow of thunder shook him from his morbid reverie. Suddenly, the latch clicked and a billowing gust forced the door open, banging it repeatedly against the wall. Ferocious winds thrashed a spiral of dust and papers across the room as Shanks Hewitt and Dub Moody pushed inside and dropped a small stockpile of picks and axes they'd been gathering. Hewitt steadied himself against the blustering winds, staring out at a squall of dust obscuring the dismal darkness behind them. The two deputies exchanged worried glances as he shoved the door closed. Moody rolled a smoke and lit it, while Hewitt headed for the cot pushed up against the wall. Not much they could do but wait.

Before Hewitt could sit, the creaking door flew back and Sheriff Chance stormed in. A shadow of hardness creased his features as he scowled at the meager collection of tools on the floor. Without preamble, he snarled crossly at the deputies, his words clipped and cynical, "That's IT? For chrissakes, that's the best you slackers could scrounge up?"

Moody cursed under his breath, dropping the cigarette from his fingers and twisting it under the toe of his boot. The huffy deputy wiped sweat from his lip with a shirt sleeve and took a surly step forward. Abruptly, he went white around the nostrils, letting his teeth snap together tight. He recognized the look of urgency on the sheriff's face and countered respectfully, "It is, sheriff. Word gets around fast when you've got demons in the mix. Most good citizens of El Paso refused to open their doors to us. How many takers you get on that posse you're rounding up? Maybe we should all give it another shot."

Vivid lightning strikes silhouetted McQuade in a blazing blue aura as he hovered in the open doorway. His graying hair was wild from the wind, but his eyes were wilder. Spurs clinking loudly on the rough wooden floors, he strode briskly into the room and slammed the door. A rigid grin split his lips into a grim smile. "I believe I can answer that, Deputy Moody. None, not a single man. Sad to say, lives of the innocents in Almas Perdidas rest in the hands of the people in this room. It goes without saying that the odds are stacked against us, but that's the way it is and we're stuck with it."

Sheriff Chance curled his hands into fists until the flesh was white around the knuckles, then raked unsteady fingers along his scalp line. "Hewitt, Moody, you're good men, always have been. You'd best know the mission amounts to suicide. Not a soul would fault you for sitting this one out."

The deputies stared at each other in open-mouthed disbelief, then answered in unison, "We're in. When do we ride?"

The sheriff grinned wide and nodded. "Thought you might be. Well, don't just stand there looking thunderstruck, boys, get the lead out! Start loading the gear on the horses, we move within the hour."

Sanchez could hardly breathe. He wrapped his arms around his knees and drew his

shaking shoulders up tight, listening hard to fragments of conversation drifting back from the sheriff's office. The outlaw ran trembling fingers across the oily strands of hair stuck to his sweaty brow. He'd heard enough to know that they would all be leaving him to starve to death in this stinking hole. Maybe they'd just decide to put a bullet in his head and be done with it.

He flinched, choking back a scream when McQuade paced

fiercely into the back room, staring at him through the bars of his cell. A good thief got used to reading a man's intentions and Sanchez was one of the best. The man was restless and reflective. Damn, if the Archbishop wasn't about to offer him a deal. Sanchez jerked his chin forward and spoke first, "What kind of hours do you people keep around here? What's up with all the chatter out there? It's keeping me awake!"

Mcquade bared his teeth in a snarl and spun the cylinder on the pistol he was holding. "That's none of your concern, prisoner. The way I see it, you have two choices here. Ride with us right now or I'll kill you where you sit."

Sanchez reckoned they must need him for something or he'd already be dead. Sweat poured from the creases in his face as he stood up and stretched, trying to look bored. His beady eyes narrowed shrewdly and he swaggered forward, leaning into the bars. "I won't be helping you with a damn thing, holy man, unless you sound off first. If you don't want to talk, then hell with you. Let them get you all!"

McQuade cocked the pistol and grabbed a handful of shirt, flattening the outlaw's face against the rugged iron bars, "Fair enough, I guess. Let's say I'm feeling charitable and you feel like breathing a while longer. Simple truth is, the innocent men, women and children of Almas Perdidas, or what's left of them, are running out of time. Turns out, you might damn well deserve to hang for your crimes, but you pulled off an unlikely escape from these demons and lived to tell about it. So you see, my problem is now your problem. Help us negotiate those deserted side streets and free the villagers. After that, if you survive, you'll ride away with a full pardon." The Archbishop's finger tightened on the trigger. "Or are we done talking?"

McQuade released his grip on Sanchez's shirt and the outlaw staggered back. He laughed hoarsely, swiping at a thin, red line of blood in the corner of his mouth. "We both know that I'm a dead man either way. What the hell, nobody lives forever. Let's get this over with."

THUNDERHEADS RUMBLED ALONG THE SKYLINE, SPITTING RANDOM slashes of lightning into the thirsty dust. The coming storm washed Almas Perdidas in a familiar sepia glare. Same damn glare that blew in before the twister back in Whiskey Lick.

Hadriel's malignant stare swept the deserted street for any sign of the souls he'd released from damnation. He should have sensed the sorry sinners by now, but he found it difficult to muster more than a cold indifference to his grisly troops. They were a weapon, nothing more. He hadn't really thought much about them at all until they turned up missing. In fact, the only thing he could feel was trouble closing in from both directions.

The wary Fallen drew his pistol and snapped it open with a flick of his wrist. He idly counted his bullets, then shook it closed and spun it back into the holster. The wormy specters had come up against something, that much was for damn certain. Fragments of the past coiled and rattled, looping the sequence of events in his fevered mind. It kept coming back to the same thing, that miscreant half-breed and his endless list of grievances. Hadriel snarled, he'd feed the little backstabber to the crows the first second he figured out how to kill those mangy hellhounds.

The wind picked up, blowing clouds of dust down the street, and anything else that wasn't secured down. Shouldering the cantina door open, the Fallen stalked angrily to the bar, bathed in a weak pool of yellowed lantern light. A dozen or so skin boys were getting loud and rowdy in back, drinking shots and playing Liar's Dice, voices jacked up at a high-pitch roar to compete with the thunder.

Slumping his weight to one hip, Hadriel bent a knee against the bar and pulled a bottle of tequila from the shelf. A nagging uneasiness prickled the hair on his arms, like an itch he couldn't scratch. Could be due to the treasonous halfbreed, or maybe the absence of birds in the air. No matter, after this was over they would butcher and eat the hostages, then get back to the revival. He took a long swallow from the bottle and clenched his teeth, facial muscles twitching. When the storm passed, there was killing to do.

"HE-YAW! GIT UP THERE!" THE OUTLAW LEANED INTO THE SADDLE, slapping his reins against the horse's flanks. Hooves burned into the ground as he cut across the desert in an unrestrained run, retracing the trail of his escape from Almas Perdidas. The other four riders charged after him, wavering unsteadily in the raging winds. When the trail curved, the outlaw slowed his racing horse to a cautious trot, picking a path through the scrub and cacti.

Mcquade stepped up his pace, flanking Sanchez on the right. The outlaw jerked his chin, indicating the direction they would be taking. "Almas Perdidas is about a mile in front of us, just over that rise. Storm or not, it would be wise to dismount about a half mile out. We'll circle behind the village and lead the horses in on foot. You and your boys best listen up, holy man, there's storms in the wind, devils in the streets and we're goin' in dust-blind. You might not want to breathe too loud, if you catch my meaning."

The Archbishop was having doubts about his take on the outlaw. The crazy bastard meant what he said when he took the deal. He'd had a few chances to cut and run back in the desert, but here he was, riding into the jaws of Hell. McQuade grabbed the whiskey from his saddlebag and took a hard pull, then passed the flask to Sanchez with a firm nod. "You're a good man, Pascual Sanchez."

Sanchez's eyebrows shot up and he snorted scornfully, "You and them lawdogs don't know nothing about me, holy man. I'm not rightly sure how God feels about thieves, but I have some cash put back, enough to buy me a place and live comfortable the rest of my life. See, without that pardon, I'd be looking over my shoulder until some bounty man collected the reward on my shifty ass. I've got your back for the time being, as long as you intend to own up to YOUR end of the deal."

Sharp-edged lightning forked across the sky and Almas Perdidas flickered in the blackness ahead of them. The riders reined to a stop, dismounting cautiously. McQuade locked eyes with Sanchez, speaking in low, even tones, "I'm a man of my word. Can't say how God would feel about a thief like you, but I do know how he feels about liars." He clasped the outlaw's hand and shook it. "Good luck, prisoner."

Weathered boards moaned and shuddered in screeching winds that battered and rattled at the rickety stables. Staggering in the cross currents, the rescue party formed a single line, bracing against the side wall. Sanchez tucked his shoulders and crouched down, inching around the corner. Apart from the storm, there were no signs of movement in the wind-torn street and no one had bothered to close the stable door since his break-out. He mustered his nerve and swallowed hard, creeping warily inside. It was empty, like before. Maybe his premonition was wrong. Releasing a shaky exhale, he crossed himself and ran back for the others.

Forced into empty stalls, the skittish horses reared and strained against the reins as the men tethered them securely. Once satisfied the animals had somewhat calmed down, no time was wasted in shouldering their weapons and gathering tools. Sanchez waved his arms, pointing at the open window he'd crawled through, then held a sweaty finger to his lips, motioning them to follow.

The outlaw foolishly gazed up at the building storm and a cold chill latched onto his spine. There was no moon. Premonitions never really went away, sometimes they just shifted focus. Staring grimly ahead into the deepening darkness, he kept moving furtively up the deserted alleyway, keeping to the shadows.

Directly, Sanchez jerked an arm up, turning to face the others with a flat, vacant look stamped on his craggy face. His gaze crawled up to meet the Archbishop's and he nudged his chin to the left. McQuade narrowed his steely eyes, nodding slow and silent, then pressed an ear to the wall. Agonized weeping and groans from those trapped inside sounded over the raging surge of adrenaline hammering in his ears.

Deafening concussions of thunder doubled in fury, concealing the frenzied impact of picks and axes smashing into the cracked and pitted facade. Jagged fissures in the wall were rotted and blistered where rains had seeped through. Weakened by decay, the moldering adobe yielded, crumbling rapidly under their aggressive onslaught.

Sanchez struck a hardened clump of adobe, breaking the stitches in his right arm open. Dark red blood oozed from the wound, saturating his shirt. Ignoring the foul, pungent smell of infection filling his nostrils, he continued to hack away with his left. Reason told him this storm meant to be a howler, so the skin boys would be sitting it out. The moon had other ideas, telling him to wrap things up with a quickness. In the grand scheme of things, who was he to argue with the moon? He swung his ax down hard to drive the point home and met no resistance. Numb with pain and fatigue, he let the ax drop from his shaking hand and exhaled sharply, excited bursts of breath swirling in the dust like smoke. A swelling barrage of thunderclaps tumbled from the blackening sky, matching the sound of his bootheels lashing out again and again at the shattered wall.

Hewitt caught the sudden, chaotic motion in his side-eye and slapped Moody on the shoulder, pointing at Sanchez. Straightaway, the others followed suit and the sagging aperture wobbled, collapsing in a dense plume of dust.

A foul stench of rot and accumulated human waste wafted out from the opening. Sheriff Chance gagged back his revulsion and took the lead, with Moody and Hewitt on his heels. The lawmen took a few stumbling steps then hesitated, swatting blindly at buzzing swarms of flies while their eyes adjusted to the gloomy darkness. Dim light issued from the waxy remains of three candles, flickering on a shabby table littered with faded fiesta banners and rancid meat. The room pulsed with a hushed silence. Chance traded white, sickish glances with the deputies. Lord knows, he couldn't fault the poor bastards for hiding, but this was no time for nonsense if they wanted to live. Outraged by the grisly conditions, they picked their way around the filth, searching for the survivors.

Sanchez paced side to side with a derelict hitch. Where the hell were these wretches he'd signed on to rescue? He closed an anxious hand over the butt of his pistol and trudged into the darkened room. Figuring to drag the damn ingrates out himself if need be, his eyes fixed on the lawdogs. Chance and his boys seemed bent on speeding things along, to no effect. Heads down and knees drawn up tightly, the horrified villagers cowered together against the wall, refusing to stand. Hollow-eyed mothers clung to dirty, starving babies, pleading for their lives in terrified whispers.

Staring into the haggard, tear-stained faces stirred the hardened outlaw's memory, details of the bloody massacre he'd witnessed. These hollow-eyed, emaciated men, women and children had been living in raw terror, waiting for skin boys to butcher and eat them. He squared his shoulders back to tell the sheriff as much when a manic, wild-haired woman whined shrilly and charged from the shadows, violently swinging a rusty machete. Her eyes shone with devout fury as she stood between her people and the intruders, making awkward jerking movements with the weapon clutched in her fist. "I am Rosa Ruiz and this is MY home! Get BACK, demons! You shall not pass!"

The Archbishop entered quietly and rested a protective hand on Rosa's shoulder. He nodded calmly, his clear voice deep with concern. "These men and I are not demons, Rosa. We mean only to free you from this nightmare. How many in the village survived and where can we locate them?"

A warm thrill rushed through her body. God had sent his messenger to save them. She slumped to her knees, head bowed. "Fourteen, Your Grace. All that remains of Almas Perdidas is in this room."

Mcquade regarded the trembling villagers with sorrowful eyes and turned back to Rosa. "Find your feet, my child, you must gather these people and flee into the desert. There is no more time to waste."

Sanchez and the deputies hung back until Rosa grouped the others together outside, then swept the smaller children into their arms and carried them through the opening. McQuade stood across from Chance and scowled. "Sheriff, I don't like this any more than you will, but it looks like one of us has to help those people out there to safety while the other figures how to get at the hostages. Father Amantino and the good Sisters are my responsibility, so you'd best step lively in that storm."

The sheriff hauled his hat off and grinned. "Gotta say it's been a pleasure knowing you, Your Grace. God be with you."

Mcquade shook the sheriff's hand and grinned back. "And with you, my son. Now, get the hell out of here before our luck runs out."

Chance slid his gun from the holster, motioning Rosa to keep the villagers quiet. The lawman looked back over his shoulder at the innocents depending on him, then stared out into the gathering squall, sizing up possible threats. Brilliant veins of lightning flashed, flooding the empty alley. Satisfied things were good as they were ever gonna get, the sheriff urged the refugees to move swiftly toward the outskirts of town.

"Moody! Hewitt!" the Archbishop furrowed his brow and growled, "You men hold position. Make damn sure those folks don't run into trouble on the way out of town. Once they reach the desert, it's in God's hands. I'm going to scout ahead, take a measure of what we're up against at the Diablo Rojo."

Nodding resolutely, Moody leaned back against the wall and rolled a cigarette while Hewitt answered for them both, "You can count on us, Your Grace. We'll catch up to you shortly."

Sanchez crossed his arms and slowly ambled over to the Archbishop with purpose in his stride. "So, what about me, holy man? How do I figure into all this?"

Mcquade half turned and his lips went tight. "Yes, of course. forgive me if it slipped my mind in the chaos. Not many would have had the guts to ride it out this far, and a deal's a deal." Without pause, he pulled a neatly folded piece of paper from his pouch and looked it over, then handed it to the outlaw. "That's a pardon, Sanchez, we're done here. Now, if I were you I'd mount up and ride out of here before all Hell breaks loose."

Sanchez tipped his hat, carefully tucking the pardon inside his jacket. His eyes narrowed to hesitant slits as he glanced first at the deputies, risking it all to defend a ragged bunch of peasants they'd never met. Then his reluctant gaze slid back to the Archbishop, heading off to do battle with the forces of perdition. Briefly wondering if he'd lost his mind, he grumbled, "See, here's the thing, McQuade, it's just not in my nature to leave a job undone, any damn job. Reckon I'll stick around a bit longer, if it's all the same to you. "

McQuade's eyebrows drew together in a solemn frown. He placed a firm hand on the outlaw's shoulder, regarding him with respect. "Your call, son. Stay here and wrap things up with Moody and Hewitt. After that, I could use an extra gun at the cantina." The Archbishop turned on a heel and started walking back down the alley. Sanchez barely heard his parting words over the clamorous wailing of the wind, "Right now, God must be feeling pretty good about a thief like you."

Thunder rumbled as the nervous deputy rolled up the last of his tobacco. A blinding shock of lightning scorched the sky, exposing the silhouettes of Sheriff Chance and his charges disappearing into the desert. Moody dropped the smoke into his pocket and clapped Hewitt on the back. "Yessir, would you look at that. It's about damn time! Let's head out before McQuade gets his ass in a sling."

Before they could move, a faint whimper drifted out from the hole they'd made in Rosa's house. Sanchez spun his pistol from the holster, and stepped over a pile of rubble at the entry. The deputies watched in alarm as he vanished from sight. Hewitt called out, "Aw come on, amigo, the wind plays tricks in these old houses. Seriously, you wouldn't."

Sanchez whispered back, already working his way forward in the pitch black, "The hell I won't!" The room was much darker now, he could barely see his hand in front of his face. A small voice piped up in his brain, "That's because there is no moon." The whimper sounded again. He inched toward it, groping his way along the grimy walls until he came across a small storage alcove. His fingers touched warm flesh and he crouched down, squinting to focus. A young girl, maybe sixteen or so, huddled against the wall, shivering in a reeking pool of her own waste. Chances were she'd been hiding, too terrified to move or make a sound since the violent massacre. Even the others had failed to notice her presence in the dismal, blanketing gloom.

Sanchez called to the others in a hoarse croak, "Looks like we missed one, boys!" Eyes tensely dodging back and forth in utter blackness, the edgy deputies started following the sound of his voice.

Without warning, three ogreish skin boys burst noisily through the opening, firing off a string of angry curses. Hewitt and Moody dropped to the floor and rolled under the long dining table, freezing stock still. Sanchez holstered the pistol and clamped his wounded hand over the squirming girl's mouth. Not daring to breathe, he quickly tightened his good arm around her waist and pressed back into the alcove.

One of the hellions thrashed around the cramped confines in wild circles, grunting and sniffing at the air like a rabid boar, while the other two hovered in the entry. A deep, gravelly voice pierced the room, "Shut them wormy lips of yours and get off my damn back, Tobias. You too dumb to know it, but I did you a solid pulling you off that Archbishop when I did. What kind of slack-witted jackass don't know no better than to eat the one man that might lead Hadriel to the Book?"

Tobias snorted and fired up a fat cigar, blowing a sour cloud of smoke into his heckler's face. "Kiss my starving ass, Shaw. I say SCREW Hadriel and his precious Book. That dumbass Fallen is a liar and a raving lunatic. Where's that big army of damned souls he goes on about? Nowhere, THAT'S where! Look around you, where's that supply of God-fearing food he promised? Nowhere, THAT'S where! Unless I eat you, I'll most likely starve!"

Shaw felt the dull ache of hunger in his own belly and regretted his decision to turn the Archbishop over to Hadriel. Seething with frustration, he shoved Tobias and screeched at the other skin boy, "The room is EMPTY, Bud! Stop it, just STOP it!"

Bud shrugged his massive shoulders and inhaled deeply. "Don't think I'll be doing that. They're in here alright. I can smell them."

Tobias and Shaw looked at each other. Something changed in their expressions and the dark, black pools of venom in their eyes glazed over. The three skin boys tilted their heads and edged slowly forward, sniffing the air. The toe of Bud's boot touched Moody's hand and the horrified deputy jerked it back without thinking.

Mercifully, darkness prevented Sanchez from watching the slobbering hellions drag the deputies out and feed, but the horrible screams of terror and agony were impossible to shut out. The unspeakable savagery rang in his ears as sharp, ragged talons raked into soft skin, ripping out organs and long, bloody pieces of flesh. After some time, the sounds gave way to guttural grunts of chewing and the crunch of bone.

For what seemed like hours, white hot rage and the pain of

loss scorched the outlaw's cheeks. Beads of sweat gathered in his eyebrows until it felt like all the veins in his head were bursting. The room was still now, dead silent. He felt certain the monsters were gone, headed back to inform Hadriel of the villager's escape. When he couldn't stand it any longer, he took a small step forward, just one small step so he could breathe. It was a foolish move. Within seconds, the skin boys were on him, going through the motions, eager to feed. It was a messy death.

STREAKS OF LIGHTNING SPUTTERED OUTSIDE THE GREASY WINDOW OF Diablo Rojo, washing the cantina in a sinister amber sheen. Watery waves of consciousness rippled in and out as Mcquade struggled to breathe and realized his nose was broken. Swollen and battered, his body was nailed to an overturned table with rusted iron spikes driven into the wood.

A squawking mob of bored skin boys formed a circle around him, hurling insults and laying bets on how long the Archbishop would live. Hadriel slowly raised his tequila-laced eyes from the dark puddle of blood congealing on the floor, spreading out around McQuade's sagging body. He thought about how it had felt to smash his fists into the pompous bastard's face and watch bright red trickles of blood spill down the front of his pretentious robes. It felt good.

A cruel sneer jerked up the corners of Hadriel's mouth as he pressed his drooling lips to MacQuade's ear and slurred, "The Book for the priest, it was that simple. Coming into MY town to just take what you want? That was some bad idea my foolish friend. You fancy yourself a righteous crusader? Your lips to God's ears! Want to know what you really are? You're a dead man, food for demons."

Fighting back the ragged edges of blackness threatening to overwhelm him, McQuade coughed and spit, whispering gruffly,

"Unlike you, Fallen, God still hears me. They'll be coming for you shortly."

Hadriel struck him silent with a brutal backhand slap, but his gut told him it was true.

## 17

---

UNTOUCHED BY GUILT, the brutal predator sank deep into the abyss, exhilarated by the searing burn of hellfire on his flesh. Throughout countless years of soul-crushing torment

and anguish, those around him fell to slavering madness, even as he immersed himself in the blistering torture. By the time Hadriel summoned the damned, he no longer remembered his name, only that they had called him the Flesher and he hungered to relish the piercing shrieks of horror and pain from victims once again.

The Flesher was first to walk free from the jaws of perdition, eager to annihilate any sentient creature crossing his path. His hooded eyes reflected an inflexible drive to obey the command as he swaggered away, tracking the given course. He was a stone-cold killer with no interest in the darkened thunderheads churning over the Zona, wanting nothing more than to watch the world burn.

Hadriel's persistent directive pulsed in his necrotic brain, spurring the Flesher toward the road to Almas Perdidas at a frenzied pace. The killer roared in frustration, staggering back when random, gale force winds swept in at a fevered pitch, erupting into dust and thunder. Briefly blinded, he stumbled over a loose pile of rock and pitched headlong into a squirming nest of enormous scorpions migrating north from the Zona in search of prey. At once, bony fingers of lightning reached down from the sky and struck him square between the eyes, shooting rolling electric aftershocks into his withered skull.

As the energy surged through him, he felt a shift of energy. It felt sadistic, ruthless. There could be no doubt that death had released his essential, indestructible body, capable of possessing more solid forms. Was it conceivable that the transfer wasn't limited to humans? He raised a bulging pincer to confirm what he already knew, squeezing the sharp, serrated claw shut with a ferocious click.

Instinctively, four of the fiendish brutes slithered away seconds before the Flesher clenched and lashed out with his poisonous, upraised tail, striking repeatedly until the convulsing monsters stopped twitching. It had nothing to do with domination. He killed because he liked to kill.

The Flesher casually snapped off a piece of meat and stuffed it in his drooling maw to take the edge off his hunger, then crawled out onto the road, resuming the directive. Drawn by the power he emanated, the surviving monsters kept their distance, creeping silently behind him. He felt the movement instantly, but they held no appeal. Humans satisfied his nature, especially the women with their high-pitched screams and terrified pleas for mercy. Of course, they were dead from the moment he set eyes on them. If they ran...he would follow.

Lightning struck deep into the road ahead of him, vibrating in the cracked arid soil. He hissed smugly, pleased with his new, sleek body. The hellhounds would be on the prowl, searching for specters. Focus on the specter...miss the scorpion.

IT HAD HAPPENED IN A SPLIT SECOND. WITH NO WORDS OF WARNING, that swaggering, high-handed vampire up and slapped the stallion hard, forcing her to run off at a headlong pace until she was long gone, swallowed by the menacing darkness. Struggling against driving wind currents that threatened to tear her from the saddle, the diminutive nun jerked doggedly at the reins slowing the frantic horse to a steady gallop.

The brooding storm stretched unbroken to every side of her, escalating rapidly. She'd been riding for some time when an upswing of wagon ruts and hoofprints told her that Almas Perdidas wouldn't be far ahead.

For the better part of an hour, Sister Anjelica had been unable to shake the uneasy feeling that something in the distance was tracking her, gaining ground. She drew in a sharp breath as an image of Creed surrounded by a pack of specters popped into her head. The greedy scavengers circled their prey, closing in for the kill. Just as quickly, she dismissed the thought. If anybody could hold his ground it was Goodnight, but it served to bring his parting words to mind. As usual, the meaning was vague. He'd promised to meet up with her on the outskirts of Almas Perdidas, but hadn't bothered to tell her exactly where. Maybe he expected her to just loiter by the town limits sign while whatever fresh breed of monster chasing after her had time to catch up. That being said, she wouldn't mind him riding beside her right about now, if only to reassure her about the skittering rumble behind her, sounding in that echoing lapse between thunderclaps.

Regardless of the danger, she needed to establish a lookout point with a long view of the road before going much further. Likely as not he would never hear her admit it, but the gunslinger was right. Riding into the village alone amounted to pointless suicide and an end to any chance of rescuing the hostages.

When the road circled around a towering mesa, Sister Anjelica urged her weary horse slowly up the steep incline.

Worn saddle leather groaned noisily over the plod of hoofbeats as she ascended the rise, leveling out onto a narrow plateau. A brief scan from the ridge revealed Almas Perdidas less than a mile ahead and a sweeping view of the road below. She blinked back the tumbling dust, spotting a blurred structure looming on her right. As she rode closer, she could make out what seemed to be a darkened church hidden in the heavy, sulfuric fog. The solitary building sat silently in an open clearing, showing signs of falling into disrepair.

Quickly dismounting, the nun crouched behind an outcropping of rocks and listened for the slightest movement. Satisfied that the church was empty, she brushed the dust from her vestments and approached the entry. The unwieldy oaken door was studded with rusted iron, demanding all of her weight to shoulder it open. A layer of dust, settled into the craggy plank floors, muffled the echo of hooves as she led the stallion inside.

Sister Anjelica tethered the animal to a sagging pew, setting aside her own troubles for the moment. It saddened her to see such a beautiful church abandoned to decay. Thick wooden arches, now draped in cobwebs, rose into darkness between delicate stained glass windows, grimy with neglect. A small apse adjoining the chapel had a plaque above the door, dedicating it to the Magdalen. Simple wooden chairs lined the walls, circling an aging stone fireplace. She lit the vigil lanterns, casting a warm light into the room. There were stacks of moldering firewood at either side of the hearth.

Of course, it was madness to think of lighting a fire knowing that the smoke could be seen by any of those fool enough to venture out in this storm, but what other choice did she have? If Creed survived, he would know where to find her. If not, she wasn't sure how, but it was her fate to rescue the hostages alone.

She crossed herself and struck the match. Flames began to flicker and billows of heady, aromatic smoke poured from the chimney wafting into the wind.

SHERIFF CHANCE STARED INTENTLY UP AT A TUMULTUOUS SKY seething with lightning. Almas Perdidas disappeared behind them in a pummeling wall of dust, leaving nothing but endless desert in front of them. Chance hadn't expected McQuade to be so direct and he didn't know what to make of it. "Once they reach the desert, they're in God's hands?" What the hell kind of bullshit was that? Seriously, he expected a bit more from an Archbishop.

His angry thoughts were interrupted when a frail, emaciated child skidded past him in the dust, caught up in a whirlwind of scrub and debris. Muttering a string of curses, the sheriff powered into the wind and snatched the girl by her shirt. He hugged her tightly as the panicked child clung to him, refusing to release her terrified grip. Chance quietly asked which of these women was her mother. The girl sobbed that her name was Maricela and her parents were dead. He pulled her closer to hide the deadly grimace on his face. It wasn't that he was afraid for himself, but for these fourteen people he'd been charged with saving. Right then, he had no idea how to manage that without food, water or a place to hole up while this son-of-a-bitchin' storm tumbled over.

Thunder and lightning eased some, concealed by the storm. It didn't make him feel any better because he damn well knew they'd kick right up within seconds. Suddenly, the acrid, over-powering scent of wood smoke filled his nostrils. He took in a deep breath to quiet the fierce pounding of his heart and squinted feverishly into the oppressive murk. Sure as hell, a dense column of smoke was rising from a mesa directly ahead. Lord only knew what vile aberration had built that fire, but six bullets in the chamber said these folks would have some kind of shelter tonight.

Thin as a rail, Tacho Macias gained a nod of respect from the sheriff by offering to stay put and boost the others up the slippery incline, holding them steady until they found their footing. With any luck, his efforts would speed things along before the wind picked up again. Chance shifted Maricela to his back while he and Rosa scrambled up first and planted themselves on the ridge, wresting the struggling villagers over as they reached the top.

Tacho dusted his hands, waiting until the last person had been pulled to safety. Gratified that everyone had made it to the top, he dug his sandals into the soft, gravelly soil and started climbing. Startled by an unexpected noise, he hesitated and spun around, catching a turbulent disturbance behind him. There was a vicious thrashing and a dense thicket of mesquite spread apart as something big moved through it at a quickening pace. Panicked, he tried to climb faster, screaming hysterically, "Dios mio! Help me! HELP ME!"

The frustrated sheriff gritted his teeth until his jaw hurt, growling, "Well hell, here we go." He drew his weapon and swung the wailing child into Rosa's arms, growling, "Get the lead out, girl! Run for the smoke and don't look back!"

Chance cocked the pistol and took aim at the lip of the mesa, but it was too risky to take a shot. He could barely make out the heaving man's form grappling to the top. Cursing under his breath, the sheriff holstered his weapon and scooted down the steep slope on his backside until he could grab an outstretched hand. Knocked off balance by the effort, Tacho's leg slipped on the loose gravel and he was yanked toward the bottom, briefly at first, then more forcefully. Chance fought to keep a firm grip, straining frantically to pull the screaming man up. Horrified shrieks for help intensified, then ended suddenly as a massive black claw reached up from the bottom and snapped shut around Tacho's waist with a terrible click. He remained alive for several seconds before realizing that he'd been severed in half. Chance gasped and released his hold, clambering furiously toward the ridge as Tacho was dragged down into the writhing darkness below.

There was nowhere to run but forward, along the narrow plateau. Chance did just that, racing wildly back and forth between mesquite and cactus like his boots were on fire. The sheriff had mixed it up with a lot of nastybottomfeeders, writing it off as part of the job, but it rattled him watching Tacho struck down like that. If he had to ask himself why, it was because he had no damn idea what he was dealing with, or how many. Whatever the hell these abominations were, they started crawling over the ridge, right about the time he caught sight of Rosa standing with a nun in the open doorway of a church.

Chance charged into the chapel without breaking stride, roughly shoving the two women backward, then muscled the door closed behind him, throwing the heavy, iron bolt. Wheezing in an effort to catch his breath, he barked sharply at the nun, "I'll apologize later Sister, but right now I need to know if there's another way into this place."

Sister Anjelica nodded calmly, pointing toward the rear of the church. "I might have seen a door behind the altar." A quick glance revealed a thin slice of darkness skirting the frame. The door was ajar.

Churning black clouds unleashed the pent up storm as the door flew open and the monster crept inside. It was a scorpion, a BIG damn scorpion! It hovered between him and the door, hissing and flashing its beady, black eyes as if threatening his escape. There was something dark and crusted stuck to its bloody maw. Chance recognized a finger, Tacho's finger!

Without hesitation, Sister Anjelica dodged the lashing tail and scrambled into the Magdalen Apse. She ripped a strip of cloth from her veil, wrapped it tightly around her hand and pulled a burning log from the fireplace. Praying that the rotten wood wouldn't sputter out, she waved the fire in front of her, edging past the monster to the open door.

She managed to heave it shut and drop the bolt just before the remaining cluster burst into the church.

The first invader jumped into the room, tail raised, reacting to a furious pounding of heavy claws at the door. It came at the sheriff fast, bloody foam dripping from its mandibles. Chance kicked out hard and caught it squarely in the head with the toe of his boot, wincing when its swollen stinger curled over, plunging through the thick leather and into his ankle. Slicing deep into his tendons, the sting throbbed horribly with the beat of his heart. Toxic venom immobilized him. For an instant, he couldn't breathe or move as the rampaging scorpion smacked against the wall with a bone-chilling hiss.

In seconds, the monster twisted to its legs and charged him again. Instinct kicked in and Chance spun the pistol from his holster. Wavering unsteadily, he clenched his shaky hand into a tight fist around the grip, then took aim, emptying the chamber into its pulsating maw until the monster stopped moving. The sheriff stood transfixed for a full minute, continuing to squeeze the trigger when there was nothing left in the chamber but echoes.

Shooting twinges in his ankle grew rapidly worse. He held his breath and squeezed his eyes shut, waiting for a wave of nausea to pass. There was no damn way he'd go out like this. He hadn't made it this far just to wind up six feet under from a damn bug bite.

After securing the back entry, Sister Anjelica had paused for several heartbeats, steeling herself, then kept swinging the flames to distract the writhing scorpion. She saw the tail whip around and plunge its dripping stinger into the sheriff's boot and had promptly called out to Rosa, with deliberate calm in her voice, "Rosa, we'll be needing a mud poultice. Collect as much soft dirt as you can and mix it with water from the canteens. Have two of the strongest men at the ready, they'll know when it's time to act."

Without waiting for a reply, the nun rushed back to the Magdalen Apse to grab a stack of blankets from the shelf, rolling them out into a thick pallet on the floor. When Chance's legs finally weakened and buckled underneath him, the men were waiting. They carried him to the pallet and braced his upper body, keeping the wound lower than the heart. Lethargically, he slid the hat from his head, spreading a stabbing pain up his leg. Beads of cold sweat stung his eyes as he slurred, "I'm grateful to you, Sister, for taking these good folks in. You should also know that I'm right sorry for my rudeness at the onset."

Sister Anjelica stooped down and yanked his boot off, pleased to see a piece of stinger tip protruding from the wound. After an easy extraction, she unsheathed the knife at his waist and tapped it firmly against her palm, grinning casually. "Put your hat on cowboy, you won't be dying today. Lucky for you, the monasterio taught me many lessons. Nobody knows better how to treat the sting of a Zona scorpion than I do."

Chance bit back a scream as she made a small incision into the wound, slashing the venom sac open. The patient nun swiped at the puncture with the strip of veil wrapped around her hand until she was certain that the sluggish flow of blood had diluted enough poison. Then, she nodded to Rosa, who applied the mud poultice to start drawing out the rest.

Soft flickering firelight held back shadows while the wind huffed and whistled at the windows. Maricela squatted beside the sheriff, protectively clutching his sweaty hand. Abruptly, her teary eyes widened in shock. She jerked urgently at the nun's sleeve, whispering in a tiny, terrified voice, "Sister! Listen!" Sister Anjelica tilted her head, mindful of the girl's agitation. Then she heard it, absolute stillness. The hammering at the door had stopped.

Chance heard it too and struggled to move, but the nun pushed him back, admonishing sternly, "YOU are to stay put until the venom has left your system!" She tugged the pistol from his shaky hand and reloaded with the bullets inside his coat pocket. Snapping the cylinder shut, she laid a reassuring hand on the girl's shoulder. "Maricela, YOU are to remain here with Rosa and these men, keeping watch over our patient. yes?" When the child nodded, she crossed herself and hugged the girl tightly.

Light from the flickering lanterns behind her cast a long shadow as she paced solemnly into the chapel. The villagers were huddled in the pews with their heads bowed, praying fervently. They stared blankly, exchanging confused glances at the nun's demand that they stop praying and look for anything that could be used as a weapon. Sister Anjelica rolled her shoulders back and clapped her hands together sharply. "Let's get to it folks! NOW! We've got trouble!"

The fear came when a skittering rumble rattled the boards under their feet. Dusty cobwebs rained down from the shuddering ceiling, spurring the paralyzed group to action.

Swept by panic, they foraged hysterically for a means of defending themselves while the clicking hiss of scorpions doubled in volume, slithering up all four sides of the church. Clicking claws drove into the aging adobe, digging their way through the walls.

Unflinching, Sister Anjelica positioned herself in the center of the chapel and cocked the pistol, ready for the first monster to break through. Suddenly, the sound of rapid gunfire boomed outside. It was the sweetest sound she'd ever heard.

Chain lightning cracked along the storm-blasted plateau, deadening the clop of hoofbeats closing in on the church. Creed and Rev sighted the frenzied scorpion thrashing away on the wall, at right about the same time. Both raised their shotguns, firing jointly, vaporizing the monster's hideous head into a fine mist. Creed drew deep on his cigar butt and squinted at Rev. "Hey kid, you ever see a scorpion tryin' to dig its way into a building?"

Rev leaned down, crossing his arms over the saddle horn.

"Naw, vampire, those bastards are too damn stupid. Never seen a Zona scorpion this far north either."

Creed sensed motion and caught two more startled scorpions in his side-eye. It would have been a simple matter to pick them off, but Rev was right, things didn't add up. When the monstrosities skittered down either side of the church and made a break for it, he figured to take care of business and sort it out later.

Scratching his jaw with a puzzled frown, he drawled, "Uh huh. You take the runner on the left." Creed reined right and Cuchillo snorted, giving chase. Feinting side to side, he quickly ran it to ground along the outer rim of the ridge. Wobbling pincers snapped at the air, as the cornered scorpion twitched backward toward the edge, boxing itself into a copse of mesquite. Creed casually pushed the hat back on his head and reloaded. "Last chance, you sumbitch, What the hell are you up to?" When the scorpion hissed, he leveled the shotgun and pumped two rounds into its head, drenching the dust in a shower of the same foul-smelling ichor that oozed out of any other scorpion. Shaking his head, Creed reined Cuchillo around and headed back to the church, grinning over his shoulder. "Nothing, huh?"

From the sounds of ruckus back at the church, Rev's belly-dragger was putting up a decent fight. Riding in a little closer, Creed hung back in the shadows. Fair was fair. He figured the kid had it coming for watching him get his ass kicked by that headless bitch, Rebecca Surette.

Rev struggled to get a solid bead on the fear-crazed scorpion as it spasmed and danced around him in erratic circles, wildly waving its pincers while releasing a horrible, grating series of high-pitched squeaks. Purely by chance, the kid's mount got smacked by a stray claw and the horse went down, spilling him from the saddle. Roaring with anger, Rev jerked the shotgun up and fired blindly, blowing the bastard a good twenty yards away.

While the horse found its footing, he lurched over and grabbed a shovel from a pile of rusty tools stacked by the door.

The monster squeaked and hissed, straining to roll over while he bashed it with the shovel until it stopped making that irritating noise. It was still quivering, so he raised the shovel over his head and brought it down with every ounce of his strength, splitting the scorpion in two.

When the dust cleared, Creed ambled over. Rev ignored the smirk on his face while he grabbed the reins and swung back into the saddle. Red-faced, the kid turned and glared at him. "How long you been lurking out there, vampire?"

Creed pursed his lips into a smug smile. "Long enough to see you get knocked off your horse by one little scorpion, kid."

The most savage souls are almost always the most cunning, a quality the Flesher prided himself in. He slithered silently across the roof of the church, crouching at the edge to size up these new intruders. Shrewder than any human or mindless scorpion, the brute was instinctively driven by detail, sensing instantly how to dispatch the threat. His intended victims, cringing inside the church, would still be there when he finished with the crusaders.

Tittering with malice, the killer scorpion leapt from the roof, shooting plumes of dust into the air with his leaden landing. Startled, the horses whinnied, pawing at the ground as the menacing monster thrashed and convulsed, clattering its lethal pincers. Creed snorted, screwing his face into an annoyed frown. "AW hell, how many of these blasted things ARE there?" Rev shrugged indifferently and jerked the shotgun up, but held his fire. Curiously, the manic scorpion coiled its whipping tail, rolling the poisonous stinger into its own body, striking again and again until it collapsed dead on the ground.

Sulfuric fog cast an evil reddish aura as the Flesher rose from the husk, a hungry specter with mad staring eyes. Pulsating with carnivorous heat, his hollow voice echoed in the gloom, "You seem to have misjudged your vulnerability, boys. So, you took out a few scorpions?" Face lethally intent, eyes dead, the Flesher slowly clapped his hands and leered, "We'll see how you match up against an unkillable force from Hell, itself."

The unlit cigar rolled from Creed's lips when he tilted his head, letting the match burn down and singe his fingers. His tongue clicked against the roof of his mouth as he shoved Rev hard on the shoulder. "Well I'll be damned! NOW it makes sense!" The two looked at each with pained expressions, then burst into fits of laughter. Rev shook his head and stifled a snicker, whistling shrilly.

Rumbling growls vibrated in the rolling fog as a legion of glittering red eyes emerged from the darkness, emanating a predatory animal musk. The Flesher ran...and the hellhounds followed.

Creed put an ear to the door, hearing a faint shuffling inside. He glanced back at Rev then grasped the handle, turning it silently until the latch clicked. Holding up his fingers for a count of three, he kicked the door open and found himself staring into the shaking muzzle of Sister Anjelica's pistol. Slowly, he cupped a hand over the gun and lowered it to her side, sighing gently, "Sis? You okay?" Without thinking, he wrapped his arms around her and hugged her to his chest.

She let herself be held for several seconds before pushing away with a stern reprimand, "You're LATE, Mister Goodnight! While I understand that the devil whistled and you had to answer, it was still reckless to send me off like that. Too much time has been lost. We must catch up on events quickly, then ride!"

Creed rolled his eyes and tipped his hat, muttering under his breath, "Uh huh. Yes
ma'am, next time I'll try to wrap things up quicker."

Rev rode the perimeter of the plateau to flush out crawlers that might be holed up in the rocks, but there was nothing apart from the growing storm to fret over. The church
door was open, so he lazily tied off the horses and scuffed inside, absently wiping his gory hands down the front of his shirt. Panic broke out, filling the chapel with horrified wails of

terror. Exhausted villagers crowded together behind the nun, pointing and screeching, "Madre de Dios! Zombie! ZOMBIE!"

Creed scowled and took a hard look at Rev's rapidly decaying visage, then busted out laughing all over again. Sister Anjelica gave the gunslinger a sharp rap on the back of his head and turned to face the group, arms outstretched. "No, no! This man is not a zombie! He is Reverend Jim, the reason we are all still alive!"

Rev figured he couldn't be that much worse than a killer scorpion-specter, and nodded politely. Sobbing quietly, the people cowered back as he followed Goodnight and the nun into the Magdalen Apse.

Creed eyed the wounded Sheriff and grinned. "Well, look at you old man, all laid out to meet the angels. That scorpion in there belong to you?"

Sheriff Chance made a weak attempt to stand and dropped back onto the pallet, grumbling, "Damn right, Goodnight. A few more hours to flush this poison out and I could take your undead ass with my eyes shut. For now, you folks best be on your way. McQuade is already in Almas Perdidas. The damn fool plans to take on the forces of Hell, along with my two deputies and a thief." Chance squinted at Rev and shook his head. "You aren't lookin' so good, son."

The halfbreed shrugged. "That right, sheriff? No matter, I aim to be feelin' much better before long." He gave a short whistle and the chapel sounded with fresh shrieks of terror as three fierce hellhounds padded into the apse. Chance and Rosa gasped when the female laid down and nuzzled the orphan's shoulder, resting her ferocious head in the child's lap.

Creed caught the sheriff's alarm and put a firm hand on his shoulder. "Most of these hounds will be guarding the breach until the Gates are sealed. Seeing as how we still have a few of those nasty specters running loose, the kid figured you could use some backup."

The sheriff nodded at Rev and tipped his hat. "Much obliged, son."

OUT ON THE MESAS, THUNDER ROARED, SPLITTING THE SKY WITH wilding veins of lightning. Fearsome black clouds swelled into a spinning behemoth, burying the road ahead in a sea of dust as the three riders galloped north, into the raging winds.

---

## 18

REVOLVING SKIES DARKENED AND LOWERED, dipping dangerously low in violent, twisting currents as the gunslinger and a half-breed kid rode into Almas Perdidas. The furious nun, riding close beside them, was shaking on a short fuse, ready to blow. It was her sacred duty to devise a way of sealing a breach in the Gates Of Hell, putting an end to the madness. The book in her saddlebag said that silver bullet was gonna be Creed Goodnight and the priest held captive in Diablo Rojo Cantina.

Streaks of lightning scraped the sky, leaving pale wash on a cobblestone street littered with desiccated corpses. Creed caught motion further up and spotted Father Amantino's transport coach, flipped to its side in a rubble of shattered wood and warped metal. One wheel teetered precariously on a jutting axel, creaking and spinning lopsidedly in the wind. He counted six rotting carcasses of what must have been a team of horses strewn around the wreckage, dismembered and partially devoured.

Rev trotted up next to the gunslinger, his narrowed eyes glued to the carnage. "Damn, looks like the skin boys aren't messing around any more." Near as he could tell, there was only one human in the mix. The skull was crushed and bony fingers wound tightly around a coach whip. Only a fool would risk riding in closer, so he nudged his jaw at the skeleton. "The driver, most likely. Seems our priest is still in play."

After initial hesitation, Sister Anjelica moved up to join them, studying the gruesome remains of the coach. Creed squinted hard at the nun. The expression on her face wasn't nearly as horrified as it needed to be.

Nothing felt right about this. Hell, given all the chimney smoke and ruckus back at the church, he'd almost expected a welcome party, but it was dead still, like someone was waiting on them to make a move. A second measure of the barricaded windows and shadowy doorways revealed all the makings of an ambush.

Creed rolled a cigar to the corner of his mouth and targeted Rev through the match glare with a brooding scowl. "Seein' how this whole mess rides on keeping that priest alive, we'd best figure out what we're dealing with before goin' off half-cocked, kid. Sheriff Chance mentioned that the last time he laid eyes on McQuade or his lawdogs was at that big hole they scratched in the wall. I reckon that's as good a place as any to start."

A rolling bank of rumbling thunderheads hung inches above the cramped dwellings. Lightning sliced into the pitch black just before a sudden, cyclonic gust sent a Saguaro cactus scudding along the rooftops, littering the narrow alleyway with sharp shards of adobe tile. Creed hesitated at the entry, squinting into the murk. Stinging winds blew dirt in his face, obscuring possible threats that were probably lurking in the shadows.

Rev raked restless fingers through his hair and came up beside him, snarling, "Assuming you want that priest breathing, I'd suggest you stop screwing around and get the lead out. I get that you want to protect the nun, but it was made clear what she signed on for." Without waiting for a response, he nudged the stirrups and rode ahead. Sister Anjelica followed close at his heels.

Shortly after, the gunslinger sighted piles of human remains blown up against the wall of Rosa's home. Reining to a sudden stop, he dropped from the saddle to get a closer look. The bones were picked clean, but a shred of cloth clung stubbornly to a blackened pool of congealed blood, flapping in the wind. He pried the scrap out of the muck, then handed it to the kid. There was a gold star, a deputy's star, pinned to the backside. Rev shifted in the saddle, passing it over to the nun with an unruffled expression. "I count two men here, maybe the Archbishop got lucky."

Creed picked up the cloying reek of skin boys, mingled with the smell of decayed flesh. Whipping winds tore at his duster as he glowered menacingly into the rugged opening, growling, "Uh huh. You two stay put, we'll just see if that's true. I don't trade in maybes." Halfway through the hole, he spun the Colt from his holster and vanished into the darkness.

Up until Creed's intrusion, the squatters had a pretty sweet deal. Hadriel bought their story about the breakout, minus the part where they'd eaten the deputies. Food had been real scarce since the massacre and the two squabbling skin boys were looking to lie low and feed off Sanchez until the Fallen got what he was after. There was a sharp crack of bone, followed by a guttural whisper, "Hell's bells, you jackass, keep quiet!" Something heavy crashed to the floor and the grating voice piped up again, "Didn't I TELL you to be quiet?"

Resentful, his sullen partner hissed back, "YOU don't get to tell me anything, Tobias!" The gunslinger heard awkward footsteps stumbling in his direction and pressed back against the wall, a black shadow silhouetted against a deeper black. When the skulker got close enough, Creed snatched him by the head and ripped his throat out without a sound, catching him as he buckled forward. He laid the body down carefully, but the bastard's knife slipped the sheath, banging noisily on the floor.

It got dead quiet while Tobias tried to make him out in the dark. At last, a weak voice called out, "Bill? Is that you?"

Creed cursed and answered, "Yeah, it's me!" then dodged left just as a bullet whizzed inches from his ear with a loud, echoing crack.

Shaken to the core, Tobias charged wildly at the spot where he'd heard the voice, bellowing, "His name ain't BILL, it's SHAW!" Creed reckoned he wasn't much smarter than his partner and stared impassively while the raging skin boy discharged his ammo into the same spot. When the gun was empty, he wound a tight fist into the screaming hellion's hair and dragged him out to the alleyway, slamming him hard against the ground. Confused, the dazed skin boy laid there a second, scratching his nails into the dirt. When the blurring faded, he eyed Creed and spat out a choked off curse.

Sister Anjelica bit her lip, paying critical attention to the hellion's blood smeared face before speaking. Lightning cast shadows in her stony eyes as she hovered over the wretch. "Can you follow me, demon? Pay close attention. I'm done with your blasphemies. There is only one way the devil can do us any good. Tell me what has become of Archbishop McQuade."

Tobias laughed coarsely and struggled to his hands and knees, wiping dirt and gore from his lips with the back of his hand. His face tightened, stretching into a leering grin, "Who?"

Rev came out of the stirrups in a blinding blur, landing a boot to the gut that snapped the weasel shut like a jackknife. He was still gasping for air when the kid opened him back up with a solid fist to the chin, snarling savagely, "The Sister asked you a question, hellspawn."

Tobias's breath rushed out in a long, quavering wheeze. He coughed up blood and teeth, then turned his head to see who'd hit him and let out a shrill, terrified shriek. His heart started hammering against his ribs. "Aw, HELL no, please NO! Look, It's ME, Tobias, remember? For pity's sake, we rode together! I ain't got no ties to that tight-ass Fallen. What do you want to know? Anything, only please, halfbreed, don't whistle for them hounds!"

Rev watched the sniveling skin boy with detached curiosity,

wondering how the hell he'd ridden with these fools for so long. His teeth clamped shut and he hissed venomously, "You got sixty seconds, scumbag, start talking."

The hellion's tongue was thick with fear, garbling words together in a panic, "Last I know, your holy man was still breathin'. I swear! Hadriel's got him nailed up to a table back at the Diablo Rojo. He ain't got nothing we need, but he damn well keeps the boys busy. Most demons never seen any Archbishop up close and survived, but THIS holy man? We got ourselves the Texas-fucking-Torquemada, sure as shit! That son of a bitch McQuade, hisself, halfbreed! I ain't lyin'.'! OH, and we got us a priest and a pair of nuns too, all trussed up in the food pantry like Sunday dinner."

Rev pinned Creed in a hard, questioning stare. A slow grin spread across the gunslinger's face. He casually struck a match on the hellion's cheek and relit the butt of his cigar. "That pretty much all of it, Tobias? Nothing more to add?"

A drool of spittle ran down the hellion's chin. He carefully licked his swollen lips, then shook his head decisively, side to side. "Nope, that covers it!" Feeling better about things, the skin boy nodded to Sister Anjelica and tipped his hat with a wink. "Glad I could help, ma'am!"

When he turned his head back around, he was staring down the barrel of Rev's gun. At first he didn't get it, but things narrowed down quickly. The kid gritted his teeth and snarled, "DON'T call me halfbreed!" Rev squeezed the trigger and the pistol roared, pumping a bullet into Tobias' horrified face.

Dazzling displays of lightning shattered the ominous overcast, charging the air with electricity. Creed held the skittish stallion's reins while the nun mounted up, then swung into the saddle and growled at the kid, "Hey Rev! Is that the kind of deranged backwash you trigger in all the hellspawn?"

Rev continued to reload and shrugged defensively. "Well, you got me there, vampire. Seeing how I've been in the wind for a while now, saving your sorry ass, I expect it is. Now that you

184 | ONE HELL OF A NIGHT IN MEXICO

bring it up, things between me and Hadriel might get a little dicey too. What's on your mind?"

Muscles twitched at the corners of Creed's mouth. "Judging from your pained

expression, you know what's coming next, kid, so I'll keep it short. Hadriel is gonna let me walk right through that door for the sole reason that he's tired of me doggin' him around.

See, back in Whiskey Lick, mine was the last face he saw this side of Hell. I'm betting he'll want me to plead my cause in the court of skin boys. That should buy me time to nose out the priest and pass the Book. I'm plenty fast enough when things heat up.

"Now, betrayal, that's another matter. No way they let it ride. One whiff of you, the whole damn cantina mobs up like a bunch of rabid coyotes and everybody dies. There's not a soul I'd rather have at my back when things get messy. All I'm asking is that you keep downwind and hang back until the bullets start flying." On impulse, he tugged a stick of dynamite from his pocket and handed it to Rev. "It's my last one, kid, use it wisely."

Rev studied his spurs, looking sideways at the gunslinger, then shrugged. "I reckon that sounds mutually beneficial. You'd best remember our deal regarding the Fallen, vampire, cause I'll be seein' you again real soon." He licked an index finger and held it to the wind, then galloped north, into the swirling dust.

Creed flanked the stallion and locked gazes with Sister Anjelica. Blood pulsed in her pale cheeks, playing up an odd, manic gleam in her eyes. Unsure if that meant trouble or not, he offered up a stern smile. "If you want a shot at sealing the rift, you gotta hand that book over...now."

Gasping in hot, shaky breaths, her sweaty hand flew to the saddlebag. "As a guardian of the Gates, I am bound to strict guidelines, Mister Goodnight! My very soul depends on it!"

He squared his jaw and shot back, "Sorry about the soul thing, but rules were meant to be broken. As guardian of the Gates, I'm more inclined to think you'd best do whatever it takes to restore balance!"

Tiles from Rosa's roof tore away, crashing into a wall behind the nun. She steeled herself, holding the Book in front of her with a false bravado, "Just so, Mister Goodnight. I suppose that was God's way of reminding me who's in charge."

Wary of the Book, Creed held the pocket of his duster out and let her drop it inside. He wanted to hug her again, tell her things would work out. Instead, his voice took on a low, comforting tone, "Trust me, Sis." When there was no snappy comeback, he reined the horses around and backtracked to the street.

The two riders crouched low into the saddle, slowly making their way to the stables. Winds had increased with a velocity that staggered the horses, growing more violent by the minute. Their former confidence that the storm would pass drained fast and dread washed over them. Figuring it would ease up was like trying to stop a speeding bullet. It was coming and nothing would change that.

The sky congested with swirling debris as they led the horses into the stables. Creed helped Sister Anjelica dismount, then tethered the stallion inside a stall. Cuchillo snorted and whinnied, calming the frantic animal down some.

They kept to the shadows, creeping furtively along shuttered facades. Gunshots rang out from inside the Diablo Rojo, followed by raucous laughter and the sound of shattering glass. Silently signaling the nun to stay put, Creed cautiously pushed at the door. It was locked.

Out of nowhere, Sister Anjelica twisted the shotgun from his hands and shoved past him. She crossed herself and fired point blank at the handle, then tossed the gun back. The aging door heaved and echoed from the concussion, pitching inward before settling back into the frame. At once, startled hellions bristled and dragged her inside, closing in around her before the dust had settled.

Lantern glare reflected on the heavy silver crucifix clutched in her pale, bony fist. She caught sight of McQuade, sagging against a bloody table. The blackened pockmarks near his body suggested they'd been using him for target practice. Outraged, the nun rolled her shoulders back and pushed a path through the posturing crowd, demanding, "Stand aside, wretched hellspawn!" Further ultimatums stuck in her throat, choked back by the reek of tainted air, coiling fast around her in a thick grid of smoke and sulfur. Suddenly weakened by the toxic fumes, she staggered back against the wall, reeling from a taunting chorus of howls and high-pitched laughter.

Creed pulled fresh shells from his pocket and reloaded, grumbling a string of curses. He damn well knew that glassy look in her eyes had spelled trouble, but what was done is done. Bitching about it wasn't gonna change things.

The gunslinger braced for battle and strode through the door, swaying to the crack of thunder. A loaded shotgun makes that certain sound when you rack it, right before the bullets start singing. Wary skin boys recoiled at the noise and emerged from the shadows. Hesitant, they collected on the fringes of the room, keeping a distance. Nervous fingers fluttered over their pistols. Their flat, beady eyes watched his hands, tuning in for the smallest twitch, but nobody wanted to draw down first.

Creed grinned wide and fanned his shotgun across the blustering mob, coming to a stop at a tall, surly figure, eyeing him from the bar. Of all the bottomfeeders in the room, he was the one that didn't fit. Thick, reddish hair fell around a handsome face, smiling back at him with flawless, white teeth. He fixed the fancy man in a focused, straight ahead stare. This one was confident and primal, amused by the shotgun pointed at his skull. Clearly, this was the Fallen and the son-of-a-bitch was stark raving mad. Another piece of bad luck, 'cause he'd promised that body to Rev and it was always the damn crazies that tended to be unpredictable.

There was a tense, ringing silence while Hadriel sized him up. The gunslinger might be a loose cannon, but that setback in

Texas was proof he was too damn smart to bust in without a plan. If they were sitting on a powder keg, chances were Goodnight held the match. That being the case, he didn't mean squat in the bigger picture, so the Fallen offered a patronizing grin. "Creed Goodnight! No hard feelings about Whiskey Lick. A job's a job, right? I've been waiting on you two since you rode into town. There's just no disguising the gagging stench of nun, is there? You know, we're the same, you and me, cut from the same cloth. What's your play in all this? She got you thinking she's holy, maybe she can save you? We both know that nothing can save you, so whatever your damn problem is, let it go. This world is ours now. If you want a piece of that, I can give it to you. If not, walk away, vampire, but the whore stays. We figure she might have a lead on a book we're chasing, is all. It belongs to us and we mean to collect what's due, and then some."

Creed rubbed the back of his neck and dropped the shotgun to half-mast. "Well, I'm right glad to hear you say that, amigo. See, the Catholic Church swore to kick in serious cash if I dropped some holy folks off at this monasterio out in the Zona. It was never specified in our deal that they had to be breathing." He pulled a cigar from his pocket, struck a match on the bloody table and jerked his chin at McQuade. "If you would oblige me by pulling the nails out of this man, he can stand witness to my story. Not to mention, he OWES me MONEY! I don't give a rat's ass what you do with the girl. She came with the job."

Hadriel sputtered, then roared with laughter, "Won't parlay with the Fallen, but crawls into bed with a damn vampire? That's worth the price of a ticket. What are you waiting on, boys? You heard the bloodsucker, pull those nails out!" He leered at Creed, flicking an indifferent hand. "Feel free to indulge yourself, Goodnight. Leave a few scraps for my boys when you're finished."

Sneering howls of contempt rattled the rafters when the Archbishop slumped to the floor, spreading his hands out for balance. Creed watched his battered face twist in pain and fired up the jeering mob with mocking grunts. Unfazed, McQuade took in a shuddering breath to steady himself, then squinted up at the gunslinger through swollen, purpled eyelids. His fierce eyes were crystal clear.

The gunslinger got the message and grabbed a fistful of the Archbishop's robes, body-slamming him upright against the bar. Arms folded, the skin boys clustered in on all sides, oblivious to the shotgun, now propped up next to McQuade's outstretched fingers. Bloodthirsty eyes honed in on the promise of violence, instead. Creed flashed a cruel smirk for the edgy crowd and lowered his head to McQuade's ear, growling, "In the end, holy man, we all get what's due us."

After Creed's grand entrance, the nun figured they'd have to shoot their way out. By contrast, all eyes remained riveted on the face-off, forgetting she was there at all. No gunfire was a good thing. It meant time to let her vision adjust to the dim lighting. By some miracle, the gunslinger had convinced them to free McQuade. She weighed her odds, then used the distraction to inch quietly along the wall to a utility pantry hidden in the shadows.

Pressing an ear to the door, she could barely make out sounds of stifled breathing. Mercifully, all the hostages were still alive, tangled together in the narrow closet. Clawing at the knots until they slackened, Sister Anjelica pulled the ropes off and extracted the gags, motioning them to remain silent. They were pasty and sallow, weak from long hours of confinement. She was afraid they might pass out, but their eyes widened in relief and they struggled to sit up. "Can you move?" she mouthed silently. "We need to move...now!" Father Amantino nodded, helping the Sisters to their feet. He leaned in against the door, gingerly twisting the handle before shoving hard with his entire body. The door screeched open on its rusted hinges and the priest stepped out into the light, flanked by four resolute nuns.

Red Bernal, a simian brute sulking alone at the bar, got a bad feeling in his gut when he'd yanked those nails out. He never liked that damn gunslinger's face from the git-go and it turned out he was right. In an instant, Red charged at the Archbishop, seething with hatred. "No WAY you get to walk away from this, inquisitor!" McQuade raised the shotgun, squeezing off a blast that blew the hellion off his feet and over the bar.

The Fallen's inky black eyes bulged with venom, fixing Creed in a cold stare. All pretense of letting him walk out in one piece was off the table. Leather snapped and the Colt spun from its holster in a silver blur, locking Hadriel in the sight. The gunslinger snarled like a hungry wolf and whispered, "Bang," then hauled McQuade across the room before anyone even saw him move. Grinning roguishly at Sister Anjelica, he arched his eyebrows and threw his duster open. The nun reached into his pocket for the Book, blushing crimson as she passed it to Father Amantino.

Outside, the rain began to pour in driving sheets. Screeching winds swept the street, hurling rotting corpses and pieces of the barricades into the air, crushing them to bits against the shaking facades. Suddenly, the back door flew open, smashing a hole in the adobe. Twitchy palms slapped leather as Rev swaggered in, slowly clapping his hands. He casually tipped his hat to Sister Anjelica, then faced off with Creed. "Wise choice, gunslinger. I can do without bullet holes in my new ride. Not that I was worried, but it got a little itchy out there, waiting on you to shake things up. In case it slipped your mighty vampiric attention, that little squall back in the desert was just a taste of what's headed this way right now."

Hadriel watched the conversation intently, without blinking. There was no change in his murderous, deadpan expression as he grunted smugly,"HALFBREED! I thought I smelled wet dog." The Fallen took a threatening step forward, but no further, shaking an accusatory finger. "YOU did this! Threw in with this useless lot, did you? Figure on taking me down with the Book? Betrayer! As of this moment, any previous deals you made with Hell are revoked. I should have killed you at birth, but it's never too late to skin those mutts and watch your whiny ass burn in the deepest pits of perdition."

Rev reckoned Hell would have something to say about cutting ties with the sole means of insurgent control, but his patience was wearing thin. He shifted his weight and pinned the Fallen in a malicious stare. "See, that's where you and these grinning jack-asses got it all wrong. It's not your call who I sell my services to and negotiations aren't over until I say they are... or he does." A brief smile cracked Rev's face as he gestured at the priest. "Your move, Padre."

Blood boiled in Hadriel's veins. He felt his lips pull back, warping his features into a rigid snarl. Flat, deadly eyes looked past the priest to the insolent nun who'd defied him. His words were hostile and bit deep, "Sister Anjelica, is it? You're a clever girl. I admire that. Not much escapes my notice, but you, little mouse, slipped right past under my nose. Now is the time to think about your companions. You wouldn't want to be a part of their ugly death, would you? Sadly, your fate was decided when you stumbled into this cantina, but there are so many varied ways to ravage a human body. If you grab the Book and toss it over, I promise to kill you first, a clean shot to the skull."

Sister Anjelica wrapped her shaking fists into a hard knot, gasping in shallow, ragged breaths. Father Amantino placed a firm hand on her shoulder and whispered, "Find your faith, Sister." The priest was a compelling presence with the unwavering, square shouldered stance of a warrior. Thick, iron-gray hair accented a rugged face, stark contrast to the stiff, white purity of his surplice. Brandishing the Book, he stepped resolutely forward.

Instinctively wary, a hush filtered through the hellish ranks and they cowered back, sizing up the opponents. Throwing in with angels, Fallen or otherwise, was like rolling dice with death. Where were the specters to back his bullshit up? That damned Fallen was surely cursed like Cain. This very minute, torrential rains were spattering the dirty street to mud, washing away all traces of his so-called domination over the priest. Smart money said maybe they should just cut their losses and make a run for it.

Hadriel squinted with irritation at the growing insurrection. The scent of raw fear sparked a hunger for blood. It was probably true what they said, cowards are the easiest to run to ground. After the book was destroyed, he might put that to the test. For the time being, his needs were better served by directing his attention to the priest, standing there all high and mighty like he was God's pride and joy.

Rain turned to hail, pelting the roof tiles so hard, it sounded as if the cantina might collapse at any second. The Fallen glared darkly at his steely nemesis and pressed a slow, deliberate step closer, hissing, "You don't need a lightning rod to know when a storm is coming. Of course, you won't win, but what do you say, Padre, shall we dance anyway?"

Hadriel grinned lewdly and outstretched his arms, sparking red hot cinders from his fingertips. At once, windows shook and shattered, raining shards of sharp glass as the floor pitched and rolled under their feet with the deafening rumble of a freight train. Liquor shelves ruptured with a fearful screech, erupting in a ferocious explosion of bottles and splintered wood. Braced for a fight, the surly skin boys quickly circled back around their leader, hands by their pistols. It was basic instinct, to the strongest go the spoils.

Father Amantino gave no indication he'd noticed the disturbances, standing by patiently until all blazing eyes focused only on him. Tension hung in the air as he removed the cap from a small vial of holy water, provoking nervous howls of protest. Undaunted, he calmly lifted his hand, tracing the sign of the cross in all four directions.

Hellish faces contorted with anxiety. Uncertain now, the confused skin boys trembled, guarded eyes gleaming with an aura of hate and malice. The Fallen snorted derisively, running a dry tongue along his blistered lips. "Heads up boys, while Father bootlicker sprinkles us with his holy hoodoo. Come on, holy man, Is that the best you've got?"

It was then, the hail stopped suddenly. Surging winds let up briefly and Sister Anjelica heard the sound she'd been dreading. A shrill, piercing whistle sounded in the distance, rapidly intensifying to thunderous, whining bellows. The nun prayed it wouldn't head their way, but it had to go somewhere. Spiraling rotations of dust lashing the street said that "somewhere" was Almas Perdidas. She clutched the priest's arm, whispering anxiously, "Forgive me Father, but you need to speed things up!"

Father Amantino scowled and gazed at the Fallen with an intensity that shone through his skin, commanding, "BE SILENT!" His deep baritone voice reverberated, vibrating like a lightning-strike as he locked eyes with the Fallen and intoned, "Almighty God, creator and defender of the human race, look down in pity on this your servant, and grant me strength to cast these unclean demons back to Hell."

The demonic hosts recoiled, wailing and foaming at the mouth. A firestorm of hot, white energy charged the room. Father Amantino traced the sign of the cross three times and began, "Exorcizamus te...omnis immunde spiritus..."

Weakened, Hadriel pushed back against the bar, spewing demented shrieks of loss and outrage. His head throbbed from this upstart priest's wretched invocation, refusing to accept what was happening to him. Being cast from Heaven may have cost him grace, but surely he was still an angel!

Rev took hold of the divine power and let it surge through him, then charged the sluggish Fallen. In an instant, a pulse of opposing forces gathered in the air around them, binding the shift of energy. He could feel himself filling the empty faith healer's body. It felt strong and vital.

At the same time, a loud rushing filled Hadriel's ears as unfamiliar, sagging flesh closed over him. He struggled to open his bloated eyes and found himself staring at his former host. Appalled by the suffocating reek of decay, thick fingers flew to his face, confirming the switch. That traitorous halfbreed would have to be dealt with later, after he escaped the compelling drone of exorcism. Hadriel took a hoarse, heavy breath, forcing the rotting flesh to move, and lumbered out the back door.

Rev settled into his new skin. He trailed after the Fallen in a heartbeat, shouting over the storm, "Go ahead and run, you blathering ass! Run until that rotten heart splits open! Hear my feet behind you? Run faster! Stop for one second and you'll be dead."

Hadriel picked up the pace, unchecked panic in his stride. He disappeared into a pitch black wall of darkness, hoping to shut the halfbreed out, but Rev could smell him. It struck the kid funny to be holding the barrel of a gun against his own forehead. He laughed hard, then pulled the stick of dynamite from his old tattered pocket and stuck it in the Fallen's mouth. It was a short fuse. He ran for all he was worth but the blast still blew him back a good ten feet, sending him skidding across the mud in a shower of meat and blood.

Creed, along with everyone else, missed the switch, but he heard the blast. Seeing how things were heating up inside the Diablo Rojo, he figured the kid could handle himself. The gunslinger scratched his head, shifting his weight as flames began licking at the soles of his boots. Sweat oozed from his pores in thick, salty beads, roasting him in the acrid stench of burning flesh now billowing around him. He cursed and tilted his head, making a wide sweeping gesture with his arms. "For CHRISSAKES, Father, I'm on your side!"

Aging walls screamed and shook, drowning out his protests. McQuade read the situation and reloaded the shotgun, then caught Creed's attention. "The way I see it, son, there's no reasoning with a priest bent on exorcism unless there's nobody left to exorcize. You real sure those hounds can round up the strays?"

The gunslinger spun the Colt from his holster, snarling through gritted teeth, "Uh huh, I reckon so." He pulled the hammer back with a sharp click, joined by the resounding ratchet of McQuade's shotgun. Fire burst from the muzzles as they drew down and fired on the skin boys. Bullets flew like fragments of the storm, engulfing the paralyzed mob.

Outside, tornadic winds swept the village, cutting a wide swath of destruction. Panic ricocheted through every hellspawn in earshot. In an effort to dodge the deafening staccato crack of gunfire, terrorized skin boys retreated out into the street, trampling each other underfoot in a primal instinct to survive. Straight away blinded by a churning vortex of dust and rubble, the mob stampeded headlong into three gigantic columns of violently twisting wind, sweeping the desert just east of town.

The gunmen leaned back on a hitching rail fronting Diablo Rojo for the better part of an hour, squinting out at the chaos just beyond the borders of Almas Perdidas. As could be expected, the twisters flattened everything close enough to swallow up, reduced it to kindling, then were gone in the blink of an eye.

Creed fired up a cigar and passed one to McQuade, killing a few more minutes. They exchanged satisfied glances as the Archbishop drew deep on the smoke, grinning ironically. "Well, that had to hurt."

The gunslinger stood, brushed off the seat of his pants and headed to the stables, calling back over his shoulder, "Yup, I expect it did."

# 19

---

OUT ON THE MESA, a high, indistinct howling of coyotes sang a mournful requiem to the ghosts of Almas Perdidas lingering in the ruins. Amber flickers of moonlight stuttered through the overcast, dancing between three wooden crosses at the top of a rutted dirt road leading to the cemetery. A resonant tolling of bells built slowly, piercing that long stretch of silence that dangles at the edge of a final amen.

The Archbishop remained at the gravesite with his rugged hands clasped in front of him while the Sisters crossed themselves and walked slowly back to the village. When they were out of earshot, the priest turned to him, his clear voice deep with concern, "Did you have more to add, Your Grace?"

The rite was complete, which made his answer puzzling. "Yes, Father, I believe I do. I'll make it fast." Whatever his reasons, Father Amantino sensed a need for privacy in the Archbishop's manner. He spun on a heel and quickly followed the nuns back to town.

Mcquade looked down at his boots, letting a few seconds go by, then laid a gold star on two of the graves and slung a cartridge belt over the third cross. Regret for not knowing these brave men better reflected in his haggard eyes when he finally spoke, "Hewitt...Moody, turns out you boys had the balls to ride against Hell itself. Sorry I never made time to thank you for that. I'd have had your back if I could and I know you'd have done the same for me." His flinty eyes narrowed to a stern squint, reflecting on Sanchez' blood-caked cartridge belt. "Son, you once asked me how God felt about thieves like you. I reckon you can ask him that yourself now,

Mcquade tugged the whiskey flask from his pouch, solemnly raising it to each of the graves, then threw back a healthy shot, rasping, "I figure you might be curious as to why I would lay you three to rest in this particular cemetery. It's like this. In Mexico there are three deaths, when the heart ceases to beat, when the body returns to the soil... and when there is no one left to remember you. I promise you, amigos, nobody in Almas Perdidas will ever forget you. God be with you."

Creed hung back in the church steeple, cleaning his gun while they filled in the holes. He didn't give a damn about the dead men, but the others did, so the least he could do was ring the bells. For him, mourning wasn't an issue, seeing how he'd been dead for a while, now. The Archbishop's elegy lent weight to the ceremony, just the same. He finished his smoke and pitched it with a flick of his fingers, then caught up to McQuade at the Diablo Rojo.

Muggy desert breezes rolled back the oppressive cloud cover, unveiling a waning moon on the edge of sunrise. Pale strings of pink and orange daylight wavered in the rising heat, promising a scorcher. Father Amantino whispered a prayer for the dead, then thanked God there would be enough horses to make the journey. Gripped by urgency, he insisted the nuns mount up and sprang into the stirrups, himself.

Creed and McQuade looked at each other, thinking the same thing. The Archbishop quickly snatched the priest's reins, growling, "God helps those who help themselves, Father. In this instance, I figure that to be devising a plan of action before charging off in a panic."

Father Amantino scowled, slowly sliding the reins from McQuade's fingers. "All respect, Your Grace, the plan is to saddle up and close the Gates Of Hell. That's exactly what I mean to do."

The gunslinger pulled a half dozen bullets from his pocket and reloaded. Getting in the middle of a squabble between holy men was some bad idea, but he saw the real trouble coming when Rev walked out of the cantina, strutting like he owned the street. One quick glance at the righteous rage burning in McQuade's eyes said it all. A deadly grin spread across the kid's face, showing every perfect, white tooth "Somebody better remind Judas Iscariot, here, that we had a DEAL!"

McQuade racked the shotgun, white-knuckling the grip. The Archbishop was all worked up and a man like that doesn't want to listen, won't listen until he hears it twice.

"Son-of-a-BITCH", Creed cursed and stepped between them, growling at Rev, "I smell gunpowder. Reckon it must be you in that bloody frock coat, Reverend Jim. You hurt?"

Rev shifted restlessly, keeping McQuade in his side-eye. "Naw I'm okay, just a few pieces of Hadriel on my shirt, is all. Would've come around sooner if a couple of high-ranking demons hadn't pulled me aside selling Hadriel's old command and talking like snakes. "Here, boy, sign this. It's a Hell of a deal." Course, I turned 'em down. There's a revival tent out there calling my name. That is, if your holy man keeps to his promises." He scowled, jerking his chin at Father Amantino. "Don't much care for the way that one is staring at me, either."

McQuade pressed an open palm forward and tossed the shotgun back to Creed. "Can't blame me for the confusion. We've all been through a bad spell, but I'm a man of my word, son."

Father Amantino glared grimly at the Archbishop, tremors of outrage hardening the lines in his face. He took in a deep shaky breath and held it as long as he could before his thoughts spilled out with a flat, hissing sound, "Blasphemers! Fallen angels! Vampires! Demon deals! Body thieves!"

Rev shook his head with resignation and mounted up. A feral sneer creased his flinty stare as he answered coldly, measuring his words, "I'm only gonna say this for you once. Won't deny being sired by a Fallen and I've sure as hell felt the fire. Thing is, I have yet to see the light, much less been cast down from it. No doubt someone in Heaven is sayin' a prayer for you, but you're lookin' at the ones who saved your holy ass. We did our jobs, Padre, now you do yours and SEAL the damn BREACH!"

Tense seconds passed while the priest regarded Rev, letting the implication play out in his mind. Finally, he broke the silence, with a direct question, "You have angelic blood, but you've never fallen? What ARE you?"

Rev looked sideways at the gunslinger and smirked, "Can't rightly say. I figure some of God's own are just naturally unruly."

Father Amantino shook his head dismissively, ending further discussion. He quickly regained his composure, demanding, "I expect we have much ground to cover and we're wasting daylight. Your Grace, Sisters," his eyebrows furrowed into a heavy scowl, "Vampire, and whatever you are, saddle up! Let's ride!"

McQuade pursed his lips into a thin line and jerked his chin toward a spiral of smoke billowing on the mesa. "Apologies Father. If I were the one sanctified to seal the Gates, it would have been done and dusted by now. As it stands, that singular honor goes to you. That being said, I have a wounded man on that ridge over there, Sheriff Quinten Chance. Seems he caught the bad end of a Zona Scorpion, which will require some serious medical attention. I aim to make sure that he gets it. Mister Goodnight, here, will see to it you and the Sisters reach the monasterio."

Creed swung into the stirrups, grinning at the priest. "Uh huh. About that, Padre, I would but it's been a while since I last ate and I tend to be wild as they come on an empty belly. Gonna stop off in Purgatorio, look in on a woman who said she'd miss me. Reckon I can get you and the Sisters that far, for which I expect to be fully compensated." The gunslinger eyed the singed flesh on his arms and locked stares with the Archbishop. "Far as your exorcism goes, McQuade, it's nothing that won't heal up, but I'll be tacking a new pair of boots to that bill. I figure the kid can take them the rest of the way. No one knows the Zona better than he does."

Rev let out a sharp bray of laughter, shifting in the saddle. "You need to be more mindful of who you offer up my services to, vampire. Seeing how the hounds have a handle on strays, I'm left with time on my hands, which got me to thinking. You might recall that revival I mentioned? Well, I'm leaning to a little truth put to organ music, mixed with a whole lot of carnival. If you need me, I'll be whistling gospel just to watch the crowds dance."

He tipped his hat to Creed and McQuade, then trotted over to confront the priest. "So we're straight, Padre, I'm no thief. The former owner was on his way out, thanks to you. Just wore out his welcome, is all. Figure I owe you for that. Now, you can take your chances with specters and scorpions, or I can have hell-hounds pick up your trail in Purgatorio, get this situation wrapped up right. Pick your poison." When the priest crossed himself and nodded, Rev spun his horse around and headed out for the border, whistling over the clatter of hooves.

Father Amantino was a righteous man, fierce and relentless. In the end, the only thing that mattered to him was reaching the monasterio where he would recite the ritual, seal the Gates of Hell and be done with it. Without another word, he spurred his horse, riding into the desert at a full gallop.

SATURDAY NIGHT WAS WICKED HOT, HOT ENOUGH TO STOP THE OLDER dogs from barking. Raw, arid winds washed in from the open desert, vaporizing breath as it left the lips. The ancient wooden doors of Rosario's were thrown open to unbridled laughter and dancing in the streets of Purgatorio, celebrating closure of the breach. Fireworks shot amber ribbons whistling skyward that burst into dazzling explosions, peppering the wastelands in light.

Overhead fans churned lazily in the dimly lit cantina, cooling sweat from the gunslinger's face. Truth be told, he'd been holed up for days, itching for a good zombie smiting or a scorpion rumble. He was dead set on heading back to El Paso, when the kid turned up and slid into a chair across the table from him.

Rev eyed a collection of empty bottles littering the floor. He laughed and leaned back in his chair, yelling over the raucous crowd, "Food! And a bottle of Mezcal for good luck!" Plum girl pushed away from the bar, balancing a greasy platter of green chili enchiladas. She swayed to the table with a deliberate slowness, placed the platter in front of him and shoved the bottle into Creed's hand without asking if he was hungry. She knew he wasn't. The gunslinger's upper lip curled over his teeth as he watched her walk away with a sensual strut. Her kind had moves that could talk by themselves and he got all worked up just looking at them.

The mood wore off on a downhill slide when a familiar voice piped up behind him, "Mister Goodnight! I suspected I would find you here!" The kid jerked up nervously as Sister Anjelica shifted her gaze his way. She dragged a chair to the table, fixing him in a stern glare. "Reverend Jim, I did NOT expect to see you. Tell me, is the revival living up to expectations?"

Rev bristled, "Yes ma'am. You'd be downright amazed how profitable mixing good intentions with a flexible code of honor can be. Now, before you get all righteous on me, I always tell the truth and everyone walks away better for it. Simply put, I trade a handful of forgiveness for a collection plate heavy with the wages of sin. Fact is, business is SO good I thought I'd kill a little time catching up with my amigo here."

Creed cracked a wide grin, creasing the corners of his eyes.

"Uh huh. That right, is it? Here I was thinkin' you were bored as I am."

Rev crossed his arms and settled back into the chair, grumbling, "Suppose I'd be lyin' if I said there wasn't some truth in that. Got something in mind, vampire?"

Sister Anjelica cleared her throat in a way that meant business. "Pay attention! This isn't a social call. Archbishop McQuade is prepared to enlist your services. You will be assisting my investigation into a rash of robberies and missing persons along the border. These desperados have the ability to come from nowhere, then vanish without a trace. My first break in the case came three days ago when the gang hit a payroll train outside of Las Cruces. They made off with cash and fourteen passengers asleep in the pullman car. Descriptions vary wildly, but most witnesses agreed about the smell. Tell me, gentlemen, what do you know about lycanthropes?"

Rev slapped both palms on the table, leaning in eagerly. "Werewolves? I know you're lucky to have witnesses. Most prey never say anything at all. Sounds like my kind of trouble. Count me in!"

Creed leaned back in the chair, propping his charred boots up on the table. He regarded the nun with a sarcastic leer, smirking, "I know to never corner something that's meaner than you are. I also know that my pockets are still empty from the last job I did for the Archbishop. All due respect, Sis, but even Satan himself has rules for doing business. At least in Hell, everybody is equally rewarded. No offense."

Sister Anjelica patted his shoulder sympathetically, then reached into her satchel for a bulging, black velvet money bag. The bulky pouch landed between his boots with a clattering chime of gold coins. The nun countered with the cynical arch of an eyebrow. "None taken, Mister Goodnight. Your reward must have slipped my mind due to the urgent state of affairs along the border. I'm quite sorry, you know, about your boots. It must have been dreadful for you." She scribbled a number on a scrap of paper and slid it across the table to him. A spark of electricity passed between them as she curled her lips into an impudent smile. "Negotiations are over now, yes?"

The gunslinger slowly unfolded the paper, then returned her smile, "Yes ma'am, I do believe they are."

# ABOUT THE EDITOR / PUBLISHER

Dawn Shea is an author and half of the publishing team over at D&T Publishing. She lives with her family in Mississippi. Always an avid horror lover, she has moved forward with her dreams of writing and publishing those things she loves so much.

*D&T Previously published material:*
    ABC's of Terror
    After the Kool-Aid is Gone

Follow her author page on Amazon for all publications she is featured in.
    Follow D&T Publishing at the following locations:
    Website
    Facebook: Page / Group
    Or email us here: dandtpublishing20@gmail.com

.

# SUNNI ELLIS

...Poet...Designer...Painter...Seamstress...and Carnival Gypsy, Sunni Ellis keeps a room in Nashville where she lives with her dog, Jax, and various ghosts.

One Hell of a Night in Mexico by Sunni Ellis

Edited by Jamie Lachance

Cover by Ash Ericmore

Formatting by J.Z. Foster

One Hell of a Night in Mexico by Sunni Ellis

Made in United States
North Haven, CT
20 March 2023

34336232R00117